Bryan's Will

by

Martin Ketley

Published in 2024 by FeedARead.com Publishing

A CIP catalogue record for this title is available from the British Library.

Bryan's Will
By
Martin Ketley

For Firefighters everywhere.

Chapter One The Reading.

"This is the last Will and testament of Bryan Michael Collins Mills. This is to be read in the presence of Charles Oscar Mills and Donald Behan Mills…"

Charlie always found the drive along the M3 and round the "bastard" M25 such a drag. He found it mind-numbing, tedious, boring, soul-destroying and any other adjective he could think of. If he was honest with himself though, were these adjectives just excuses? Excuses as to why he'd hadn't been back to Essex that much in years (Apart from visiting or picking up his Dad, he very rarely went into the town itself.) Although Chelmsford was his home town, where he grew up and spent his 'formative years', he usually managed to find an excuse or two for not going back there. Unfortunately, there was no getting out of it this time….

"I, Bryan Michael Collins Mills, being of sound mind and in reasonably good health, bequeath my worldly goods and belongings as instructed in this document: - "

(The M25 ~ The notorious motorway that encircles London. Originally considered to be a 'deadly racetrack', now more likely to be referred to as 'Europe's biggest carpark'!)

As he approached the junction to join the "bastard" M25, Charlie's heart sank. He'd tried to stay on top of the traffic situation via his Sat-Nav, but it was virtually a 'Catch 22' moment. If he went clockwise, he would encounter congestion round near the M11 junction (according to his Sat Nav). But.. if he went anti-clockwise, he was bound to be held up at the 'Dartford Crossing'. This gave him the excuse or perhaps prompted him to have a rant, out loud, to himself, "like a nutter"-

"How come, they've taken the toll booths away from this side of the tunnel and the traffic STILL slows right down? There's STILL bloody hold-ups! AND… why do we still have to pay a charge? What's it called? Oh yeah, Dart bleeding Charge. They said that once the tunnels were paid for, it would be free! I remember when it was just ONE tunnel, for all the traffic both ways. There were never these many delays and now there's TWO tunnels going north and a fuck-off great big bridge going the other way!..."

Charlie then realised that he was talking/ranting out loud. This often happened when he was driving. It didn't seem to take much to get him to do this. Normally, it would be someone would didn't thank/acknowledge him when he let them through or, someone who drove too close behind or, drove too slowly and held him up OR.... any number of other road related ineptitudes.

He understood that it was considered healthy to talk to himself. He did this a lot at home (he lived alone) He remembered reading about this in a 'men's health' magazine and decided it was true (using his logic of agreeing with theories that suited him and dismissing ones that didn't) It was a 'toss-up' so he decided his route. Logic said that there was a guaranteed hold-up if he went clockwise so he'd take his chances the other way (where there was just a 'chance' of it)

"My two sons are my only living relatives; my assets and possessions are to be divided between them as follows: -
My flat (66 Eagle Way, Tile Kiln, Chelmsford) is to be sold and the profits of which will be divided equally between my two sons.
The furniture and belongings contained within the flat are to be sold and any monies made are to be divided equally between my two sons. The only exception is my writing desk and contents. This is to be given to my son Charles with my request for him to deal with the paperwork contained within.
My car (mark three Cortina registration number STW 402M) I leave to my son Charles. It is to be maintained, nurtured and the ongoing restoration work to be continued to ensure that it is roadworthy.
My two motorbikes (FS1e registration JFM 66L and Triumph Bonneville registration EWC 36X) I leave to my son Donald. These are also to be maintained and kept roadworthy"

On the approach to the Dartford Crossing, Charlie was resigned to the fact that, once again, the lack of toll booths, the two tunnels and the fuck-off great big bridge did nothing to prevent the congestion. Charlie swore, had another rant (out loud, to himself) then joined the queue of traffic that shuffled towards the tunnels under the Thames.
Eventually, he turned off the "bastard" M25 onto the A12 and (if his memory served him correctly) he was almost there. No. This dragged too, no traffic problems, just boring.
Since Charlie moved to Poole, he rarely ventured far. He'd not long turned fifty and wanted to feel settled and

content. The Dorset coastline and countryside were enough for him so any motorway journey, (particularly around, through or near London) was going to make him miserable and stressed. It was bad enough that his Dad had died but he was dreading the fact that he had to see, spend time with or 'liaise' with his brother Don. They really didn't get on. Since their teens, Charlie found Don to be domineering (Don is three years older) self-opinionated, arrogant and a bit too 'shouty'. Don, however, always accused Charlie of being their parents' favourite and seemed to enjoy trying to humiliate him. Their mother, Katie, had passed away when Charlie was nineteen so when it was just the three of them, the atmosphere was probably partly responsible for Charlie wanting to get away.

Their Dad, Bryan, was a bit of a character, a joker, life and soul etc and didn't seem to take much in life seriously. Whereas Don seemed to become more and more 'assertive' and, some would say, almost aggressively domineering.

"My savings are to be distributed as follows: -
£30,000 in my bank account is to be divided between my two sons - £15,000 each.
The remaining £2,000 is to be shared between my two favourite charities – 'Focus Ireland' and 'Respond'. Details of these charities and how to donate to them are contained in my writing desk. There, my son Charles will find specific instructions on how to do so.
In the writing desk, Charles will find numbered envelopes, that are to be opened in order, containing very specific instructions on duties that I require to be carried out, people that need to be contacted and certain gifts that need to be distributed.

I entrust these duties to my son Charles and require them to be carried out to the best of his abilities. My funeral arrangements have all been taken care of. My solicitor has all the details and an insurance policy I took out many years ago will cover the cost."

Charlie eventually got to the outskirts of Chelmsford. He noticed the (brown heritage) signs for Hylands House (A restored stately home surrounded by green belt land) This brought back some memories. Memories of wandering off in the grounds with Elaine Robson from school on that hot summer's day. He laughed when he remembered his pathetic, embarrassed fumblings with a condom, then realising there was a strange-looking bloke watching them from the middle distance. He laughed at the memory of Elaine leaping up, pulling her skirt down and running off and of him trying to run next to her, pulling his jeans up and stumbling. Happy, carefree days? Or just rose-tinted spectacles?

He arrived on Parkway, a road that divided Chelmsford, en route to the city centre.

"Just as I thought," he exclaimed "Loads of traffic, nowhere to park! They can never get the bleeding traffic system bleeding right in this town! It's always been like this!"

Chelmsford, the county town of Essex, was now a City. It's ever-expanding population was really putting a strain on it's infrastructure. It was notorious for it's traffic problems. There always seemed to be congestion, especially during rush hours and school run times (even worse if it was raining!) Charlie wondered if every town/city was like this but concluded that Chelmsford was particularly bad.

Luckily, as usual, Charlie was (almost ridiculously) early and got parked in the aging multi-storey carpark just off Parkway. A short walk through the crowded city centre (It was sort-of familiar, didn't seem to have changed much?) and he came onto Duke Street where he found the solicitors' office. He paused outside, looked up at the sign 'Elsworthy and Holland Solicitors', a feeling of dread came over him. Not only was there going to be the reading of his Dad's Will, he also had to be in the presence of his brother Don. He sighed, ambled in and introduced himself to the receptionist. He knew that Don would be late. He was always late, the world had to wait for Don.

Chapter Two The Fleece.

"Just as I expected! You get more than me! I bloody knew it!" Don was becoming more obnoxious and getting a bit 'shouty'-
"I knew you'd be looked after and do alright out of this! Mummy and Daddy's favourite little boy comes up smelling of roses.... again! What's with this writing desk business? I bet there's some valuables in it, just for you. AND you get the car!"
Charlie was also getting angry. How can his brother put this ridiculous spin on this? For Christ's sake, their Dad had just died and all Don was bothered about was who got what.
"Hang on, hang on! What are you going on about? You've got TWO motorbikes; I get that knackered old rust bucket of a Cortina!" Charlie immediately felt guilty about saying that as the car was his Dad's pride and joy. His 'project'. His hobby.
"And the writing desk business sounds like it might be a pain in the arse. Anyway, stop being so bloody mercenary. Dad's just died and you're being all materialistic. You've got to admit that, as usual, everything just drops in your lap. You don't have to do anything; you don't even have to pretend to be nice!"

When the solicitor had finished reading the Will, Charlie had sensed an atmosphere developing. He knew that his brother was prone to blowing his top and for shouting over anyone who disagreed with him. Charlie had quickly suggested that they come out of the solicitor's offices and, once outside, was frantically looking for somewhere 'discreet' to go and 'discuss' the contents of the Will. In the absence of somewhere discreet, he spotted The Golden Fleece. The Fleece, as it was known colloquially, was an 'old-fashioned pub', right in the City centre. It hadn't changed much in many years. All dark wood panelling, stained glass windows and traditional fittings. At least they could go in there, off the street, sit down and talk calmly like sensible adults. Some hope. Fortunately, it was just after the lunchtime rush so there weren't many people in there. Charlie bought them both a drink and they sat in a cubby-hole area. It didn't take long for it to kick-off.

"What do mean 'pretend to be nice'?"

Don had bitten on that one.

"I'm sorry for being able to stand up for myself now and then. Just because you used to creep round Mum and Dad…."

It was getting more heated, Don was beginning to raise his voice, raising it to the level so that other people in the pub were comfortably over-hearing.

"Look" said Charlie, trying to calm things down.

"It is what it is. That Will was what Dad wanted, whether we agree with it or not. I think the least we can do is to go along with his wishes. To be honest, it seems pretty fair to me, having said that, the writing desk is an unknown, it might be quite involved"

Don was still fiery -

"Oh, poor old you. Might have to make some effort. I notice you haven't made much effort in coming to see Dad lately!"

"I saw Dad a bloody sight more than you! You can hardly talk" Charlie snapped back. Straight away regretting getting involved in the sort of tit-for-tat slanging match that his brother seemed to thrive on.

"Besides, it's a lot further for me to come. You're only in Hatfield. Bloody hell, I'm right down on the south coast."

Don was starting to get spiteful -
"Well, if you'd bothered getting yourself a decent job, a career, you might have been able to afford to stay in this area. The good old prosperous south-east. Instead you're still just an admin dogsbody for a Mickey Mouse council!"
Charlie took a moment; he took a deep breath. He so did not want to get into this petty, one-upmanship crap that Don always resorted to.
He thought of things that he could respond with (but wasn't going to, at this time) He COULD say that he's very sorry that he's only a 'admin dogsbody for a Mickey Mouse council' and that he wasn't a 'high-flyer' like Don. Don worked for a security firm and was the supervisor for the security arrangements at the Lister hospital in Stevenage. Charlie always thought that although Don had a reasonably well-paid, stable job, it didn't really make him the 'Mr. Big' he thought he was. Let's be honest, all he was, was a glorified security guard – was what Charlie chose NOT to say right now.
Don's wife, Carol, had inherited a nice little sum when her father died and Charlie felt that they were the epitome of nouveau-rich. They paid off their mortgage, bought a couple of flash cars and became, in Charlie's opinion, unbearable with their, thinly disguised boasts and barbed comments. At social gatherings and family get-togethers, Don would appear to be so generous, throwing his money around but Charlie came to believe that this was just showing-off. He felt that Don could easily afford to be like that, he was always loud and attention-seeking. It seemed like they were 'please like me, please notice me' gestures.
Charlie was surprised that Carol didn't attend the reading of the Will. He thought that she wouldn't be

able to contain herself to find out what she and her husband would be getting.
He had to control himself. He desperately wanted to tell Don exactly what he thought of him but he knew that, in a couple of days, there was the funeral to come and they still had to go to the flat to sort Dad's effects.
He took a deep breath then calmly said -
"Let's not get into all that now. I don't think this is the time or place. We really need to be talking about the funeral and Dad's flat."
"Oh yeah" said Don "How much do you think that's worth now? I know Dad had no mortgage on it."
"Bloody Hell, it's not all about money and how much we get!"
"I know" Don was slightly taken aback "I was just wondering. This all seems a bit sudden. Did you know Dad was that ill? He never really let on. He was from that generation that always said 'Oh, I'm alright' and soldiered on."
Charlie was relieved that Don had calmed down a bit.
"When he was round mine at Christmas, all he said was that he had a bit of a problem with his lungs and that. You know, coughing and that. He also said that his 'ticker wasn't what it was'. I just thought that the cough was due to all the years of fire-fighting. He never let on that it was, you know, terminal."
It went quiet for a moment. They were both deep in thought. Different thoughts, though.
Don piped up -
"He was round yours Christmas day, was he? I didn't know that."
Charlie couldn't resist -
"Yes, I came and got him. He was round mine EVERY Christmas day since we lost Mum and I moved away.

You must have known that. You NEVER had him round on Christmas day."
"What's that supposed to mean?"
"Look, you didn't even know where he was last Christmas, or probably any Christmas. I don't think you were even interested. You NEVER saw him at Christmas. You give it the 'holier than thou', 'Mr perfect' act in front of everyone but don't forget, I know what you're like."
"What the fuck are you on about? It's always you that pretends to be all caring and thoughtful. We noticed that you were always creeping round Dad, making out you're Mr nice guy. You weren't even here when he died, were you?"
Charlie knew when Don was really riled. That's when resorted to nastiness and often fabricated things in an attempt to hurt or get a bite.
That one did hurt. Charlie was haunted by the fact that he hadn't seen his Dad for a few months and that he died, sort of alone, with no family around him.
"Neither of us were there, Don. I feel terrible about that. I don't know what his final days were like. I'd spoken to him on the phone, I don't know how long before and he never let on that.... you know.... that he didn't have long. I'm the same as you. When I got that call from the hospital, it was a real shock, it knocked me for six."
The wind had been knocked out of Don's sails -
"I know. It was a terrible shock. I can't help thinking that all of us could have done more. You can always do more. We have to live with those regrets, he's passed away, we can't change that, we just have to deal with it."
"Yes, we do" Charlie was glad of the moment of clarity. "That's why we have to respect his wishes with

the funeral and his will. That's the least we can do. Let's try to get through this without any more bust-ups. We've still got to go through the stuff in the flat."
"Yeah, I know" Don was calm "I bloody hate funerals. Let me know when you want to go to the flat. Obviously, me and Carol will be at the crem, if you want to go to the flat before that, I can always pop down. I don't imagine you'll be going home. Where are you staying? You could always come to ours."
Charlie hoped that the horror that he felt inside at that prospect, wasn't shown on his face.
"Oh, it's ok, thanks. I was going to book in at the Premier Inn. I think I need to be round here for a bit."
"Well, you're always welcome. What about work?"
"Oh, they're alright. I've got compassionate leave but my line manager is great. He said that I could take as much time as I like and we'll sort it out when I get back. I've got plenty of leave. Pretty good for a Mickey Mouse council, don't you think? I'm joking! I'm joking!"
He saw that Don was just about to pounce on that one! Instead, he gave a wry grin -
"Don't know what I'm gonna do with those two old motorbikes."
"Dad left instructions about them. Bloody hell, we've only just been to the reading. Have you forgotten already?"
Don grunted -
"I haven't got time to sod about, titivating two knackered old bikes. I reckon he's given me them as some sort of punishment, a penance, if you like."
Charlie refused to bite -
"Well, you're stuck with them, I'm afraid. Gift horse, mouth etc! I reckon I'll have a go at sorting that Cortina out. Get it on the road. They were great, that era of

Fords. The Cortinas, the Granadas and that. I reckon it will have a, sort of, retro/vintage charm when it's on the road."
Don returned to his obnoxious self -
"People will take the piss out you! Driving around in something like that. Me and Carol prefer a bit of luxury. We like new. You can't beat that 'new car' smell."
Charlie refused to rise to that one -
"Let's see how it goes with them. Dad took care of everything, didn't he? All the funeral arrangements, the Will, everything. I'm intrigued as to what I'm going to find in that writing desk. Those instructions and the like."
Don was straight in -
"Glad you got lumbered with that. I don't have time for loads of instructions, errands and sodding about."
Charlie thought (but didn't say) -
"Don't have time? My arse. Can't be bothered, more like. He'd only be interested if there was something in it for him."
A voice piped up -
"Charlie? Charlie Mills? Is that you?"
They both looked round. It took a moment to sink in.
"Bloody Hell" said Charlie "Steve? Stevie Gates? Long time and all that. How are you doing? You remember Don? My brother Don?"
"Yes" Said Steve "I remember. You alright?"
Don sort of grunted something.
Steve turned back to Charlie -
"Haven't seen you in ages, years, probably. I didn't know you were in town. Bloody hell, good to see you. Mind if I join you? I'm getting them in. What are you two drinking?"
Don seemed agitated -
"Thanks anyway Steve, I've got to get going. Got to get

back to Hatfield." He turned to Charlie "Like I said, let us know when you're going up to the flat, otherwise me and Carol will see you at the funeral. Good to see you, Steve. Bye."

With that he was gone.

Charlie looked at Steve. Just seeing his face brought back so many memories. Memories of school, of chasing girls, of playing football, of being drunk many times.

"How's it going, Steve? Are you alright?"

"To be honest Charlie, I never really cared for Don."
Charlie had sort of already sussed this but didn't let on. He was hoping to do some digging, hoping Steve would give him some gossip or ammo.
"I did sort of get that impression just now. I sensed a bit of an atmos."
"Oh, you got that, did you? I wonder if he did. Actually, I don't really give a shit, to be completely truthful, I bloody hated him. He was a bully-boy, a loud-mouth and I always sensed that he wasn't genuine, you know, a bit of a phoney. And I tell you something, he didn't half pick on you, you know, he was always on your case. Everyone noticed that."
Charlie had been hoping for more actual dirt but he picked up on what Steve said -
"Do you know what, I never really noticed that until round about the time I left school. A couple of lads mentioned it to me and it was only then I properly realised. I can only think that I sub-consciously considered it to be normal and just accepted it. It was only when I left home and moved to Bath that it hit home. I became a bit more confident, a bit more relaxed, I could actually open my mouth and speak, actually have an opinion without Don's voice in the background tutting and calling me thick."
"Yup, that was Don. Always putting you down. Not just you, mind. He was always so opinionated and thought he was so clever and everyone else was stupid. Listen to me! Talking about him in the past tense! He's still here, he was sat just there a few minutes ago! He might have changed, he might be different, he might be more agreeable."

"NO, 'fraid not. Don will always be Don. He's hardly changed. Now he's got a bit of money behind him, he's often more obnoxious."
"Thought he might be" said Steve, nodding. "Still, it's not as if you see him much these days or have much to do with him."
"That's true, I'm relieved to say. He lives in Hatfield and I'm in Poole in Dorset. We've had to communicate and get together because Dad's just died and we've got to sort stuff out."
"I heard about Bryan, err, your Dad. Really sorry mate. He was a bloody good bloke, such a laugh. He was always so good to me when I came round. He would take the piss and all that but not like your brother, with Bryan it was always in a good way, it was always funny and you couldn't take offence. He had a way about him."
"Yeah, he did. He was a popular bloke. I remember I came back for his retirement do, when he left the Fire Brigade. Bloody Hell, what a turn-out. There was loads of people there. They all seemed to have a genuine affection for him, they said some lovely things about him, in speeches and to his face." Charlie started to get a bit choked-up. "I wish I could have seen more of him in the later years. I honestly had no idea he was so ill. I'll always regret that."
Steve could sense Charlie's emotions -
"Oh mate, you can't dwell on that. You weren't to know. And besides, it's not as if you were right on the doorstep, was it? I know you moved away. Where was it you went? Did you say Bath?"
"Well" Charlie explained "Do you remember Lisa, Lisa Ramsey? I had a bit of a thing going with her. I met her in Dukes Nightclub. Remember Dukes? Of course you do. It was crap really but it was the only nightclub in

town so they had a bit of a monopoly, didn't they? We only went there to try and meet girls. Anyway, I met Lisa. Back then, I was just plodding round, doing shitty, dead-end jobs and she kept on and on about how wonderful the city of Bath was and how much cheaper property was (than here) you know, standard of living and all that. Well, eventually she persuaded me to move there with her. We got a rented flat and I got a job with the local council. Don't get me wrong, it IS a lovely place and it Is cheaper to live than here but I soon realised that she only wanted to be closer to her family there and she wasn't that bothered about me."

"Oh mate, what a pisser. You uproot and go all the way there and that happens! Bet you were gutted."

Charlie was philosophical -

"At first I was. When the relationship went downhill, I was a bit lost. I didn't know what to do. We were just like flatmates rather than being loved-up and in a relationship. The thing was, I started to adapt and I soon realised that, although the situation wasn't perfect, I was just so glad to get away from home, you know Chelmsford and Don. My parents had been on my case about 'getting a proper job' and all that."

"So, are you still there then? In Bath? Or was it Dorset, you said?"

"Yes, I moved on again. I got a bit bored and got into this online dating business. God knows how but I sort of hooked-up with this girl, Wendy from, of all places, Bournemouth."

"Nice and local, then?"

"Exactly. Anyway, we were backwards and forwards between Bournemouth and Bath, spending a fortune on petrol and train fares. So, guess what. She talked me into moving in with her. I know, I never bloody learn, do I? It was actually pretty good for a while. We were

all over each other, I got a job with Dorset County Council, it all seemed fine and dandy. That's when things usually go tits-up for me."
"And they did?"
"Yup, I caught her having a 'thing' with our plumber, it all kicked-off and that was that."
"Shit! You don't have a lot of luck with women, do you? You're nearly as bad as me!"
"Oh, I think you used to do alright."
"Used to, exactly."
"Anyway, she was full of guilt and decided to be 'fair' about everything. I didn't bugger off immediately. I really liked the area, had a cushy job (still got it) so I hunted around, found a nice little flat in Poole and that's where I am now."
"Look mate," said Steve "If you're gonna be here for a few days, where are you going to stay? Do you have family or anyone?"
"No, I'm going to stay at the Premier Inn. Don't know for how long."
"Mate, you don't need to do that. You can crash at mine; I've got plenty of room. It'll be like the old days. Well, the VERY old days!"
"That's bloody good of you Steve. That would help me out big time. You're still in Hillary Close, aren't you?"
"I am. When my Dad pegged it, he left the house to me (No mortgage) There are some advantages of being an only child! Seriously, come round. You can stay as long as you like, it'll be a laugh."
"Cheers Steve, I'll take you up on that."
Steve lived in a large, ex-council house in Springfield on the southern side of Chelmsford. It was close to the primary school, the secondary school, the local pub and all the places and people they remember from the 'old days'.

They made their separate ways to Hillary Close. On the drive there, Charlie felt that he was on a real nostalgia trip. It had been a while since he'd been over this side of Chelmsford and although a few things had changed, the memories of his childhood and teenage years came flooding back.

When he got to Hillary Close, he straight away noticed that Steve had converted the front garden into a driveway. That helped, as commuters would park obnoxiously all over the place then walk to the station, leaving the residents with nowhere to park.

Charlie pulled up next to Steve's car and wandered in.

"God, this takes me back. I came round here a lot in my schooldays. Your parents always looked after me. They fed me and put up with me. I didn't particularly want to be at home much. They must have thought I was a lodger!"

"I was glad of it" Steve joked "Being an only child and that, I was glad of the company!"

"Mate, you weren't lonely, I seem to remember. You did pretty well with the ladies."

"'Did' Not so much in recent years. Anyway, come in mate, make yourself at home."

Charlie went in. There were black and white photos of Steve's late parents, there were some primary school photos of Steve in his Tyrrells uniform. Charlie was slightly relieved that he didn't appear in any of them. The house had been done-up really well inside. Steve was always pretty handy (He was a mechanic) He could turn his hand to anything.

"Like what you've done to this place Steve, you seem to be doing ok, motor mechanics pays well, does it?"

"I do ok" replied Steve. "I've always had work. A few years back, me and Paul Phillips went into partnership together (I don't think you know him) We're doing pretty well. Got a couple of lads working under us…FOR us, I mean and business is pretty good. Can't complain. I like it because I can be flexible with my time (like today) I can go in and do my bit though, when it's required."

"I'm glad to hear it mate. It's funny, isn't it? When we were at school and choosing our options, we were told 'You must get your English and Maths. Get some good O' levels in geography, science or commerce and the like.' All so we could get a good 'respectable' job in an office or bank etc. At that time, all the drop-outs, wasters and non-academic types (no offence) did Building Construction or Motor Mechanics, like you did. We were supposed to look down our noses at you lot. 'They'll never amount to anything' and so on. That's the crap we were fed. And yet, you so-called wasters acquired a trade, a good trade, have always earned good money and never been out of work! And, us so-called academic types, have been in and out of work and been in low-paid, dull office jobs. We were fed some shit at school, weren't we?"

"Yeah, I'm glad I took the path that did. I just really enjoy tinkering with cars. I do wonder about some of those in our year at Boswells, where they ended up, what they ended up doing for a living. The only career talks we ever got were The Army or engineering for boys and secretary or nurse for girls. What a joke."

Tyrrells was the local primary school and Boswells was the secondary school. People who lived locally all made the progression through both. Charlie noticed that many of them, after they leave school, never leave the area. They move house locally and marry another ex-pupil from the Tyrrells/Boswells combo. Charlie thought that this was a bit incestuous and was glad that he got out of it.

Charlie moved his bags in. Steve's house had three bedrooms, the small room, he'd converted into an office and the spare room (the guest room) was done up well but, to Charlie's horror, there were more old school photos on the wall and he did feature in some of them.
"Can't believe you've still got all these old photos, Steve. Christ, I look a right dick-head in some of them!"
Steve joined him and studied the photos -
"We've all aged mate. Look, there's you, next to Sharon Butcher. There's David Milton. There's Cheryl Milburn, remember her? I went out with her for a while. She was bloody lovely. Wonder what she's up to now."
"I remember her." Said Charlie "Like I said, you did alright with the girls."
"I had a good spell." Joked Steve "Look, there's Elaine Robson. You were with her for a bit, I remember. You spent a lot of time with her."
"We went out for quite a while. I was still seeing her after we'd left school. I think we sort of drifted apart. My fault really. I went a bit weird after my Mum died. Became a bit distant, a bit withdrawn."
Steve felt a bit awkward -
"That was a shocker though. You hear about those fatal car accidents but you don't expect someone you know, or his Mum to be killed in one. That would affect anyone. Here, I know what Elaine Robson is doing now. She married Terry Portman. Remember him? He was two years above us. Word is that they're not happy. You want to get in there mate. Rekindle the old flame!"
Charlie laughed. Elaine was great, in the old days. That was it, it was a long time ago. Besides, she's married, that means she's well and truly spoken for.
Steve and Charlie chatted about the 'good old days' for so long that they lost track of time. Steve ordered pizzas

to be delivered and kept a steady supply of beers coming from his 'beer' fridge.

Whilst they were waiting for the pizzas, Charlie thought that he'd better ring Don and tell him that he was going over to Dad's flat tomorrow and give him the option to join him. Don was all -

"Ooo, I'm not sure, err…hang on…."

It went quiet and Charlie knew what was going on. He could just make out Don's voice, all muffled then he could hear Carol. Her voice seemed more abrupt, more forceful. Charlie always thought of Carol as 'the Ice Queen' and him and Dad used to joke about her. Dad once said that if she gave you one of her stares, you would turn to stone. He said that he could never warm to her, "Hardly surprising" he would say "considering she has ice running through her veins!"

Don came back with what Charlie knew was a load of crap. It was all about how they had too much on, Carol had some things to attend to and they had to work because they were taking the following day off for the funeral.

Charlie was relieved. Although he could do with another pair of hands and he was sure that they could reminisce when they were sorting Dad's stuff, Don and his attitude could really get on his nerves.

Steve was enjoying himself. Charlie guessed that he hadn't had a beer and nostalgia evening for a while. When they knocked about together at school and for a short time after, Steve was what was considered a 'pretty boy'. He had a mop of jet-black hair, always seemed to be tanned and he'd grown a thin 'Midge Ure' type moustache. Girls seemed to pursue him. Charlie remembered being in Dukes nightclub with him and literally getting pushed out of the way by girls who wanted Steve's attention. Sometimes Charlie would

think his luck was in, when girls approached him, only to find that it was Steve that they were interested in. "Will you get your friend to dance with me?" "What's your friend's name? He's lovely." Charlie could have been miserable about all this but his philosophy was – Steve's been a bloody good mate so I'm pleased for him.
"'Course I remember that time" Steve laughed "I have to admit, it went to my head a bit. I'm not proud of how I treated some of them. When I think of the birds I rejected…bloody hell, wouldn't mind some of their attention now!"
Steve still had a mop of hair, greying slightly around his temples. He had a bit of a beer belly (or middle-aged spread, depending on how you see it) no Midge Ure anymore but he still had that tanned look and that glint in his eye. Charlie thought that Steve could still be a bit of a charmer, if he put his mind to it, he had that 'cheeky-chappy', gift of the gab.
Steve was telling some great stories involving booze and women and he had Charlie in stitches. Steve wouldn't bullshit him so the fact that they were all true, made them all the more shocking or funny -
"I met this girl in Dukes, one Saturday night, don't know how I pulled, I was SO pissed! Anyway, I sort of remember getting in a taxi with her then I must have fallen asleep. I don't recall going in her house or much else. Thing is, I woke up, or stirred, should I say, I was in this bedroom, the small light was on, I was laying there, still with my shoes on, with my trousers and boxers round my ankles and this girl was twanging, pulling and flicking my wedding tackle, trying to get it going! I was WAY too pissed! I almost said something like "Good luck with that, love!" and I reckon I passed out. Anyway, bright sunshine coming through the

curtains woke me up in the morning and I felt like shit, a blinding headache and that. She was sparko next to me. I had to get away so I carefully and quietly got dressed, (bearing in mind, my boxers and trousers were still round my ankles AND I had my shoes on) tip-toed down the stairs and out the front door. Trouble was, I had absolutely no idea where I was! I could have panicked but I just laughed. I wandered round a bit, along some streets until I sussed it. I was in Galleywood!"
(Galleywood is a 'village' joined onto Chelmsford on it's south west side.)
"I found the main drag then waited ages for a bus (no mobiles in those days to call a cab) and went home with an almighty hangover. That's not the end of it, mind. There's a punchline. Couple of months later, I met up with Johnno, do you remember Simon Johnson? In the year below us? Anyway, he worked for an insurance company in Chelmsford, it was his birthday so they were all meeting in The Ship for lunchtime drinks and he invited me along. I was minding my own business, talking to Johnno, over a pint when I suddenly realised….one of the girls in the group from his office was that girl from Galleywood! They were stood right behind Johnno at the bar. AND, guess what, he only introduced them all to me! I must admit, I went all hot and was almost lost for words. She clearly remembered me. I don't know who was more embarrassed, me or her. We exchanged some small talk but the 'incident' was never mentioned. Lucky cow, I showed her a good time!"
Steve was full of stories like that. Charlie was loving it and could have listened to him all night. It ended up a late one and they eventually crashed out. Even then

there was a “Remember that bloke?” and “What about when” or two shouted through the bedroom wall.

Chapter Four The Flat

Surprisingly, next morning, Charlie didn't have too much of a hangover. He didn't drink that much those days so he was expecting one. He was just a bit tired and thirsty (pizza and beer will dry you out) He hydrated in Steve's kitchen before he set off (two cups of tea and a pint of water) It was mid-morning so the traffic wasn't too bad, Steve had left for work about nine-thirty (the perks of being the 'boss'!)

The Tile Kiln area of Chelmsford was on the other side of town, on the way to Galleywood. When Charlie saw the sign for Galleywood, he chuckled to himself as he remembered Steve's amusing story from last night (one of many)

A wave of sadness came over Charlie as he got nearer to Eagle Way. Obviously, he'd known, for a short while, that it was going to be like this but just now it started to hit home. He was going round to his Dad's flat, as he's done so many times before but…his Dad wasn't going to be there. He will never be there again. He got really choked with his eyes welling up when he faced the reality that he'd never see his Dad again. He kept telling himself that everyone goes through this when have a bereavement or lose a loved one but that was no consolation right now. Right now, he was grieving, he was hurting.

The small block where Dad lived was just inside Eagle way, a cul-de-sac and, as Charlie drove past the flats, on the way to the access road that ran behind them, he glanced up at the window of his Dad's flat on the first-floor. He could almost picture him standing there, waving as he did every time Charlie drove away. "Shit" Charlie muttered out loud "This is not going to be easy."

He pulled into the allocated parking bay (the one that only visitors used because his Dad had packed in driving a few years back.) "If only he could have got that Cortina on the road" thought Charlie "Maybe he'd have wanted to drive again." He sat for a moment, supposedly to gather himself.

He fumbled for the bunch of keys that the solicitor had given him. He couldn't understand why there were so many keys. It became obvious to him when he went through them that there were two, sometimes three copies of each key (his Dad was almost anal is his obsession with being organised) When Charlie went through them, he read the little plastic tags attached: -

Flat main door (x3)
Flat front door Yale (x3)
Flat front door deadlock (x3)
Lock-up #66 (x2)
Lock-up #68 (x2)
Desk (x2)

Dad was one of those blokes who thought of everything, he never seemed to miss anything, he had a real attention to detail.

Charlie began to work things out. He thought -

"Dad had obviously 'acquired' next-door's lock-up. He must have needed more room for storage. Of course! He had his 'project/hobby' Cortina AND the two bikes AND his tools AND his other 'stuff'. I bet that writing desk in the flat is all tidy and organised (AND locked-up!) Can't wait to go through the 'numbered envelopes' with their 'instructions'. Could be intriguing or fun. Or it could be, as Don said 'A pain in the arse'. Only one way to find out!"

He now realised that he was sub-consciously, now consciously, putting-off going into the flat. He knew

that just going through the front door was going to be tough. He decided to go and peep in the lock-ups.
He unlocked the huge padlock on Lock-up #66 and pulled open the heavy wooden doors. There it was. THE Cortina.
The first thing that he noticed was, obviously, the bonnet. It looked surprisingly good. It was a shiny light blue colour and looked to be in very good condition. Charlie flicked on the light switch and went in. The lights consisted of four bare light bulbs, two hanging close to the ceiling at the front and two at the back. The bodywork looked good, initially. The bonnet, the boot and all four doors had obviously, he thought, been replaced and looked pristine, almost. On closer inspection however, as he walked around it, he noticed that the wings, the roof and the panels along the lower part of the car were not so good, a bit rusty and tatty, all the way round. He was then wondering what condition the engine was in.
"No point in even opening the bonnet" he thought "I know sod-all about cars and the running of cars." He only really looked at the bodywork and some of it was not so good, some was almost immaculate, especially the doors.
He noticed that these were good sized lock-ups. Probably just as well as his Dad needed plenty of room for his stuff. Along each wall and along the back, on shelves, was a variety of tools, plastic bottles and tubs and, what Charlie could only assume were, spare parts. Everything was laid out in neat rows and (he presumed) were in a logical order. He smiled -
"Good old Dad, SO organised, 'Everything in its place and a place for everything'" He could hear his Dad saying that. More emotions.

He kept thinking that he'd love to get that car out on the road again but it would be quite an undertaking, especially for him, who didn't possess the appropriate skills to 'do it up'. He so wanted to honour his Dad's wishes.

He undid the huge padlock on Lock-up #68 and opened it up.

"Plenty of room in this one!"

He found the light switch and once the lights came on, he realised why. Right at the back were the two bikes, both covered in brown dustsheets. Either side of them were large wooden boxes, almost like trunks. When Charlie looked inside them, he found spares, lubricants and liquids and bits, all appropriate for the bike they were placed next to. He pulled back one of the dustsheets. There was the moped.

"It doesn't look to be in bad nick" he thought "but, what do I know?" It looked reasonably clean, no too much deterioration although a little out-dated or old-fashioned.

The other bike was a slightly different story. Under that dustsheet, he found the Triumph and it was looking good. "A classic" he thought "Oh yeah, like you know what you're talking about!" All the chrome or metalwork that he could see was gleaming. Even to someone who was not into motorbikes, like Charlie, it looked impressive. He tried to not get too carried away as he, obviously didn't have a clue how it was mechanically, how any of them were. Still, the bikes were Don's problem - "'Problem'? Is that the right word? Bloody hell, Don's been handed these on a plate, without him or his wife having been that good to Dad. I've got the Cortina 'problem' but I'm happy with it and grateful. The thing is, how the bloody hell do I fix it up? I don't have the know-how. How do I get it home? It doesn't even have an MOT. It probably doesn't even drive! I'll have to cross that bridge etc…."

After securing both lock-ups, Charlie turned and knew that he had to face the inevitable. He had to go in Dad's flat.

He found himself walking slowly towards the building, emotions coming to the fore again.

Once he was through the main door to the flats, he couldn't help noticing how clinically clean the stairs were. The décor was like a hospital, he thought, very white walls and they were shiny white. He'd never really thought about it before, all the other times he'd been in there. He smiled to himself as he thought that this was just how Dad would have wanted it.

As he climbed the stairs up to the first floor, he was conscious of his footsteps echoing down the stairwell. Perhaps it had always been like this or was he imagining it?

As he was unlocking the front door to Dad's flat (Yale and deadlock) he thought about the immaculate, shiny red gloss on the door. Fire engine red?

He went in, closed the door behind him, turned and paused. He let out a big sigh. He tried to pull himself together - "Come on" he said, out loud "Stop feeling sorry for yourself!" His voice cracked on the word 'sorry'. He looked down the hallway. In the half-light he could still make out the photo frames lined up along the walls. There were a couple of family groups, there were photos of him and Don on their respective first day at school. As he moved along the hall, he got to Dad's Fire Brigade recruit squad photo (It seemed to be from another time, the uniforms, the hairstyles, even the faces, well, it was nineteen sixty-three!) By the time Charlie got to his

Dad's retirement do's picture, he had tears running down his face. He sniffed -
"Oh, bloody hell."
Wiping his face, rubbing his eyes, he shuffled into the living room. It was like a show-home.
"That's Dad" He smirked, nodding "Always tidy, always spotlessly clean."
He was aware of more photos. Why had he never paid much attention these before? All of them must have been in their 'places' for years (maybe) and he'd never really studied them.
There was one of Dad's favourites of Mum. He thought it was taken on their last holiday together in Salou, Spain. She was looking suitably tanned and happy in her very 'nineteen eighties' clothes. It was nineteen eighty-eight. The accident happened later that year.
He spotted another family photo. He guessed that this one was taken on their last family holiday all together. He seemed to remember that it was in Puerto Pollensa in Majorca. He looked closer. Don's face was full of 'attitude'. He recalled that Don did not want to be there, thinking he was too mature and too cool to go on holiday with his parents and his 'stupid', 'annoying' little brother.
Charlie thought that Don took after his Dad (in appearance, that was. God knows where he got that temper and that obnoxious behaviour from. Neither of his parents ever behaved like that.) Don had a jawline like his Dad's and the same hairline. They both had jet-black hair and a very pronounced widow's peak whereas Charlie had a receding hairline and his hair had always been light brown, like his Mum's. He looked at the faces in the photo. Don – attitude. Mum and Dad – big grins. Charlie – How would you describe that? His face seemed to say 'fake smile, troubled, a sadness in

the eyes'. Perhaps Don had moaned at him or criticised him just before. He couldn't remember (thankfully) Despite the analysis of the faces (mainly his and Don's) just seeing his parents looking so happy, set him off again. They were both gone. Gone. He sobbed, sniffed, wiped his face. Although he was a confirmed atheist, he so hoped that they were now together in some way, if not in an after-life, then some other way.

He looked around the room. The immaculate three-piece suite, in front of the settee the shiny coffee table, against the wall the small drop-leaf dining table with two chairs and, in front of the big window, there it was. The writing desk. THE writing desk. He knew that his Dad enjoyed sitting at it, organising household bills and 'correspondence' but since the Will reading, it had taken on, an almost 'mythical' quality. Here it was. The desk that contained Dad's plans for his legacy.

He could picture his Dad sitting on the black faux-leather swivel chair in front of the desk. It was on wheels/castors and it could be tilted back a tad. When Dad was deep in thought, he would push it back from the desk a foot or so, lean back, tilt his head back and organise his thoughts.

The desk seemed so out of place. He recalled that Dad picked it up from a second-hand furniture store. It was 'weathered' or 'well used' with one or two marks and scratches around the edges. Dad would say it had 'character' and he would polish it so the surfaces always gleamed. It consisted of two fairly large drawers that would be by Dad's knees when he sat there.

"Handy for paperwork, correspondence and pens and stuff" his Dad would say. Above the drawers was the lid. In it's closed (and locked) position, like now, it tilted from the front of the drawers, inwards until, at the top, above it, there was a six-inch surface (Polished and shining) On the shelf, Charlie homed in on one of Dad's most prized possessions. It was the axe, mounted on a plaque that his mates at the Fire Station had clubbed-together and presented him with, at his retirement do. It was a Firefighters' small axe, almost impossibly shiny and on the plaque was a breathing apparatus tally that they adapt for such a gift. Charlie looked at the dates on the tally. 'Time in - January 25th 1962, Time out - March 9th 1993'

Dad did just-over his full thirty years as everyone knew he would. He loved his job; he loved being a firefighter. Charlie sat on the swivel chair and paused. He looked out the big window. How many times had his Dad sat like this, looking out? Mum died years ago so Dad lived here on his own. That thought made Charlie choke up again. He tilted the chair back and sniffed back some tears.

He took a deep breath then sorted through the bunch of keys until he found one of the 'desk' keys. When he unlocked the front of the desk, (the lock was at the top of the fold-down) he smiled and thought that there should be a fanfare or some dramatic music to accompany this moment.

He pulled down the lid (that then became the desk surface) and low and behold, there was the neat pile of A4 envelopes.

Charlie laughed -

"Good old Dad, he thought of everything."

He then started to try and work things out. He knew that an ambulance had to be called to take Dad in at the end but Dad must have known, before that, that he didn't have long. He organised his Will (no surprise there) but these envelopes and instructions must have taken some planning. Dad must have known that he was dying and had come to terms with it, accepted it.

Charlie looked through the pile of envelopes, trying to focus through misty, tear-filled eyes. There were six envelopes, each numbered in their top right corner, with, what Charlie assumed was, a permanent marker. Envelope number four was different to the others. It was a padded envelope, a little larger (a 'jiffy bag'? Charlie thought) and it was a little heavier.
He took envelope #1 from the pile and as he started to tear it open, said out loud -
"Well, here go then, let's see what he's got in store for me!"
Inside was one sheet of A4. It had been hand-written. Charlie read it (out loud)
Envelope #1
Charlie, I'll start by saying - thank you for following my instructions.
As you're doing this, it means that I'm no longer around.
You've always been so good to me. I was so proud that you're my boy. I knew I could rely on you to do things for me. I hope I've not imposed on you too much (over the years AND with these wishes in these envelopes.)
This started Charlie off again. He sobbed, tears now dripping off his face. He struggled to read on.
Please follow the instructions in each envelope.
Please DO NOT open the 'next' envelope until everything is finished in the previous. I hope this will all make sense to you as you go along. Sorry to be a pain but it means a lot to me, knowing I can rely on you to do things properly.
Take care of yourself, Charlie. Have a good life.
Thank you for all your kindness and all you've done for me. I hope you have many great adventures in

your life and I hope you enjoy carrying out my wishes.
I love you, son.
Bryan.

Charlie slumped forwards, his head resting on his arms, on the desk. He was sobbing uncontrollably -

"I love you, Dad" he whispered.

He pictured his Dad, smiling.

He could see him laughing with his friends.

He could see him in his Fire Brigade uniform, so proud.

He could see him, a broken man, at his wife's funeral.

He pictured him, in The Tulip, sat in his favourite chair, chatting with the other regulars.

He pictured him, last Christmas, at his flat in Poole, dozed off on the settee with his paper Christmas cracker hat half over his face.

"Oh, bloody hell!"

It took him a while to 'pull himself together'. As he was wiping his face down with his handkerchief, he vowed that he would carry out all the instructions, all the requests that his Dad had given him. It was the least he could do, his Dad was a wonderful man, a great Dad and a thoroughly decent human being.

He put Envelope #1 to the back of the pile then picked up Envelope #2.

"Christ, I'm belting through these!" he joked "This is easy!" He tore it open.

Envelope #2

Out came another hand-written sheet of A4, about twenty-five photos and a wad of banknotes in a small envelope.

Charlie picked up the sheet of paper and read.

COFFs - Chelmsford Old Firemen Friends.

Please find below, a list of dates of the next few meetings of COFFs at Chelmsford Fire Station. (I put a few down – don't know how long I've got!)
I would like you to attend a meeting, introduce yourself, and socialise with those lads. Trust me, they're the salt of the earth, great lads, the sort of blokes you'd want beside you when the chips are down.
The money – I'd like you to present it to them. They can all have a drink (or two) on me. (I will hear them toast me, wherever I am!) The rest of the cash – I'd like them to put it towards their latest charity fundraising.
The photos – I'd like you to give these to the secretary of COFFs, Martin Whymark. He collects old photos and memorabilia and I know he's got an album for them.
Thank you,
Bryan.
P.S. Please check the dates of the meetings. If there isn't a COFFs meeting imminent, (they're usual once every couple of months – sometimes more frequent, if they have an event) please proceed to envelope #3.

Charlie chuckled -
COFFs. Dad loved going to those meetings. COFFs was an organisation set up at Chelmsford Fire Station as a club that welcomes anyone who's ever served there, past or present. It was mainly old boys, like Dad who didn't want to, or couldn't, let go, once they retired. They met, Charlie recalled, probably once every couple of months at Chelmsford Fire Station. They'd created a 'pop-up' bar in the recreation room and the 'meetings' were pretty well attended. Dad had told

Charlie all this but Charlie, obviously, had never been to one.

COFFs was quite a witty name, Charlie always thought. Dad was 'old school' and according to him, firemen (nowadays known as fireFIGHTERS) were 'smoke-eaters'. They rarely used their breathing apparatus (quite basic equipment, compared to now) and therefore took on a lot of smoke, hence the cough joke. (A sad irony now as it was Dad's lungs that probably finished him off, as well as his heart)

Charlie had a look through the photos. Some black and white, some colour. It was Chelmsford Fire Station, or Dad's watch, through the years.

There was one (in black and white) of a group, posing in front of a fire engine. There were two rows, the back row, all stood very upright, arms folded. The front row, sat, also upright, hands on knees. His Dad was in the back row, second from the left.

There was (another black and white one) of a youthful looking Dad, with some others, in uniform, in Chelmsford High Street, collecting for charity. Some members of the public putting coins in Dad's helmet.

He found pictures of his Dad, (and others) in front of Chelmsford Fire Station, all stood round a brazier, on a picket line.

There were pictures taken at various fire calls (or jobs, as Dad would call them) They had various scenes of devastation and destruction with Dad and his mates all covered in soot, dirt and filth. There were some that showed the aftermath of horrendous road accidents.

Charlie laughed out loud at another that he found. It showed Dad and two of his mates, out the front of the Fire Station, next to a giant snowman, they'd obviously built. It was a wintery scene, with heavy snow all around. Dad, and his mates were all naked, apart from

their boots and their fire helmets, which were held to strategically cover their 'embarrassments'.
"They'll love these" Thought Charlie "Glad that they'll go in an album for posterity, for all those lads to see."
He looked inside the envelope containing the cash - "Bloody hell, there's a fair bit in here!" He counted it. Five hundred pounds, all in twenties. "I reckon they WILL have a drink or two!"
He thought he'd better check the dates that were listed, to see when the next COFFs meeting was.
"I do not believe it! That's Dad. He's done this. He's somehow made this happen. It's tonight! On the eve of his bloody funeral! The next meeting is tonight!"
Charlie decided that it was meant to be. He had to go. (If he put it off or 'bottled it', the next meeting wasn't until over two months' time AND he'd have to come all the way back here)
He gathered everything together and had a wander round the flat (more emotions) before heading down to his car, trying to work out what he was going to say at the Fire Station later.

Chapter Five COFFs

The Fire Station was on the north east side of town and although Steve had offered him a lift, Charlie decided to get a taxi. There was no way he was going to drive; he knew what these firefighters were like as regards their drinking.

As he walked up towards the 'visitors'' front door on the office block attached to the Fire Station, he paused. He couldn't remember the last time that he came here. He came a few times as a boy. Dad would bring him down and he'd sit on the fire engines wearing a helmet that was way too big for him. So exciting and awe inspiring for a child. He guessed that Dad may have been slightly disappointed that he had never joined up but Dad never once said it or showed it.

He took a few deep breaths before pressing the doorbell. He wasn't that confident, if anything, he was quite shy (unlike Don, who was very over-confident) and was getting anxious about the evening that awaited him.

Eventually, the door was answered. An older man, huge mass of grey/virtually white hair, unshaven (white stubble) over-weight, his cream pull-over was straining to stay covering his large frame.

"I've come for the COFFs meeting"

Charlie tried not to appear nervous.

The old bloke looked him in the eye and squinted. He was probably trying to see if he recognised him in some way - "Come in, fella! We're all upstairs. How yer doing?" He was quite loud and very cockney.

As Charlie followed him, he noticed that the old bloke (early seventies, he guessed) was quite bow-legged and walked with a limp.

Charlie was struggling to think of what to say. Whilst they were climbing the stairs, he heard himself blurt out -
"I've come here to talk about Bryan Mills."
The old bloke paused -
"Millsy? Yeah, cracking bloke Millsy. Really sorry to hear about him. Really sad. Knew him well, we were on Blue Watch together, years ago. We got into some scrapes, we did. We had some laughs. Bloody good bloke, Millsy, or Diesel, as some used to call him"
"Diesel?" asked Charlie. That was a new one to him. "How come he was called 'Diesel'?"
"Well" said the old bloke, leaning in "When he was younger, they say he could pull anything! Haha!"
"Oh right"
Upstairs, as they were going through the door into the recreation room, the old bloke turned back to Charlie -
"Anyway, how did you know Millsy?"
"I'm his son."
Although Charlie was aware that his Dad was a bit of a charmer and had a bit of a reputation of being a 'ladies' man', he wasn't wild about the revelation of that nickname. However, he thoroughly enjoyed the look on the old bloke's face and how uncomfortable he obviously was.
The room was pretty busy. There were chairs placed against every wall and there were groups of 'older' people sat all around the room. There were husbands and wives and, Charlie guessed, some firefighter widows.
As he approached the first group, he decided to introduce himself properly, hoping to avoid any more 'Diesel' moments. (He glanced back at the old boy who had let him in. He was still hovering in the doorway, on

his own, with a big frown on his face, probably trying to figure out how to remove his foot from his mouth)
"'Evening everyone, my name is Charlie Mills. I've come along tonight to talk about my Dad – Bryan Mills."
The group all replied together. Charlie could make out a mixture of words like "Really sorry", "Millsy" "Condolences" and "Nice fella"
"Thank you" replied Charlie "Dad asked me to come along to this meeting to meet you all and present COFFs with a couple of things."
He gradually worked his way around the room, chatting to little groups of 'older' people. He detected some real fondness and affection for his Dad. They were very sympathetic and said some very kind words. A few of them told him that they were going to the funeral on the following day.
Eventually, he remembered the instructions and asked one of them if Martin Whymark was there. When Martin was pointed out by a firefighter's widow, Charlie realised that he'd somehow bypassed him as he'd 'worked the room'.
Martin was a tall, solidly built character. Despite his slightly receding hair, his youthful face disguised his actual age. (Charlie discovered later that Martin was in his early sixties)
"Excuse me, are you Martin Whymark?"
"Guilty as charged."
Charlie let that 'quip' go.
"Nice to meet you Mr. Whymark. My name is Charlie Mills. I'm the son of Bryan Mills." He couldn't get himself to say "the late Bryan Mills."
"My Dad requested that I talk to you at this meeting."
"Good to meet you, Charlie and please, it's Martin. Really sorry about Bryan. Very sad. I regarded Bryan

as a good friend, as well as a colleague. We were on Green Watch together, right from when Green Watch was created in nineteen seventy-eight until he retired. Ninety- three, wasn't it?"

"Yes, it was." Replied Charlie, impressed with the man's memory. He later found out that Martin Whymark was a bit of an 'anorak' for facts and figures, names and dates. He was almost, what you could call, Chelmsford Fire Station's historian. "Dad wanted me to give, err, I mean, present you with these."

Martin was visibly taken aback. Although he was thrilled with the cash, (for charity as well as booze!) he was so excited about the photos.

"Bloody hell, that's me, next to Nosher Lambert, and there's Bryan! Did they actually have cameras in those days? Shouldn't these all be in sepia? Weren't the fire engines pulled by horses back then?"

They stood together for a while as Martin went through all the photos. He laughed, he gave descriptions and names and got quite emotional at times. He shook Charlie's hand and told him that he should really tell all the members about this. Apparently, he usually made a speech of some sort at these meetings.

"Can I have everyone's attention please? Excuse me! Thank you."

Martin had moved to the end of the room where he could see everyone.

"Welcome to you all, thank you for coming. It's a really good turnout which is so good to see. It's great that you're all supporting COFFs because, as well as our fundraising efforts, this is all about socialising, keeping in touch, meeting up with some old faces. Some older than others! Now, I'm sure that you're all aware, we lost someone recently. We lost a former colleague, a bloody good fireman, a COFFs regular and, most of all,

a very good friend. Bryan Mills, Millsy, to many of you."
"Or 'Diesel' to some of you." Thought Charlie, hoping that would never come up again.
"Bryan was a lovely fella" continued Martin, his voice cracking slightly. "He was an integral part of this station for many years. He served all his time here, on Blue Watch and then, ever since it was formed, on Green. He was an original Green Watch member. He was a union official, on and off, over the years, right through some difficult periods, like two or three strikes that we had. I reckon he must have stood on EVERY picket line in front of this station, sometimes on his own, in all weathers. He loved his charity work, always at the forefront of fundraising stunts and efforts. Let's not forget, he was Father Christmas at all this Station's kids' Christmas parties (sorry to spoil that for you believers!)"
Charlie twigged, he thought -
"I knew it! I bloody knew it! When me and Don were at those parties, Dad would always 'disappear' when Father Christmas was due, then reappear later, after all the presents had been given out, saying that he'd been busy and he was sad that he'd missed Santa. I never realised for years!"
Martin continued -
"He retired in nineteen ninety-three and had been a COFFs regular ever since, still so keen with his fundraising efforts. He passed away last week, quite suddenly, although, as it turned out, he'd been ill for some time and, typical Millsy, he never complained. In fact, hardly anyone knew that he was poorly. Charlie, on behalf of everyone at COFFs, may I offer you our sincerest condolences to you and your family. I'm sure, as you've chatted to people here, you've realised how

popular and loved that man was. By the way, everyone, in case you haven't met him yet, this is Charlie, Bryan's boy."
Charlie felt himself blushing slightly.
"Hello everyone" he mumbled.
Martin was still going -
"Bryan requested that Charlie came to this meeting and I'm happy to say that he asked him to present COFFs with five hundred pounds, to have a drink on him and to go towards this year's adopted charity."
A murmur of approval went around the room.
"He's also sent a load of wonderful photos for our album, we are now on volume sixteen, incidentally. Well worth looking through them. As well as being a great record of this station's history, I know that some of you will recognise yourselves in them as well as some other familiar faces. Yes, believe it or not, some of you were young once! Charlie, thank you so much for coming here tonight and carrying out your Dad's wishes. Perhaps you'd like to say a few words......?"
"Bollocks" thought Charlie "I was hoping he wouldn't say that!"
"Of course," he heard himself say, as he stepped up, next to Martin.
"Thank you, Martin, and thank you to all of you for your kind words. I know Dad loved this club and he loved coming here. The Fire Brigade was so important to him and after he retired, I'm so glad he had this. He never really wanted to let go, so this was brilliant for him. You can probably tell that I wasn't prepared for a speech and I'm not used to this! Some of you have mentioned that you remember me and Don coming here with Dad for visits, many years ago and to the annual kids' Christmas party. By the way, Martin, thanks for ruining the Father Christmas magic for all of us! I

always thought it was the real Santa! Dad was Fire Brigade through and through and was so proud to be a part of it. I'm sure you all feel the same. Sorry, I'm waffling a bit here! I'd like to propose a toast, this was Dad's idea, he said that, wherever he is, he'd hear us. To Fireman Bryan Mills!"

Charlie choked and barely got the toast out.

Everyone raised their glasses -

"Fireman Bryan Mills!"

Then came spontaneous applause. This nearly set Charlie off, he struggled to hold it together.

He realised, throughout the evening, that these were thoroughly decent people. They were so kind and thoughtful. He didn't actually buy a single drink all evening as people almost queued up to get him drinks.

As the evening wore on, the crowd thinned out a bit until eventually there was about a dozen left. The hardcore. Charlie thought that some of them were great characters and had some fabulous stories to tell. Obviously, towards the end of the night, they were all a bit 'tipsy', including Charlie and the conversation got louder with plenty of laughs.

He knew, from experience, that firefighters are generally renowned for their story-telling, their funny story-telling. They love to relay tales of humorous things they've experienced or heard about.

When Charlie later looked back at that night, he could remember some of the 'Bryan stories' but really struggled to remember which old boy told which story. He knew that the 'Diesel' old boy was one of them. He remembered one or two 'Bryan stories' told by various blokes: -

"Remember that Adrian Suggett? He was a right twat. Came on Green as a recruit in the early nineties, I think. Did himself no favours. A bit too gobby.

Thought he was Mr. tough-guy, called himself 'the hardest man in Billericay' and was full of bullshit stories about how 'hard' he was. Well, Millsy got the measure of him straight away. He slaughtered him. Nothing nasty but I reckon it drove Suggett mad, brought him down a peg or two, thankfully. He got the Green Watch Guvnor, Eddie Crawford in on a wind-up AND he got Headquarters' control in on it. It was a classic. One night duty, when Suggett was duty-man, Bryan got control to send a message to the station tele-printer spinning a yarn that a train had passed through Chelmsford railway station and it had a Nuclear flask on one of it's carriages. It was suspected that the flask was leaking slightly and there was a fear of contamination. Eddie, Station Officer, got Suggett into his office and explained the 'procedure'. He told him that it was standard procedure, in these instances, that the duty-man (Suggett, in this case) should take regular readings on a dosimeter to check for any increase of radiation levels in the area. He told him that the readings had to be taken on the hour, every hour, all through the night AND had to be taken from the top of the drill tower! Suggett fell in! Millsy, totally dead-pan confirmed all this and explained how he should carry this out without disturbing anyone else. Well, on the hour, every hour, Suggett climbed all the way to the top of the tower and took readings. All night. In the morning, he was knackered, a really disrupted night. That wasn't the end of it though, Millsy told him about the 'set-down' safety procedure that he should follow. Get this – he told him that he should wait three days then take a urine sample in to his nearest Fire Station for analysis, just in case he had become contaminated. Bloody brilliant. Obviously, we weren't there for the punchline but, just picture that twat Suggett, walking into Billericay Fire Station, carrying a Lucozade bottle, full of his own piss, asking them to check it for contamination! The lads there ripped into him! What a pillock."

"Millsy got him again, a few months later. Suggett had a side-line job as a nightclub bouncer, obviously because he was so 'hard' and he kept mouthing-off about how many blokes he'd beaten-up and thrown out etc. He seemed to get quite well paid for this, although we suspected that Mummy and Daddy looked after him financially. Anyway, one night shift, he drove into the yard in his brand-new Ford Sierra. Anyone else, I reckon we'd have been pleased for them, a brand-new car, but Suggett was full of it, boasting, taking the piss out of everyone else's cars and properly giving it the big-un'. For a while, Millsy didn't tell anyone what he did to him later on. That night, when no one was about, Millsy sneaked into the yard, and, in a watering can, had a mixture of water and oil. He poured it out underneath Suggett's brand new Sierra. Next morning, Suggett went mad -

"I don't believe it! I just drove it out of the showroom yesterday!" He was ranting. Apparently, that day, Suggett drove home and was crawling underneath, trying to find the 'leak'. And failing. The following night, after listening to a few more hours of Suggett bullshit, Millsy did the same again with the watering can! Next morning, Suggett lost it. He went MAD - "That's it! I'm not having this! I'm taking it back to the showroom and I'm going to let rip! I ain't having this!"

Once again, we weren't there for the punchline but I'd love to have seen him at the showroom, ranting and raving about a leak that didn't exist!"

Not all of the stories were about Dad's 'triumphs', in some of them, he was the 'victim' of pranks or wind-ups.

"There's a great story about when Millsy was a recruit. It's been passed down as it was a long time ago. Basically, the Guvnor at the time, Frank Nelson, or 'Lord' as he was obviously known, was in on a great wind-up. The watch had been doing a lot of basic, by the numbers training. So, the gag was, in front of Millsy, the rest of the lads would moan about the Guvnor 'taking the piss' and 'exploiting' them. They even got the two leading firemen to join in (I forget their names) Anyway, everyone made out that they were so mad that they were going to refuse to do their drill training on the next morning. Poor old Millsy. He'd only been on Blue watch a few weeks and was a young lad. Next morning came and they'd arranged it brilliantly. The watch stood in a line with Millsy at one end. The leading firemen and the Guvnor had a pretend row about the situation in front of everyone. The leading fireman announced that all the lads were in agreement and they were refusing to do their drills. Lord, the Guvnor, then turned to the line-up and said -

"I want to find out if this is true. I will ask you individually."

He went to one end of the line of blokes – the opposite end to where Millsy was standing. He asked that bloke -

"Are you refusing to drill today?"

"Yes, sir, I'm refusing." Came the answer.

He worked his way along the line, the same question and response from everyone -

"Yes, sir, I'm refusing."

He eventually got to Millsy. Millsy was very nervous. The Guvnor asked - "Are you refusing to drill today?"

Millsy tried to be confident -
"Yes, sir, I'm refusing."
"Right" said the Guvnor. "This is not on. I'm not having this. I'll ask each of you one more time and I'm warning you, there could be disciplinary charges over this!"
This time, he started at Millsy's end of the line-up.
"Are you refusing to drill today?"
Millsy, all sheepish -
"Yes, sir, I'm refusing."
The Guvnor went to next man -
"Are you refusing to drill today?"
"No, sir, I'm prepared to drill."
He turned to the next man. Same question, then -
"No. sir, I'm prepared to drill"
All the way along the line, it was -
"No, sir, I'm prepared to drill."
They reckon you could see the colour drain out of Millsy's face as he realised that he was now, the only one to refuse! When they suddenly started laughing and they turned to Millsy, apparently his face was a picture of relief!
Mind you, that just shows what Millsy was like. For the rest of his career, he would always stick together with all the lads in a dispute. He was fiercely loyal, a cracking union man and he wasn't afraid to have 'words' with senior officers whenever they came down to bullshit the lads."
"There's another classic Millsy story that's been passed down over the years. Blue had another wind-up that they used on new recruits. As he was the latest recruit, it was Millsy's turn. On his first night shift, in the dormitory, they made sure Millsy's bed was right up one end, away from the door. Anyway, after midnight, when they were all in bed, they shocked Millsy. There

was a bloke on the watch known as, get this, Kevin the nonce. I know, not a very PC nickname. It was daft really. Kevin was, by all accounts a really nice bloke. The thing was, he was very well educated and had a well-spoken, posh accent. Apparently, this justified the nickname 'the nonce'. Amazingly, it didn't seem to bother Kevin, it was water off a duck's back. Kevin though, knew that he had this ability to creep people out when he wanted to and he exploited this. So, when everyone was tucked-up in bed and settling down, Kevin came in the dormitory. He stood in the doorway and said, in his best creepy voice - "I've come to say goodnight to everyone."

With that, he went over to the first bed, bent over the lad there (who was obviously in on the joke) and said - "Goodnight" and 'kissed' him, making a 'kissing' noise. Then he moved on to the next bed and proceeded to do the same-

"Goodnight" - 'kiss'. He carried this on, all the way around the dorm. The brilliant thing about this wind-up is, you have to imagine what was going through the recruit's mind.

"Oh shit, he's working his way round here. What do I do? Do I resist? Do I hide under my blanket? Do I 'kiss' him back?"

Imagine the panic as he awaited his turn. Kevin the nonce went around the entire dormitory, doing his thing, 'saw to' Millsy, then got in his bed, next to Millsy's. I asked Millsy, obviously years later -

"What did you do? Did you resist? Did you kiss?"

Typical Millsy though, he would always say -

"Of course. Me and Kev had a bloody good snog, tongues and all!"

"Do you know what, probably a year or so later, Millsy got his own back on Kevin the nonce. He only did the classic 'sandbag and fishing wire' trick."
Charlie remembered asking -
"What on Earth is that?"
"Oh mate, everyone seems to think that it's an urban myth but Millsy actually did it and, amazingly, it worked a treat.
The trick was, or should I say, what Millsy did, was, he waited until Kevin had made his bed up in the dormitory. (Most people did that when they had a moment during the evening so that it was done and they didn't disturb anyone later) Anyway, Millsy brought in some fishing wire and tied it round the bottom corner of Kevin's blankets and sheet. He loosely trailed the fishing wire along the floor, up the wall and out through an awning window (The small window above the bigger one) He then leant out the bigger window next to it and attached the fishing wire to a sandbag that he'd balanced on the outside windowsill. He then attached another fishing wire to the sandbag, hooked it around the sill then back through the big window and trailed it across the floor, terminating by his own bed. That was it, it was all set. Later that night, everyone was coming in and getting into bed, including Kevin. It was all about timing. Millsy waited. Kevin, and everyone else, settled down, it was all quiet and Millsy timed it perfectly. He reached down, grabbed his end of the fishing wire, gave it a yank. The sandbag was pulled off the sill outside and fell into the yard below. The attached fishing wire went taut then.... Kevin's bedding shot across the floor then flew out the window! Kev was left lying there, on his bed, only in his y-fronts, looking horrified! It was hilarious. Everyone was crying with laughter. Good old Kev saw the funny side too,

after he got over the initial shock. I think people were impressed that Millsy had pulled it off (literally!) because, like I said, up until then, it had always been an urban myth."

Those lads had so many stories. Charlie accepted that most of them have worked together for many years, thirty in some cases, they were close, like family. They work, ate, trained, relaxed and practically lived together for roughly half that time so it was obvious that they'd have some great memories.

Not all the stories were about pranks and jokes and laughter though. For each of these light-hearted tales there was probably fifty or so about fire calls that could be quite horrific, quite unpleasant, hardly surprising when you consider what they did for a living.

In the taxi, on the way back to Steve's, Charlie head was buzzing. He was so glad that Dad spent all those years with those good people. They were like a brotherhood. His Dad was right, they're the salt of the earth and Dad was one of them. He felt so proud. He felt very emotional (again) It was probably the memories of Dad but the belly-full of (free) beer may have contributed something.

Chapter Six The Funeral

By the time Charlie got back to Hillary Close, Steve had already turned in. Luckily Charlie had the spare key but, as usual, because he was very tipsy, the more he tried to be quiet, the clumsier and noisier he got. Every step he took on the stairs seemed to sound like a bass drum from a military band. Even getting undressed appeared to be so loud. Each shoe, as he took it off and dropped it, in his mind would have measured on the Richter Scale.

After the 'world's longest' wee, which to him, sounded like Niagara Falls, he tip-toed across the landing from the bathroom, successfully finding every creaking floorboard then slid 'gracefully' under the duvet. Although he thought that he felt sleepy, he realised that it was just beer induced. In reality his mind was still racing. It was a combination of Dad dying, sorting Dad's affairs, apprehension about the funeral tomorrow and anything else that sprang to mind as he lay there in the darkness.

He so wanted to get to sleep, bearing in mind the sort of day he was about to have, however, one thing kept cropping up in his mind. The last person he'd spoken to at the Fire Station was Martin Whymark. Martin was pretty sloshed by the end of the night and was embracing everyone as they left. When he got to Charlie, he paused -

"Listen son, I need to talk to you before you go. I don't want you to have the wrong impression. I'm sorry, I know you've had to listen to a lot tonight, I just want to keep things real."

Charlie stepped to one side to allow some others to leave and waited to get some privacy with Martin. He had no idea what Martin was going to come out with.

Apart from the fact that Martin was clearly drunk and might ramble, Charlie had no clue as to what 'keep it real' or 'the wrong impression' meant.
Eventually, it was just the two of them left in the Recreation room (although there were still some voices coming from downstairs, that seemed merry and loud)
"Sorry to drag you back like this, err, Charlie. I just didn't want you to get the wrong idea."
"I'm not with you, Martin, wrong idea about what?"
Martin paused for a moment -
"Look, I'm sure that you're well aware that firemen love to tell stories, funny tales, far-fetched yarns, if you like."
"Yes, I did hear a few of them tonight. Bloody funny, some of them, they had me in stitches."
"Yes, I know you did and I'm as guilty as the next man when it comes to telling Fire Brigade funny stories. I don't know if you know, it's also known as 'swinging the lantern'. Quite a good expression, I think. My point is, being in the Fire Brigade is not just funny stories. I don't want to give you the impression that we're like The Keystone Kops and it's just laughs and japes and that. You have to remember what the job is really all about. We are an emergency service. The official line is that we 'Save lives, save property and render humanitarian services' however in reality, we all understand that generally when members of the public call for us, they're desperate. We are their last resort and we can't let them down."
Charlie was slightly taken aback at Martin's change of tone. From being quite jovial all evening, he was now getting more serious and intense. Even though he was a few years retired, he was still passionate about the job.
"Oh, I totally understand that." Said Charlie "Dad would let us know about some of the type of incidents

you go to. I know how important it is that the firefighters are professional and efficient."
Martin, even though he was 'preaching to the converted' continued, getting more fervent -
"I don't think that people outside the job, you know, members of the public and the like, have any idea what it's like, what we have to go through, what we have to see, to experience. You imagine, right, getting called to a house fire. By the time you get there in your fire engine, the fire's really taken hold, it's very hot and the house is full of smoke. You and your buddy put on your breathing apparatus sets and go in. You know that someone's still inside but you can't even see your hand in front of your face. You search by touch; you battle your way up the stairs and eventually find the bedroom. There on the bed, you find the old boy that you've been searching for. You and your mate grab him, drag him out the room, carry him down the stairs, out the door into fresh air. You rush and hand him over to the ambulance or paramedics, only to be told that he's already dead. The smoke killed him long before the fire even started going up the stairs. Just imagine how that must feel.
Think about this one then – You get called to a road traffic accident. You and your mate are using all your equipment to cut the roof and doors off this smashed-up car to try to release the casualties. In the back, in a child seat, is a toddler crying and screaming for her Mummy. You know though, you know, that Mummy is still in the driver's seat, dead, virtually beheaded. How do you reckon that must feel?
The thing is, I don't HAVE to imagine. I know. Because that was me at those incidents. And my buddy each time was Millsy, Bryan, your Dad. We were there.

We went through that. And many others like it, over the years.
In that recreation room tonight, every bloke in that room has seen things like that. It was our job. It was what we did. You'd only be human if, at some stage, something like that got to you, affected you, stopped you sleeping or even gave you bad dreams.
Do you know what, sorry to bring this up – I thank God that Millsy wasn't on duty the day that Katie, your Mum died. Thank God he was off, playing football. It doesn't bear thinking about but just imagine if he had been. We get called to a road traffic accident at the Army and Navy roundabout, we get there and Millsy, Bryan recognises your Mum's car, and he finds that in the wreckage...I just thank God. You know, it's not so far-fetched. We've heard of cases where that has actually happened, in other parts of the country. Think about it, if a fireman lives and works in his home town, there's a fair chance that at some time in his career, he's going to go to a job involving someone he knows or is related to. All these things can get to you, it doesn't make you weak or a poor fireman, it's just one of those things.
This is why fireman use so-called gallows humour, they have some pranks and japes at the station, it's just their way of dealing with these things. Members of the public just don't get it."
"I get it" said Charlie "I know about some of the things Dad had to face. Not all, obviously because I'm sure he didn't tell us everything."
Martin paused then went on -
"I bet you didn't know about that job your Dad went to in the early nineties, I think it was. One of our appliances got called to a neighbouring town where there was a really bad house fire going on. I was on

leave but Millsy went. By the time they got there, although the local retained (part-time) crew had done their best, the house had been gutted and three children had been killed. If that wasn't bad enough, Millsy was the one who found two of the bodies and, oh, it gets worse. Millsy had to help recover all the bodies, once the fire was out. That really got to him and, I remember him telling me, what made it even more haunting for him was, the following evening, on the local TV news, they showed the school photos of two of the dead kids. Now that would get to anyone. I believe that there's counselling available these days but it wasn't really a thing in those days. You just felt like you had to 'man-up' and get on with it. So, people should hopefully realise why firemen indulge in a bit of horse-play, let their hair down, use a bit of dark humour. It's just their way of coping. It really is such a unique job, there's nothing else quite like it and no one outside really, fully understands. It's probably only people in the military and the services where it's a bit similar but I don't think people realise that we see such horror, death and destruction. Tonight, right now, in this Fire Station and in Fire Stations all over the country, there's firemen who, at any minute could go to an emergency situation. It will never stop. It's always like this."

Martin was in full rant mode and Charlie really did not wish to interrupt.

"Sorry Charlie. I went on a bit there. I think it's just tonight and talking about Millsy, your Dad, brought a lot of things back to me. (and I've had a few!)"

"It's ok, Martin, I understand. I know you're very passionate about this and I totally respect that."

After some small talk, and words about the funeral, a handshake led to an embrace. Martin was clearly upset about Bryan, it wasn't the booze talking, it was genuine.

Charlie laid there, in the darkened bedroom, a bit fidgety, kicking the duvet around, very restless. Martin's words kept taking over his thoughts. He was so proud of his Dad and the things he went through. Then he thought about all those old boys who were there this evening and how they'd all been there too. He knew that he was going to struggle to get to sleep. Too much going on in his head. He thought -

"Sod it. I might as well give myself more to stress about!"

He sat up, turned on the bedside light, reached in his bag and pulled out envelope number three.

<u>Envelope #3</u>

Charlie tore it open.

It was quite similar to the previous envelope in the fact that in it there was a smaller envelope containing cash, a few photos (although not as many as in the COFFs package) and a single sheet of A4 paper with hand-written words.

<u>The Tulip – My Wake</u>.

By the time you read this, my solicitor would have already been in contact with Mick Hamilton, the Landlord of The Tulip to sort out arrangements for my wake (following my funeral – well, you wouldn't have it before, would you?!)

When I/we lived in the area, The Tulip became my 'local' and I represented the pub at football for a few years. They were good times and I made some good friends.

In this envelope, you will find some photos, mainly of the football team but also some of the pub and the regulars. Please present these to Mick to do with

what he will (hopefully a couple might make it on to the wall of the public bar!)
You will also find some cash. Please also present this to Mick. It's to cover the cost of the nibbles that the pub is laying-on and so that everyone can have a drink on me. Again, I'll be listening-out for when you all toast me!
Hopefully there will be one or two people there and hopefully one or two will remember me!
Thank you,
Bryan.
Charlie smiled. He was well aware that Dad had been very sociable and very generous. He admired the fact that Dad wanted to take things back to The Tulip. He did frequent it a fair bit, years ago and, as he said, he played football for them. Since Mum died, however, he never really went in there that much and, besides, he moved to the other side of town so it wasn't really his 'local' any more.
With all that had been going on since Dad died, Charlie hadn't even thought about a wake. He was all set to go to the Crematorium and just assumed that would be it. He felt re-assured that Dad had taken care of all the arrangements. It made feel a bit more 'relaxed' about tomorrow. (Only a 'bit' more relaxed.)
He thought that he'd go through the photos and count the money tomorrow as he was so tired now and it was getting late.
He laid back and eventually dozed-off. It was a restless night. He woke a number of times, the first time, he swore and turned off the bedside light that was 'blinding' him.
This time, Steve insisted on giving Charlie a lift. The Crem was on the other side of town, not far past the Fire Station. Steve thought that if he could chat to him

on the way he could try to keep his mind off things, if Charlie had driven himself, he'd be alone with his thoughts.
It was an overcast day, not raining though. Charlie felt that most funerals that he'd been to, seemed to have drizzle there, just to make things more miserable.
When they'd parked-up and were wandering across to the Chapel (obviously, ridiculously early) Charlie decided that he really did not want to do the 'meet and greet' business as 'guests' arrive. He just couldn't face it. He knew that they'd all file past him (and Don) afterwards and he'd have to endure that but all that 'meeting people on their arrival' thing felt wrong to him.
That was exactly what happened at his Mum's funeral, all those years ago. His memory of that day was a bit sketchy. He knew that he'd found it quite traumatising and had assumed that his mind's 'defence mechanism' had suppressed some of the memories. He could only remember certain parts of that day. He remembered feeling so terrible, fighting back tears all throughout the day. He remembered that people came up to him, meaning well, offering words of sympathy and that just made him feel worse and he didn't know how to respond to them. However, his worst memory, that will forever haunt him, was to see his Dad, a broken man, sobbing uncontrollably, barely able to function. That vision would always haunt him.
He looked at Steve, just as Steve was kicking a stone that was in his path. They were so ridiculously early that the previous funeral was just 'finishing up'. Steve and Charlie waited in the foyer until everyone had shuffled out the other door.
Whilst they were waiting there, Steve turned to Charlie and said - "Not a bad day for it!"

"What? Oh, right, yeah."
"Sorry mate, it's difficult to know what to say. It's shit, I know. Remember, I've done this twice myself. Mind you, this is number two for you, isn't it? You know what that makes you? An orphan, just like me."
Charlie knew that Steve was just trying to 'lighten the mood' because everything about it felt so awkward. Steve continued -
"You know what my mate at the workshop said to me after my Dad's funeral? He said that I was a 'Rice Crispy' orphan – Snap, crackle but no pop! Bloody hell."
Charlie couldn't help but chuckle. However, he knew that there was no way anyone could lighten the mood today.
Once the Chapel had cleared, they wandered in. Charlie sat on the front row, Steve just behind.
"I imagine Bryan will have a good turn-out, he was a popular bloke." Said Steve, not enjoying the silence.
"I hope so" Said Charlie, twisting to sit sideways on his chair "I'd like to think so but you just can't predict it. I reckon there'll be a few old faces here."
He wasn't wrong. The rows of seats behind them gradually began to fill. As Charlie was twisted round in his seat talking to Steve, he got see who was coming in. Some of the 'guests' gave just a polite wave to Charlie (that he reciprocated) some came forward to shake his hand. The place was filling up.
He recognised some of the faces. There was a few of the people who were at the COFFs meeting the previous night. He spotted 'Diesel' man and also amongst them was Martin. Martin came forward to see Charlie. When they shook hands, Martin came in close and whispered "Hello Charlie, good to see you. Nice to

see an excellent turn-out for your old man. He deserves it."

Charlie appreciated the kind words but he didn't appreciate Martin's breath. It was that stale beer, morning after, breath. He thought he was looking a bit rough too. Hardly surprising as he was pretty hammered the night before.

There were some faces that seemed familiar to him but he couldn't place them. There was a group of old boys that, he found out later, were from The Tulip. There was Stan, Dad's old neighbour from Eagle Way.

He did a proper double-take at a lady who came in and did the discreet wave.

He thought for a moment until the penny dropped. It was one of those 'you forget that other people age too' moments.

"Bloody hell" he thought, "That's Barbara Robson! Of Barbara and Derek fame. They were really good friends of Mum and Dad years ago. The two couples used to knock about together a lot, mainly when I was a child or teenager. I remember hearing, after I'd moved away, that Derek had died. They're Elaine's parents. Shit!"

His heart seemed to pound "Is Elaine here?" He scanned the seats either side of Barbara. "Doesn't look like it. That's a shame, I'd love to know what she's like, what she looks like, meet her and that. I know, I know, she's married and that but you know…"

He almost had to check that these were just his thoughts and that he wasn't saying all this out loud.

He recalled that, thankfully, Barbara and Derek and his parents seemed to stop being so close and always socialising, around about the time that he and Elaine got together and started going out with each other -

"That was a relief" he always thought "That could have been awkward!" It was good of Barbara to come.

He knew that it was almost time. He knew that it was going to be horrible when they bring the coffin in. He looked to the back of the Chapel and, through the glass doors, he saw it. The hearse. The pall-bearers were organising themselves at the rear doors of the vehicle. He then noticed, just beyond the hearse, a fire engine parked-up. With that, three firefighters came through the doors and stood behind the back row in the Chapel. One of them was carrying a radio and he adjusted the volume on it.

"Oh, bloody hell. That's so good of them" he thought, getting a little choked "Showing respect like that, to an old firefighter who they probably didn't even know. Dad would love that. I wonder if they could get a fire call come in during the service. That would be really cool. Almost fitting. Dad would be so pleased.

I remember once, when Dad took me and Don to the Fire Station...Hang on, Don! Where the bloody hell is Don?"

"Oh, for fuck's sake!"

That last exclamation actually came out loud. Not REALLY loud but a loud enough 'whisper' for Steve to hear it.

"What's up, mate?"

Steve assumed that Charlie was getting overcome with grief.

Charlie was fuming. He angrily thought, (to himself this time.) - "I should have bloody known. I should have bloody known he'd be bloody late. Today of all days!"

He looked to the back of the Chapel and through the glass doors again. The pall-bearers had just picked up Dad's coffin and placed it on their shoulders, ready to come in and...low and behold, beside them, Charlie

saw him. Don scurrying along to get in front of the procession, with Carol trotting just behind him.
Charlie realised that he should have expected this. He could recall so many times that Don had done this in the past. Charlie, and so many other people, would get so stressed out when Don would turn up for things at the last minute or late.
"So bloody ignorant and selfish" he thought "He could have turned up on time just this once, for a change. Oh yeah, 'Don will be Don'." He was sick of hearing that over the years.
Don was wearing, what Charlie would call 'a flash suit'. It was a deep blue colour, almost shiny and he had on, what appeared to be, a black leather-look tie. The buttons on his jacket were under severe strain. Carol was wearing, what she often referred to as, her little black dress. However, black made her look even more pale than she already was and, as it was quite tight, she looked painfully thin, almost anorexic.
Don and Carol came in the Chapel and, with, it seemed, no sense of urgency, walked between the seats, all filled with mourners and shuffled along next to Charlie.
Charlie thought that at least Carol had the decency to look a bit embarrassed whereas Don had a stupid smarmy grin on his face. His, usual, insincere apology came. The one where the word "Sorry" sounds like it's being sung.
Charlie had no time to react because the congregation all stood as the coffin procession came in. The accompanying music kicked in. 'Fire Brigade' by The Move. Once the pall-bearers had placed the coffin on the stand at the front of the Chapel, it all fell silent.
The priest came forward to the lectern and began -
"Good afternoon everyone, thank you for coming. I

welcome you all as we gather to pay our respects to Bryan Michael Collins Mills."

Looking back on that day, Charlie couldn't remember much about the service. It was the expected:

"As you can see by this turnout, Brian was a popular man…"

"…Loved by many..."

"…Fine career serving as a firefighter…"

"…he was so proud of his two sons, Don and Charlie…"

One moment did stay with Charlie. It was when the priest spoke about Mum -

"I'm sure many of you know, Bryan lost his beloved wife, Katie in a tragic road accident and he was obviously devastated. When he later retired from the Fire Brigade, he knew that he was going to miss his wife as he was living alone. That year he joined COFFs – a retired firefighters' club and became an active member and had been ever since. That same year, a song came out that Bryan said gave him great comfort when thinking about Katie and he always said that the lyrics really hit home. We will now play that song 'Some Fantastic Place' by Squeeze."

Obviously, after the priest's words, everyone tuned in and listened to the lyrics. Very poignant. There wasn't a dry eye in the house.

When the song had finished, it all fell silent again, apart from the sound of some sniffing from grieving members of the congregation.

The priest came forward -

"I believe Bryan's son would like to say a few words."

Charlie panicked slightly. He didn't remember this being mentioned before. He glanced at Don. Don stared ahead, poker-faced.

"Looks like it's me then" he thought as he gingerly rose

to his feet and walked to the lectern. He guessed that there had been some wires crossed somewhere as neither of them knew of this.
As he turned to face everyone, he took a moment to try and gather his thoughts. He looked around the Chapel, at the sea of faces in front of him.
He noticed the very blue shirts of the firefighters, stood at the back. He noticed the group from COFFs. He noticed Barbara Robson; she was one of the many women in the congregation who were clutching handkerchiefs to their faces as they had been weeping. He, again, wondered about Elaine. He saw Steve, good old Steve. Finally, his eyes fell on Don and Carol. He was still angry about Don's punctuality. When he looked at Carol, he almost felt some amusement. He suddenly remembered his Dad saying to him, in confidence, that Carol usually had a face like a smacked arse! He didn't know why on earth he'd think of that right now, he just assumed it was Dad having a joke with him.
"Err…Hello everyone. Thank you all so much for coming today. It means a lot to me, err, us" He remembered Don. "I'm sure Dad would be thrilled by such a good turnout wherever erm, when, err… I'm sure you all appreciate how difficult this is"
He was aware of murmurs of understanding and sympathetic faces in front of him. He was floundering a bit so it became a very disjointed 'speech'.
"Thank you to the firefighters for being here, Dad was so proud to be in the Fire Brigade. He loved it. He used to say 'It's a brilliant job, ruined by people at the top' Is that right?"
The firefighters, at the back, laughed and nodded.
"He also loved COFFs. Thank God for you guys. I reckon you saved him from going to pieces when he

retired, with not having Mum around and that. We were worried about him, living alone, so that club, all Fire Brigade related and that, was a godsend. Hey, how about that Squeeze song? You can see how those lyrics helped him, couldn't you? Thank you for coming Stan. He said you were a good bloke to have as a neighbour and you used to look out for each other. Also, I'd like to say thank you to Barbara for being here. I know you and your Derek were really good friends to Mum and Dad when we were kids. We have great memories of those days. Sorry everyone. I know I'm rambling on here. It's difficult. It's like the priest here said, it's such a good turnout, it shows how popular Dad was. This is a really good send-off for him."
Charlie thought -
"Oh my God, I'm talking such crap, just waffling."
He tried to think of what to say, to wrap things up. He heard himself saying - "If anyone's interested, we're going to The Tulip, in Springfield, after this for a sort of, you know, wake. You're all welcome to come along and have a drink for my Dad, ON my Dad. There will be nibbles and suchlike. Erm, hope to see you there."
He felt that this was getting worse. He felt he was now talking UTTER crap and was getting embarrassed about it. With that, he just walked back to his seat next to Don. He felt like saying -
"Thanks a bundle for your help, you bloody ignorant..."
"Glad you did that" whispered Don "I hadn't prepared anything so it's a good job that you did. Christ, when that priest said..."
"Neither had I! It was sprung on me. Wasn't it obvious? That that wasn't prepared?"
"Oh, right" mumbled Don. Charlie knew that Don would never say anything like "Well done" or "You did

really well there" because Don would never give him any praise. For anything. Usually, it was just criticism. Tutting and calling him thick or stupid.

They both then paid attention to the priest who officiated over that awful part when the curtains close and the coffin disappears. There was silence apart from some of the gathered people sniffing back tears and the quiet whirring of the mechanisms. Charlie felt so painfully sad as he watched his Dad's coffin disappear forever.

Once it was over, Charlie, Don and Carol stood in a line, just outside the side door of the Chapel. Dad had chosen 'The Irish Rover' by The Pogues and the Dubliners to 'play people out'. He was always true to his Irish roots. They stood there as the entire congregation filed past, shaking their hands or kissing them, giving words of sympathy. The firefighters were first, (they couldn't risk being blocked in) then COFFs, (Martin's beer breath) then Barbara (she gave him a big hug whilst she wept) then some people he couldn't quite recognise, then Stan, then finally Steve.

The congregation then gathered in a covered area, where any flowers given were displayed. Charlie, Don and Carol followed them. This is where, usually, people engaged in small talk and most people felt awkward about how long they should stay there before leaving. No one wished to appear rude by going too soon, on the other hand no one really wanted to the last lingerer there.

It was no different that day. There was small talk aplenty. Charlie did his best to thank people individually and tried to get round the group. He had a chat here and there and was glad that most people indicated that they intended to go back to The Tulip afterwards.

He was approached by Stan, Dad's neighbour from Eagle Way. He often saw Stan when he came to visit Dad and he seemed like a nice old boy. Charlie always thought that Stan looked a bit like Ronnie Corbett and he and his Dad used to joke about it. His Dad would do a great impression. He'd adjust some imaginary glasses, and say things like -

"As I said to my producer…" or "And it's goodnight from him"

Stan had clearly been upset and wanted to talk to Charlie.

"I'll really miss your old man, you know. He was a lovely fella and a really good neighbour to me."

He was still holding Charlie's hand that he'd been shaking as he obviously wanted Charlie's attention.

"Whenever I needed help with anything, Bryan would be there, he was so kind. I can't help thinking about that awful evening, a week or so ago…"

Charlie was then worried about what Stan was going to say to him but he HAD to know. As Stan started, Charlie happened to glance over Stan (not difficult as Stan was 'Ronnie Corbett' sized) He noticed Barbara Robson walking away from the covered area, towards her car. He really wanted to talk to her but she was going and he couldn't be rude to dear old Stan. He was so disappointed. He wanted to talk to her about the old days, about how her and Derek being friends with Mum and Dad and mainly, he wanted to (subtly) find out about Elaine. He saw he get in her car and drive away. Stan went on -

"I don't know if you know but I feel you should know."

Stan was obviously uncomfortable with what he was about to tell Charlie and he was floundering somewhat.

"Your Dad was round at mine, on that evening. He was helping me move some furniture. I had a new bed

delivered so I had to re-arrange everything in my bedroom. I couldn't manage on my own so Bryan…"
Charlie wanted him to get to the point.
"Bryan was helping me. Anyway, we'd virtually finished and I said I'd get him a cuppa. While I was waiting for the kettle to boil, he sort of staggered into the kitchen behind me. I turned round and he was a right funny colour and he was sort of, hanging onto the doorframe to stop himself from… I said -
'You alright, Bryan?'
And he said -
'I don't feel that great!'
And with that he, sort of, slid down the wall a bit and luckily managed to get himself half on my kitchen stool. I thought 'bloody hell!' and told him I was gonna call for an ambulance. He said no, but I did anyway. They were quite quick. They were really good, spot on, knew their stuff. Anyway, they gave him the once over and then they took him out, down the stairs in one of those chair/trolley things. Off they went. I didn't know what to do or what was happening or how long he'd be. I made sure his flat was locked (I had a spare key, for emergencies, you know) I waited a bit then I rung the hospital. They wouldn't tell me nothing ('cos I'm not family, you see) so I got the bus. It took me a while to get to the hospital and it's bloody huge so it took me a while to find where to go. When I finally found the right place and managed to speak to the right doctor… it was too late. I'm so sorry, Charlie. Your Dad had passed. "
Charlie noticed a single tear roll down Stan's face.
Stan tried to continue -
"I can't help thinking, if only I'd done the bedroom myself, if only I'd called the ambulance quicker, if only I'd known that he wasn't well…"

Charlie interrupted -
"You can't think like that, Stan. No one knew that he was that sick. You did all that you could. In a way, I'm glad he was with you on that evening. You've always been such a good friend and neighbour to Dad, he spoke very highly of you."
"Thank you, son. That means a lot. I tell you what, I'm gonna miss that bloke."
"We'll all miss him, Stan."
"I hope you don't mind me telling you all that. I just felt that you should know. You've been a good son. Do you know what? I'd forgotten that Bryan had another son, your brother. I've never met him or seen him and Bryan never really talked about him. It was always 'Charlie this' and Charlie that'."
Charlie did not know how to respond to that.
Gradually the crowd thinned out and Charlie said to Don (with Carol) - "We might as well head off to The Tulip. You two coming?"
"Yes, for a bit." Replied Don, glancing at Carol. "Do you need a lift?"
"No, I'm ok thanks. I've got a lift with Steve"
However, he thought "Thank God. I do not want to get in one of their brand-new cars, get bull-shitted to by Don and have Carol give me regular filthy looks (OR turn to stone!)"

Chapter Seven The Tulip

Charlie got in Steve's car and they drove slowly, along the driveway, through the memorial gardens that led to the exit of the Crematorium.

By now, there was hardly anyone left so Charlie didn't feel awkward about heading off. He'd noticed, in the car park, Don and Carol were faffing. They were taking an age to sort themselves out, to get in Don's Range Rover and to pull away.

He thought that might explain why Don was always late – perhaps he spends too much time admiring his car but he came to the conclusion that Don is just an ignorant knob who didn't care what anyone thought about his lack of punctuality.

Steve was being a good mate -

"You okay, Charlie?"

Charlie sighed -

"Yeah, I'm okay mate. That's probably the worst of it out the way. I hate it at the Crem. It's always so awful and depressing."

"Well," replied Steve "Of course it is. It's not meant to be a 'fun' place. It's always going to be depressing. Someone's died and you go there to pay your respects. That's how it works. That's what it's there for. Mind you, it wouldn't bother me if, the next time I ever go there, I'll be in that wooden overcoat and it's my turn to sizzle!" He glanced at Charlie "Sorry mate, bad timing. You know what I mean."

"It's okay Steve. I'm the same. Hate funerals. I know, we're meant to. I hope my next one is my own. Hopefully, when I pop my clogs, I'd like to be about a hundred years old, just finished spending my vast fortune and it should happen at an orgy, when I would be squashed between two busty, twenty-year-old nymphomaniacs!"

Steve laughed. Charlie knew that he'd enjoy the sexual reference and, besides, someone needed to lighten the mood a bit.

Steve obviously thought too deeply about it.

"Well, I hope you do acquire your vast fortune, when you do, don't forget about your old mate Stevie. And that goes for the orgy too, don't forget about me then either! Mind you, an orgy at a hundred-years-old? Bloody hell, that's going some! No wonder it killed you!"

As they pulled out of the Crem onto Writtle Road then onwards towards the city, Charlie just happened to notice Stan. As they drove past, Stan was at a bus stop, flagging down a bus. Charlie felt awful. "Poor old Stan" he thought "Going back to Eagle Way, on his own, to his flat, no more laughs with Dad. They must have been good company for each other. Now I get it. That's why Stan was so anxious to tell me all about the night Dad died. He's off home, he's not coming to The Tulip and, I imagine, he thinks he might not see me again."

Charlie felt for the old boy. He wished that he'd been more thoughtful outside the Crem and asked Stan how he was getting home. They could have given him a lift. (It was a bit out of the way but that would have been alright.) Now he kept picturing Stan, on the bus, all alone, looking sad. Of course, Stan doesn't have a car, Dad was using his lock-up for the motorbikes.

Steve was right, someone (in this instance, Dad) has died and everyone is meant to feel sad, as a mark of respect. But, that's just it, (depending on what you believe) the person who has died is out of it. Often, it's an end to their suffering, they've 'gone to a better

place' It's the people who are left who now suffer. They suffer the pain of grieving, the sense of loss, often loneliness is inflicted on them. They're the ones that Charlie always felt for. As if a funeral isn't bad enough with the loss of someone you knew, it always set Charlie off when he saw the distraught and grieving relatives in tears, especially if it was youngsters.
"As usual" he thought "A bereavement or a funeral always makes people (namely me!) start philosophising about life, death, mortality, the afterlife even religion! I need to get to The Tulip and have a drink. I think I could do with one now."
It (surprisingly) didn't take too long to get across the city to the Springfield side. All the way there, Charlie was observing the buildings, the parks, the roads, all the changes. It was another nostalgic journey.
Steve pulled up on his own driveway. The Tulip was only round the corner, no point in parking there and, he correctly assumed, he was going to sink a few, in memory of Bryan.
As they walked the short distance from Hillary Close to The Tulip, they were both wondering what sort of an afternoon/evening it was going to be.
"Your Dad played football for The Tulip, didn't he?" asked Steve, breaking the silence.
"Yes, he did" replied Charlie, he then thought about the photos that he hadn't gone through. He was relieved that he'd remembered the envelope. **Envelope # three.**
"He had some good years there, hopefully they'll remember him and a few will be there today."
They were both satisfied when they went in The Tulip. The saloon bar was pretty busy and Charlie guessed that most of them were there for Dad. He looked around. He saw people who'd been at the funeral, they gave him nods and smiles when they noticed him. The

area in front of the bar was quite crowded and Charlie was pleased. He wanted people to have a drink or two, to remember Dad but not be too morbid or melancholy. He noticed, on a couple of long tables by the front windows, an array of 'nibbles'. There seemed to be a fair amount there and he thought that there was always too much laid on at such functions, loads seemed to be binned at the end, a bit of a waste. Mind you, there was a quite a few people there drinking, hopefully they'll want to soak it up.

Martin Whymark was the first to greet Charlie -

"Good turnout for your Dad, he was a popular bloke."

Charlie was getting déjà vu. Didn't Martin say something very similar earlier? That wasn't going to be the last time that happened that day. Charlie accepted it. He realised that it is so difficult to know what to say to someone who has had a bereavement. Some people really struggle so the repeated 'good turnout' or 'proper send-off' remarks were understandable. People were being kind and thoughtful and it was good of them to be there.

The white-haired retired firefighter (of 'Diesel' remark fame) thrust a pint into Charlie's hand without saying a word. Within seconds, a spontaneous toast went around the room -

"To Bryan!"

Charlie looked around the room. He spotted Don and Carol in one corner, sat on a couple of high-backed wooden chairs, behind a big table.

"They look like thrones" he thought "That would be about right for them! Hang on, how did they get here before me?"

He realised that they must have made their grand entrance whilst he and Steve were walking up from Hillary Close.

Once again, Charlie did his best to circulate. It felt a bit strange though because most of the people he recognised were COFFs members so he'd done just this just last night at the meeting, he did this again with them at the Crem and now he was doing the same chit-chat. It was alright though, they were good people and their warmth towards him and his Dad's memory gave him comfort.

He felt the envelope in his non-drinking hand and remembered that he'd better hunt down the landlord as per Dad's instructions.

The bar was busy so it took him a few moments to get the barmaid's attention. "Excuse me, could I speak to a Mick Hamilton please?"

When Mick appeared, Charlie thought that he looked like a stereo-typical pub landlord. He was a stocky bloke, he seemed to be early seventies (Charlie guessed that he was probably a bit younger but the 'beery' lifestyle and unsociable hours may have aged him prematurely) He had a shiny face with a fairly large, red nose. What remained of his grey/black hair was arranged in a poor sweep-over attempt. He wore an ill-fitting stripy shirt and, as he had a big beer-belly, the stripes were 'uneven' around the buttons on the front. The buttons were straining and struggling to do their job.

Charlie felt bad at being slightly judgemental. Mick was a lovely bloke, so friendly, sociable and he was the sort of man, you'd know, that would do anything for anyone.

"Yes sir, can I be of service to you?"

He called out in that 'smokes twenty a day' gruff voice.

"Hello Mr. Hamilton. My name is Charlie, I'm Bryan Mills' son…"

Before he could continue, Mick was all over it.

"Hello Charlie, great to meet you. Sorry it's under these circumstances. Look, it's noisy here, come through."
He lifted a section at the end of the bar and beckoned Charlie through.
They both squeezed past the barmaids and through a door at the back of the bar. They emerged in a store-room/office and Mick pushed across a hard-plastic chair for Charlie to sit on.
"By the way, it's 'Mick', the only people who call me Mr. Hamilton are the brewery and the wife's bastard solicitor when he's about to shit on me again (I'm going through a crappy divorce)"
"Oh, sorry to hear that."
"That's okay son, despite the fact that she's fleeced me, I've got fuck-all left and now she probably wants the shirt off my back, I'm actually happier without her! No more GBH of the ear-hole!"
Charlie laughed, not at Mick's proclamation but at the thought of anyone wanting that particular shirt, the one Mick was 'wearing' and was under considerable strain.
"Really sorry about your Dad. I've been guvnor of this boozer for years and Bryan was a regular here. He was a bit of a star of our football team. I know he changed a bit when he lost his wife and when he moved across town he wasn't in here so much. Still popped in from time to time though, always good to see him"
"Thanks Mick. I know he loved it here. He still called this place 'his local' even though he lived in Tile Kiln. He always said that he enjoyed his football with this lot more than anywhere else. Thank you for laying on that spread out there. I think I've got something here to cover that. He left a number of envelopes of instructions for me to follow, including one for you."
"Bloody hell, you're joking! That's good of him. He didn't need to do that, it was my pleasure. Besides, it's

not as if it will break me. Look at all those people here for him this afternoon!"
Charlie re-opened the envelope. He read the message to Mick.
"Jesus, good old Bryan" Mick was sniffing, struggling to hold back tears. He wiped his nose on the sleeve of THAT shirt. "He was always so generous, stood his round, looked after his mates. Let's have a butcher's at the photos."
Charlie shook the photos out of the envelope. He glanced at them as he handed them to Mick.
"Here, look at this one" Mick was excited "That was taken out there" With a nod of his head, he gestured to the rear of the pub. "That was in the old beer garden, before the extension. Look at that. Look who's with Bryan. That's old Ted Roberts. He's no longer with us, terrific fella. And that's Colin Woods. Bloody good player, a winger. I think he's here today, I'm sure he came in earlier. He'd love to see this."
He shuffled through the different sized prints.
"This one is of the first season we had a football team here. It was before the first game of the season, at Melbourne Park. Lovely sunny day, too hot for football. We won four- one, Bryan got two goals. And that one, it was taken just after we won the divisional cup. I think it was at The Marconi Club. Cracking day. We won two-one, Bryan set-up the winner. I remember it like it was yesterday. Bloody hell, it was years ago"
"I know," said Charlie. "When it was a man's game! Dad used to 'lecture' me nearly every Christmas, when he'd had a bit to drink. How did it go? Oh yeah, Man's game, you were allowed to tackle properly in those days, proper leather ball, weighed a ton when it was wet or caked in mud, the laces would cut your head open when you headed it. Not like the beachball they play

with now. Err... there was more, oh yeah, they used to wear big, solid boots back then, not the ballet shoes they wear now. It's certainly not the same now, now it's all lager-tops, perms and earrings!"
"Yes! He was right. Good old Bryan. He's taught you well."
They were both enjoying their memories. Good memories.
"He wanted you to have this"
Charlie held out the small envelope of cash.
Mick took it, peeped inside and then flicked through it.
"Jesus! There's a few hundred quid in here! I can't take this!"
"I'm afraid you have to. It was his request, or wish, that you do. So, you have no choice. You can do with it what you will. Cover the cost of the nibbles, buy the regulars a drink, whatever. He wanted you to have it."
Charlie thought, but didn't say -
"You could always buy a shirt that actually fit you, not one that's bursting at the seams!"
"I don't know what to say. Bloody good of him. I'll see that the regulars get something out of it. Listen Charlie, there's a lot of people out there, all here for your Dad. Would you like to say a few words to them? I think it would mean a lot to them, and he wanted you to toast him, didn't he?"
Once again, Charlie heard himself say -
"Of course" He was actually thinking "For Christ's sake! Another bloody speech. Sorry Dad but I'm so crap at this."
Mick stood -
"You're in luck Charlie, the P.A. is still set up from the bingo last night, you can use that."

Charlie laughed to himself -
"Oh, bugger me, it gets better. A microphone. A microphone to amplify my dull, pathetic words."
They both went through to the bar, under the raised section and then worked their way through the crowd up to the end of the room near the toilets. Here Charlie noticed a mike stand and muttered to himself -
"Bloody hell, I'm not bleeding Liam Gallagher!"
As they passed the tables, Charlie glanced at Don and Carol. Don was holding court with a small group around him.
Charlie overheard him say -
"…Me and Carol kept an eye on Dad, we had to, what with Charlie living so far away…"
Charlie was fuming -
"Bloody cheek!" he thought "What bullshit. '…kept an eye on Dad…'? I can't believe he can sit there and say that. He hardly ever saw him, hardly ever called him. And as for the ice maiden…"
"I'll switch it on for you, Charlie. The volume should be okay"
"Great, thanks Mick."
Mick 'fiddled about' on the floor behind the mike stand. Charlie took the microphone off the stand. He suddenly thought that he felt like a stand-up comic. He felt that he should have a fag burning, lean on the stand and say something (in a northern accent) like -
"My mother-in-law, my mother-in-law is so bloody fat…"
"There you go, Charlie, that should be ready to go now."
Charlie felt nervous. He blew on the end of the microphone then tapped it.
"Hello? Can anyone hear me?"
This was accompanied with a loud screech of feedback.

Charlie saw people in the room flinch with screwed-up faces, it was deafening.
"Sorry, Charlie, I've got it. I'll sort it."
Mick got down on the floor behind Charlie and 'fiddled'.
"Well, I've got their attention now!"
Charlie laughed to himself.
"Mick called (from the floor) -
"Try that, it should be okay now"
Charlie gulped -
"Here we go again, then."
"Hello? Can you hear me? Is that okay?"
He seemed to have everyone's attention. He noticed some of them moving across from the bar are so that they could see him.
"Hello everyone, yes, it's me again. For those of you who might not know, I'm Charlie Mills, son of Bryan Mills. For the rest of you, I know, you're sick of the sound of my voice by now"
No reaction.
"Err…I just wanted to say a few words. Thank you all for coming, we're all here to remember Dad, err, Bryan and I know he'd be well chuffed with the amount of people here. He loved this pub. He still referred to it as his 'local' long after he moved away. I've just been talking to Mick here about the old days when err, Bryan played football for The Tulip. I don't know if there's any old team-mates of Dad's here."
Murmurs from the bar.
"Dad specifically requested that I come here today. He wanted his wake here. He's given me some old photos to present to Mick, err, to the pub. I'm sure some of you will enjoy looking at them. He's also sent some cash for Mick and the regulars to have a drink on him."
Slightly more positive murmurs from the bar area.

"Sorry, I'm not too good at this speech lark. I should be getting better, I'm getting some practice, the last couple of days! Anyway, thank you to all of you who came to the Crem, err, the Crematorium today. That meant a lot."

Charlie paused, trying to think of what to say. His eyes darted around the room. He noticed Don sitting there (probably feeling smug that, once again, he didn't get the speech duty) then, for some reason, he thought of Barbara Robson. He looked around the faces that were looking back at him and couldn't see her. He would have quite liked to have talked to her.

"Anyway, err, once again, thank you for paying your respects to my Dad, err, our Dad. I hope everyone would like to join me by raising your glasses. To Bryan!"

The entire saloon bar seemed to join in.

Mick took the microphone from Charlie -

"Thanks a lot son, that was very good, very apt. Listen, go and have a drink and a voo low vent" (his pronunciation) "Have a chat with some of them over there, it'll make you feel better."

Charlie wandered down the room towards the bar area. He overheard Don again -

"…Carol loves her BMW whereas I prefer something a bit bigger. Hence the Range Rover…"

"Oh, bloody hell…"

As he reached the large group of people gathered around the bar, another pint was handed to him. He looked up and the provider was an older man, quite tall, dressed in a suit that seemed 'too young' for him. Charlie noticed the man had his hair swept back with a wet look (gel or Brylcreem?) He had a serious look on his face.

"I don't suppose you remember me, do you Charlie?"

Charlie studied his face to no avail.
"I'm Bobby. Bobby Cooper. I played football with your Dad. I was the goalkeeper. I can remember you coming along too, when you were a toddler. I reckon you were too young to remember. This is Colin. Colin Woods. He was in the same side. We were pretty good then, if I say so myself"
Next to him was another older man. He was quite short, balding wearing thick glasses. He looked to be in very good shape, even muscular.
"Oh yes, Mick mentioned you. You were a winger, weren't you?"
"That I was" replied Colin "Like Bobby said, we had a pretty good side in those days. Your Dad was a bit of a star. We were in the side that won the divisional cup. What a day that was!"
Charlie replied -
"Mick was just telling me about that. Dad sent some photos in today and there's one of that team, just after the final. He said Dad set up the winner."
Colin seemed pleased at the memory -
"He did. He did. He laid it on a plate for me. And Bobby here, he saved a penalty in that game. Mick's got a photo? I'd love to see that. Here Bobby, I bet you've got the same hairstyle in that picture!"
Bobby came straight back -
"And you might actually have some hair, seeing as it was a long time ago!"
Colin continued -
"It was a long time ago. We did have some good times though, didn't we? Some right laughs"
Charlie laughed to himself. He knew what was coming. These two blokes were going to reminisce, they were going to tell some tales, some legendary stories involving their time with Dad. It was a similar feeling

to the feeling that he had at the Fire Station with the COFFs people. It was good though. He didn't mind, in fact he thought it was wonderful. These people (COFFs and Tulip) obviously had great memories of their time with Dad. They obviously thought a great deal of Dad and he must have made quite an impression on them. He touched all their lives. This gave Charlie some tremendous comfort and made him feel so proud of his Dad.

He was correct. Those two blokes began to look back. They began to recall some adventures that they'd had with The Tulip Football Club.

Bobby seemed proud -

"That Divisional Cup win was probably the best highlight we ever had on the field. The standard in the league that season was pretty high so that really was an achievement. We had a hell of a night in here afterwards. Mick loved it. I can still see your Dad, dancing on a table over there, all he had on was two jockstraps – one he wore properly, the other one on his head. Bryan was quite a character. He was always the life and soul, such a laugh."

Charlie said -

"Yes, I've heard that a lot recently."

Bobby continued -

"You know, once, when Mick was busy out the back, Bryan sneaked upstairs and put loads of washing-up liquid in the hot water tank in Mick's bathroom. Jesus Christ, when Mick had a bath, you should have seen the mess, the suds were everywhere. Mick went mental! Thank god he never found out it was Bryan!"

They all laughed.

Bobby was in full flow -

"I'll never forget what Bryan did, that day we played over at Chelmer Park, I forget who we were playing.

This big defender had been kicking lumps out of Bryan the whole game. You see, Bryan was old school. We used to talk about this. In those days, if, during a game, someone boots you one, the LAST thing you'd want, is for them to know they've hurt you. I've lost count of the times Bryan would get a whack then jog on as if nothing has happened. When he'd moved away, so to speak, he'd probably wince and go -
"Bloody hell, that hurts" but not so the other bloke knew it. Bryan would be in the dressing room, after some games, and his legs would be covered in bumps and bruises, sometimes cut. He never complained. When you think of these tarts that play these days. You only have to breath near them and they go down like they've been shot. Rolling around, screaming. Makes me laugh. Anyway, on this day, at Chelmer Park, this big lad was roughing up Bryan. Second half, about ten minutes to go, Bryan is put through on goal, chasing a bouncing ball. He lobs the goalkeeper and we all thought he'd scored. The big lump of a defender charged back, did an unbelievable clearance off the line and the ball sailed away for a throw-in. However, that big lad couldn't stop and his momentum took him on and he clattered into the goalpost and went down. He was lying in a heap in the goalmouth. Bryan went running over saying -
'Oh, bloody hell, hang on everyone, hang on!'
and, same as everyone, we thought he was going to see if that big lad was okay. Anyway, Bryan stepped over him and went up to the goalpost. He put his left hand on the post and, with his right-hand fingertips, tapped the back of his left, moving it up and down the post (like a Doctor does when he's checking your chest cavity) He then turned round and shouted -
'It's okay everyone, it's fine!'

We cracked up. Even some of their lot were laughing. The ref, however, didn't find it funny. He called on their trainer to check on their bloke and then booked Bryan. Bryan wasn't bothered at all. He said it was worth it - 'The bloke was a thug and, anyway, it got a laugh, didn't it?' Typical Bryan."
We were all enjoying the amusing stories.
Colin then looked thoughtful -
"Do you remember that girl that used to come to most of our matches? She came back here after the games and hung around with all of us. No one seemed to know who she was with or who invited her along. What was her name? Jane something, wasn't it?"
Bobby knew -
"Linighan, Jane Linighan."
"That was it. Jane Linighan. I mean, she was alright. Nice enough girl. It's just that no one knew where she had come from. As you might expect, a couple of the lads took advantage of the situation. She was, (how should I say?) generous with her affections. I know of at least three of them that, err, indulged."
"Well, I wasn't one of them!" Bobby interjected.
"Me neither," said Colin. He glanced at Charlie "Oh, err, neither did Bryan."
Charlie smiled and thought to himself -
"I wouldn't have been surprised though, seeing as he had this reputation of being a bit of a ladies' man. 'Diesel', wasn't it?"
Colin continued -
"You know who she ended up with, don't you?"
"Yes, I do." Said Bobby. "Alfie George. They ended up living together. They seemed really happy. Lost contact with Alfie. He was a good bloke. Hard as nails though. Good, solid, no-nonsense defender. Took no shit from

anyone. Here, do you remember that day he got sent off?"
"Which time?" Colin quipped.
"We were playing away in Witham, I think it was…"
Colin remembered -
"Oh yeah. That one!"
"Can't remember who we were playing, they were a pretty good side though. Anyway, a couple of them were full of it. All gamesmanship, wind-ups, niggly sort of behaviour, cynical fouling, you know the types. Obviously, it was getting to Alfie. He was getting more and more angry with them as the game went on. Early in the second half, he was shielding the ball, seeing it off for a goal-kick, when this pillock forward came right up behind him, shoving him and snapping away at his ankles. In a way, he did ask for it. Well, Alfie had had enough. He spun round and I reckon this left hook started somewhere from down near the back of his knees. He caught this pillock an absolute beauty. Bang! Knocked him off his feet. That was it. It all kicked-off. All this pillock's team-mates came rushing over to attack Alfie, all our lot went rushing over to stop them. It took a while to calm things down. Bryan was a pretty good peace-maker, he had a way about him, he managed to diffuse the situation. Anyway, the ref took Alfie to one side and as he started to tell him that he was sending him off, Alfie just turned round and walked over to where our manager was, at the side of the pitch (the ref was still talking by the way) Alfie, didn't break stride. As he walked past our manager, he bent, grabbed his big kit bag and kept walking. We watched him walk right across the field to the car park. He got straight in his car, all muddy, still in his football boots and all and drove off."
Charlie laughed. He loved these old stories.

Colin took over. "That's not the end of it! I know we got beat that day. I think we would have lost with eleven on the field so Alfie being sent off didn't affect the result really. So, we're all sat in the changing room after the game, knackered. It was a tough game. Just then, the bloke that Alfie laid out came storming in, shouting -
'Where's your number six?'
I thought, thank God Alfie had buggered-off because I reckon he'd have thumped him again. Bryan told this twit that he'd gone. How he didn't see him drive off… maybe he was still a bit stunned by that left hook, you know, seeing stars. Next thing you know he starts ranting - 'He's chipped my tooth! Tell him I'll see him in court!'
and you know what he did? He waved his warrant card at us. He was a bleeding copper! What a prat. When we got back here, we told Alfie and he just laughed."
"Did it end up in court?" asked Charlie.
"No, we never heard another thing about it. When we played them again later in the season, sorry, LOST to them again later in the season, that gobshite copper was nowhere to be seen."
Just like COFFS, these lads were full of stories and memories.
Bobby went on -
"We had to play at some remote places in rural Essex. Some of these villages, I'd never heard of. Probably wouldn't find them, even now. This one time, I think it was either Great Totham or Tolleshunt something or other. Anyway, we set off in a sort of mini convoy of three or four cars. By the time we got there, we'd lost one of the cars. I know Teddy Roberts was driving, can't remember who was in it with him. No mobile phones in those days so we couldn't ring him. And no

sat-navs either. There was nothing we could do. The game kicked-off and we started with eight men. Ted's car didn't arrive until, it must have been a good twenty- or thirty-minutes in. They rushed and got changed. We were all laughing and taking the piss. Guess what, when they arrived, we were two-nil up! (Bryan got both goals) Told them we didn't need them!"

Colin nodded -

"We did play at some strange, remote and unique places. Do you remember East Hanningfield?"

"Oh god, yes!"

"East Hanningfield was a unique experience. When you pulled up there for a game, they would literally be shooing the cows off the football pitch into the next field, so we could have a game. Then…the changing rooms consisted of a double-decker bus. Yes, you heard me. A double-decker bus. The lower deck was for the away team, the upper deck was for the home team and the 'conductor's area' was for the referee."

"No showers?" asked Charlie.

"Showers? Bloody hell. Most football clubs didn't have showers. I lost count of the times I've driven back all caked in mud. We used to put dustbin bags all over the seats of the car to protect them. Anyway, also at Hanningfield, there were electricity pylons at either end of the pitch. Bobby here, he had a huge drop-kick on him. Quite a few times, when he kicked it, the ball would bounce off one of the cables above the pitch. Some blokes were worried about their safety, they thought they might get electrocuted or something."

Bobby piped up -

"I wasn't worried about being electrocuted. I was more concerned about the cow shit on the pitch. I didn't want that all over me or anyone who would be getting in my car afterwards. No showers, you remember. Didn't need that stink in my car."

The two blokes were enjoying themselves with their memories. Charlie loved it. Obviously, Dad had passed away but the fact that people loved him and respected him meant that they were getting together and sharing stories.

It was another evening where Charlie didn't have to buy a drink. He almost wished that he was more of a 'bigger' drinker so he could take advantage of it more. The footballers, COFFs members, Mick and Steve kept him well supplied. (As well as people he didn't recognise)

Don didn't stay that long. He approached Charlie (with Carol hovering behind him) to let him know that they were leaving -

"Better hit the road, we've got a long drive home. Both got to work tomorrow."

Charlie had a feeling that this was coming. He wasn't bothered though. He preferred it when Don wasn't there. Don would either be boastful and mouthy and show off or he'd do his best to belittle Charlie. Charlie had had enough of Don's 'tuts' and 'stupid idiot' muttered under his breath, to last a lifetime. Carol just nodded, waved and mouthed "Bye"

Looking back at that night, Charlie was fairly sure that he never made it until closing time. He reckoned it was much earlier when he left. He wasn't used to drinking this much and it was the third night in a row that he'd 'had a few'.

It was a good job that he did have a 'voo low vent' or two, some curled-up sandwiches and some pineapples and cheese on sticks etc. If he had carried on with an empty stomach, there could have been some dire consequences.

Some of the people had gradually drifted away and Steve had found Charlie, sat on Don's 'throne', stuffing his face with some quiche.
"Charlie, mate. Have you had enough? What do you reckon? Shall we head off?"
Charlie looked up, burped and did a quick scan of the room to see who was left.
"Yeah, okay mate. Might as well call it a night."
He said his goodbyes and his thanks to whoever was left (and probably to some complete strangers who'd popped in for a drink and didn't have a clue who he was.)
He said goodnight to Mick accompanied with a hearty, two-handed handshake across the bar. Steve and Charlie wandered outside for the short walk to Hillary Close.
Charlie's stomach was suffering. It was the alcohol. He had a sort of feeling of indigestion, it felt hot and uncomfortable.
"I'm feeling quite dyspeptic." He announced.
"What?" asked Steve "What are you on about?"
"You know, dyspeptic, bilious. My stomach is all hot and churning."
"Oh, right" Steve sort of understood. "Look, when we get in, I'll heat up some pizza, I've got some left from the other night. And, I'll give you a big glass of milk. That should settle you down. It usually works for me. If that doesn't work, then it's Andrews"
"Who's Andrew?" shouted Charlie, who thought that his quip was really funny.
Steve looked after him when they got in. They sat in the kitchen for a bit, eating soggy pizza that was blisteringly hot, straight out of the microwave. They chatted about the day's events (probably with non-sensical drunken slurs) Charlie was fairly pleased about

how it had gone. Although it was quite ‘final’ as regards his Dad having a funeral and a wake, he knew there was some unfinished business with the envelopes and Dad’s wishes. Charlie doesn’t remember actually going to bed that night. Steve reckoned that Charlie probably drank over a pint of milk (on top of all the beer) and was slightly concerned that Charlie might wet the bed, seeing as he wasn’t much of a drinker. He was glad that he could help his old mate out, that he could ‘be there’ for him, not just with his grieving but by putting him to bed when he was tanked-up.

Chapter Eight Barbara

This time, Charlie DID have a hangover. When he woke, the next morning, he knew straight away. His head was pounding. Although he was bursting to go to the toilet, he did not want to move. At all. He laid, for a while, just staring at the ceiling, observing the Artex patterns.

"Oh, bloody hell. I suppose I deserve this. Had to happen. Oh, my head. Jesus, I feel rough."

His mouth was dry, de-hydrated. He could still, just about, taste the salty greasiness of the pizza as well as that stale beer taste that lingers. He felt his stomach gurgle. He re-assured himself that this wasn't a 'head over the toilet, throwing-up for hours' type of hangover. That would be embarrassing in someone else's house. There's no dignified way to throw-up. No, this was a 'headache, feel like crap, gut-rot' type of hangover.

He heard Steve moving about downstairs. He was pleased that Steve hadn't gone off to work and left him. He was pleased, in a selfish way because Steve would probably do him something to eat, something for his hangover, something to make him feel a bit better.

He was, however, reluctant to move. It was a thumping headache. He tried to sit up. He was sort of shuffling himself then he raised his torso. It was then that he noticed something laying across his lap. He realised that he must have been curious as he went to bed but must have fallen asleep before pursuing that feeling. There on his lap was...**Envelope #4.**

He slid out from under the quilt and stood. "Oh, bloody hell, my head!" He hated this feeling. He slipped on some jeans, every movement seemed to aggravate his pounding headache and his 'unsettled' stomach. He

cautiously and slowly put on his shirt and as he ambled towards the door, picked up the envelope.
He shuffled into the bathroom and had the presence of mind to place the envelope on the lid of the laundry basket before he stood, swaying slightly, over the toilet.
"Point my Percy at the porcelain"
he heard himself say for some unknown reason. When he was done, he risked a glance in the mirror. As it was Steve's shaving mirror, it was magnified -
"Oh my God, I look like an extra from 'The Walking Dead!"
To him, it felt like it took him and age to get down the stairs. Every step was an effort, every step seemed to exaggerate his hangover symptoms. As he got half-way down, he said out loud -
"Good old Stevie! What a lifesaver!"
It was half-way down when he smelt it, just after he could hear it. Steve was preparing a fry-up.
As Charlie wandered into the kitchen, Steve was stood over the cooker, poking and moving sausages, bacon, fried potatoes etc with a wooden spoon in, what seemed like an enormous frying pan.
Steve turned -
"You alright mate? Bloody hell, hope I don't look how you feel!"
Charlie, in his rough state, couldn't even work that one out.
"Just doing you a cooked breakfast, thought a fry-up would be just what you need, make you feel better."

"You're a bloody life-saver mate. That is just what the doctor ordered."
Steve excelled himself -
"I heard you moving about so I've done you a mug of tea. It's there on the table. Sit yourself down."

Charlie plonked himself down on the chair in front of the table. Steaming hot mug of tea in front of him. He placed the envelope on the table then slid it over to one side. He was worried about spillages or getting some fry-up grease on it. He had responsibilities, it was important to his Dad.

Steve served him an awesome fry-up. A Full English. It had all that Charlie could have hoped for. Fried slice, sausages, eggs, bacon, mini fried potatoes, hash browns. It had two 'sides' – baked beans and bread and butter. Charlie polished off all that, plus another huge mug of tea and it seemed to start off his recovery.

"Mate, thank you so much for that. That really hit the spot. I'm sorry, I hardly drink much these days so, a sniff of a barmaid's apron and I'm legless."

"You're welcome, mate. Should do you a power of good. There's the message then. Drink more and you won't feel so bad! I read somewhere, or someone famous said, that he felt sorry for someone doesn't drink because when that person wakes up in the morning, that's the best he was gonna feel all day!"

"Well, right now, I wish I didn't drink. I know, the standard remark from a hangover victim, 'I'm never going to drink again!' but we all forget, we all do it again."

"In fairness, you did hit it a bit hard last night. When you think about it, you've been on it three nights in a row. Tell you what. That was good yesterday, if you know what I mean. All those people coming together for your Dad. The Crem and The Tulip were both busy. All people remembering and saying good things about him. That must make you feel a bit better, you know, give you comfort."

"Yes, it does. He was a popular man. And as send-offs go, I reckon that was a pretty good one."

"It certainly was. Anyway, I'd better show my face at work, make out I'm interested and keen. Do I spy another one of your Dad's envelopes there? What number is that? It's different to the others. Bigger. Must be quite exciting. The intrigue, the mystery."
"It sure is. This is number four. I don't know why this one's different, I'll soon find out. I suppose it is a bit exciting, the not knowing."
Steve insisted on washing up before he left for work.
'What a legend'
The house was silent.
"Well, here goes"
Charlie reached over for the envelope.
The first thing he pulled out was the 'usual' hand-written message on the A4 sheet.
Barbara Robson.
I'm sure you remember Barbara Robson. She, along with her late husband, Derek, were very good friends of your Mum and I.
We all went through a lot together and at one time, we were all very close.
Please find enclosed: -
Two envelopes.
and
A small jiffy-bag envelope.
Please visit Barbara and present her with these UNOPENED.
I'm sure you remember her address; she is still in their family home in Hill View Road. She has lived there ever since she and Derek got married.
I would be grateful if you visit Barbara, sit down and have a chat and a cuppa with her. She's been through a lot over the years.
Please give her the unopened envelopes.
Thank you again.

Bryan.

Charlie sat back and thought -

"Oh my God. Barbara. She was at the funeral. Never got a chance to talk to her. That'll take me back, going round to Hill View Road. Oh, bloody hell, Elaine. It's made me think of Elaine again. Bloody twit, I keep obsessing about her. Let it go. It all happened years ago. She's married now. Move on."

Once again, his head was spinning. He pulled himself together and struggled to get going. He showered, shaved etc and thought that his head was beginning to clear from the hangover but now his mind was racing, thinking about Hill View Road.

He tried to work out what was going to happen. Firstly, Hill View Road was definitely within walking distance (not a near as The Tulip but walkable) however, the hangover and late nights meant that he had no energy and just couldn't be bothered to walk. It did cross his mind that he might still be over the limit to drive so he didn't leave straight away. He actually had a nap on Steve's sofa. Even though his mind seemed to be racing with anticipation, he did doze off and had quite a good nap.

When he felt a bit refreshed and a bit recovered, he decided to go. As he backed off Steve's driveway, he glanced at the envelope on the passenger seat beside him and wondered -

"What is this one all about? Why the three sealed envelopes? Out of all the people he knew in this area, why has he singled Barbara out? I suppose all will be revealed." Then, for some reason, he pictured Elaine again. "Oh, for Christ's sake, stop it!"

It really was a short drive to Hill View Road. He parked up and looked across the road. The Robson house was situated facing a green. You had to go down a walkway to get to the front door. There were eight houses facing this green, four on either side. The Robson house was one from the end on the right-hand side. He laughed when he thought 'The Robson House', he used to come around here to meet Elaine. Although that relationship wasn't a secret, he used to feel a bit awkward as they were friends of the family so he used to try to be discreet. He'd only go in if Barbara and Derek were out and if they were in, he'd arrange to meet Elaine on the street (roughly where his car is parked now)

He scooped up the envelope off the passenger seat and, for some reason, walked very slowly along the walkway, almost savouring the nostalgia trip.

He remembered the gate at the end of the front garden. All those years ago he was paranoid about how noisy it was when he dropped Elaine off and as she was going in. He was always so worried about Barbara or Derek hearing. Daft really as they were such nice, friendly people.

The gate was still just as 'noisy'. Walking up the garden path, he could not remember anything about the garden or the porch. He had no memory to compare it with. He couldn't understand why that was. Now, the front door was definitely different, it was definitely a newer front door, or was it?

"Oh, sod it."

He rang the doorbell. It chimed the tune 'Oranges and lemons' and when it stopped, he suddenly felt very nervous as he waited for the door to open. It seemed like an age until he could sense movement indoors (it probably wasn't that long at all) Through the frosted glass he could just make out a grey-haired figure coming down the hall.

When the door opened, Barbara peeped through the gap, looked a bit surprised then opened the door fully, smiling.
"Hello Charlie! This is a lovely surprise!"
Even though he had seen her the previous day, he still felt as though he was looking at an 'older version' of Barbara. Of course it was. All his memories of her were from years ago.
"Hello Barbara, hope you don't mind me coming round like this, out of the blue, unannounced. I need to talk to you before I go back."
"Oh Charlie, don't be daft. It's lovely to see you. Please come in."
As he went in, he gulped. What memories. Funny how the hallway seemed so small now. The living room was pretty much how he remembered it. It was always immaculate. Spotlessly clean. It looked like new furniture. Charlie was slightly relieved that it wasn't the same three-piece. He would have felt very awkward if he sat down on the same sofa that he and Elaine first had sex on! (when Barbara and Derek had a weekend away)
"How have you been Charlie? I haven't seen you in such a long time (apart from the funeral yesterday, obviously) So sorry about Bryan, how are you coping?"
Looking at her, Charlie recalled that Barbara was always a very attractive woman. When she was younger, he often thought that she was very good looking (the old adage 'look at your future wife's mother, that's what your wife will look years from now' used to come to him in the days when he was with Elaine.) She had grown old gracefully, her black hair had turned to grey but she was still in pretty good shape. She was well-dressed, she always was. It was

just, as he'd thought a moment ago, an 'older version' of the Barbara that he used to know.
"I'm okay, thank you. It was a bit of shock when I found out Dad had gone but I'm coming to terms with it, as time goes on. Thank you so much for coming to the funeral yesterday."
"Oh, Charlie, I had to be there. I'm so sorry I didn't hang around afterwards. I really don't like funerals. That Crem has some bad memories for me (for most people, I imagine.) Wonderful turnout for your Dad though. Lovely send-off."
Charlie nearly laughed. He thought -
"There's that expression again!"
"It's okay Barbara, I understand. Yes, there was a lot of people there, even more at The Tulip after. It was quite an evening. We drank to Dad's memory, a bit too much, in my case!"
"I couldn't face going back there either. I hope you understand, Charlie. I know your Dad loved that pub."
Yes, he did. I've also been to the Fire Station as well. Some of them were there yesterday."
"Oh, that's nice. That would have meant a lot to him. He was so proud to be a fireman. Bryan was quite a character, as I'm sure you know. He was always a larger-than-life personality. He always enjoyed himself, he loved life. When I think of some of the antics and daft things he got up to…"
"Here we go" thought Charlie "Barbara will be another person who will tell funny stories about Dad. Everyone seemed to have a few of those. I shouldn't moan, it's good that they've got happy memories of him and that they want to share them. Besides, Barbara and Derek were very close to Mum and Dad at one time."
To his surprise, she didn't elaborate. She reflected for a moment then continued.

"So, where are you living now, Charlie? How long are you here for? Are you having to sort out your Dad's affairs?"
"I'm only here for a few days. I live in Dorset now, Poole. Yes, I have one or two things to sort out. Funnily enough, that's sort of why I'm here today. Typical Dad, Mr Organised. He's left a load of instructions with his solicitor. I've been given a pile of numbered envelopes to give out to certain people. There are special instructions in each of them and gifts and stuff."
"Ooo, that's exciting Charlie. Yes, Bryan was always so organised. He planned for every eventuality."
"He did. And guess what, Barbara. There's an envelope here with your name on it."
"Oh, my goodness, really?" She went bright red. "For me? Are you serious?"
"Quite serious" Charlie held up the big padded envelope. "This one's for you"
He handed it to her, she took it very slowly, nervously, like she was handling an unexploded bomb. She studied the envelope for a bit, almost reluctant to open it, it seemed.
When she finally got around to opening it, she pulled out the A4 sheet that Charlie had already read.
"Oh, that's so nice. How lovely."
She then tipped up the big envelope and the three smaller ones fell out onto her lap.
The first one she opened was the small padded envelope. Again, she shook it. Out, onto her lap, slid a watch, a medallion (of some sort) and a small, shiny spoon. She examined them, one by one.
"Oh my, oh my. Oh goodness."
Charlie could see that she was beginning to get a bit emotional.
She put the items on the small table next to her chair.

She then opened one of the smaller envelopes. Out came about ten photos of varying size, including a strip of 'photo-booth' pictures. She went through them all, studying each one, not saying a word.
Charlie felt a little uncomfortable with the silence. The only sound was the ticking of a clock from the hallway. Once she'd looked at all of the pictures, she wiped away a tear or two then put the photos in a neat pile next to the other bits.
She then opened the final envelope. She pulled out the contents. She unfolded a sheet of A4 and, what looked like a cheque, fluttered to the floor by her feet. When she picked it up and looked at it, she gasped. She then proceeded to read the hand-written message on the sheet.
More silence. Charlie looked around the room. Dotted around, on the walls, on the tables and on the sideboard were many family photos. He noticed, what was probably one of the last ones taken of Derek. Derek didn't look great in it but he was smiling and holding a glass of wine. Derek looked pale, he was bald on top and had some, thinning hair around the 'back and sides' of his head.
Charlie scanned the room. He saw pictures of Elaine from various stages of her life. A baby photo. A primary school uniform one (Tyrrells) A teenage one, with her eighty's clothes and jet-black hair. (That was when she was with Charlie, he loved that photo) He then spotted her wedding photo. She looked fabulous. Really fabulous. Her hair piled up, immaculately made-up, tasteful and stylish wedding dress. Charlie didn't even look at 'the bloke' next to her, the groom.
He had to say something. He had to break the silence. "So, how's Elaine these days? How's she getting on? It would be great to see her again."

He could have kicked himself, or bitten off his own tongue.
Barbara was crying. She placed her hand over her nose and mouth and was sobbing -
"I'm sorry, I'm sorry!"
She put the letter down on top of all the other items. She stood and then, with a bowed head walked into the kitchen.
"You'll have to excuse me for a moment!" she sobbed. "I'm sorry!"
Charlie froze. He was never comfortable around people crying and this one, in particular, was really awkward. He tried to decide if he should go after her and try to comfort her or stay put and wait for her to calm down.
"Oh. Bloody hell, bloody hell! This is great. What the bloody hell do I do?"
He could hear Barbara, in the kitchen, moving about, sobbing.
He stood and found himself pacing up and then down the living room, indecisive and flustered. It was then that his eyes fell on the table next to the chair where Barbara had been sitting. The contents of her envelope were just there. He glanced at the door to the kitchen then back at the items. He was so curious. He had to look at them. He went over to the table, sat in the 'Barbara's' chair and picked up the items.
The first thing he looked at was the cheque. He obviously knew Dad's handwriting. It was made out to 'Mrs. B. Robson' and it was for five thousand pounds. The date was left blank.
"Christ! That's generous" He thought.
Next was the pile of photos. The first one he looked at was of Barbara and Elaine. It looked it was Elaine's first day at secondary school, she had her brand-new Boswells uniform on. Her and Barbara were outside in

the sunshine, stood in front of the front door.
"I was right" thought Charlie "I knew that was a new front door!"
Next photo was of Dad and Barbara sat on a bench together at the seaside somewhere.
Then, there was an 'official' school photo of Elaine from Tyrrells primary school.
The next one was of Barbara looking amazing in, what looked like, a ball-gown. He continued to go through the pictures, fully aware that he could be interrupted at any time.
He saw a photo of Elaine and Barbara on a foreign holiday, both looking tanned and happy.
There was a picture of Barbara, probably on the same foreign holiday, wearing a summer dress and holding a cocktail, sat on a balcony.
Charlie was puzzled.
"Why would Dad have these particular photos? They all seem to be of Barbara. Or of Elaine. Or of Elaine and Barbara. And…he's in one or two of them."
The next one puzzled him more. It was Dad and Barbara, with their arms round each other, stood in front of Dad's old car.
"Well, they were good family friends" thought Charlie, confused.
Then, he came to the 'photo-booth' strip. Four black and white pictures of Dad and Barbara, their heads pushed together, big smiles. The fourth picture, (at the bottom of the strip) shocked Charlie. They were kissing. They, were, kissing.
"They were good family friends" said Charlie, unconvincingly.
He put the pile of photos down slowly. He looked round at the kitchen door. He could still hear Barbara weeping.

He looked back. There were the items of jewellery on the table. He picked up the medallion. It was a Saint Christopher. A good quality one, too. He turned it over, perhaps to look for a hallmark and noticed the inscription. It read:

May we guide and protect our children.

Charlie thought for a moment

"Is that written on all Saint Christophers? Or is that a 'special' inscription?"

He picked up the watch. Again, it seemed a good quality item. He wondered. He turned it over. On the back, was another inscription:

This time-piece can never really measure the time that we had together.

"What the bloody hell does that mean? Why would Dad have that? Why would he want Barbara to have it? And…what's with those photos?"

He remembered the small shiny spoon. When he examined it, he noticed that the handle was shaped like a baby, wrapped in a shawl of some kind. He guessed that it must be a christening spoon. The sort of gift people used to give at christenings. On the back were the initials **ER**. "Well, I don't think that's meant to stand for 'Elizabeth Regina'! It's 'Elaine Robson'! ER! What the bloody hell is going on?"

All that was left was the letter. Charlie was actually scared. Almost too scared to proceed. But…he had to. Following yet another glance at the kitchen doorway, Charlie slid the letter out from under all the other bits and held it up.

Barbara,

I've instructed Charlie to give you this letter and some other items.

As you're now receiving them, I'm sure you must be aware that I'm no longer around.
Please don't be too sad. I had a wonderful time, I enjoyed my life and, apart from losing Katie, it was great fun.
I know it's been hard for you on your own so I hope that the enclosed cheque will help you. I know that you're a proud lady and would always refuse it (if I was there) but now you must accept it!!
The photos and the other bits always meant a lot to me. I've always treasured them (in a 'special' place, in my desk) I thought that it was only right and correct that you should have them now.
Those photos always brought back many happy memories of our time together (and our 'legacy') I know what we did was wrong and improper but it happened. It was special at the time, not cheap and tawdry. We made the right decision as we knew that we couldn't go on the way we were. I believe that we've behaved correctly and appropriately ever since.
I think that we have done well to keep everything that has happened a secret, as we had to do. It's comforting to know that something special will always be there as a result. Our legacy. I hope that will always give you comfort too.
Please remember me fondly and protect our gift.
Yours
Bryan.
Charlie was stunned. He was so confused.
"What the bloody hell was that all about?"
Maybe he had suspicions or theories but maybe he was in denial. He tried to re-read the letter but he couldn't focus on the actual sentences.
Certain words seemed to leap out of the page at him.

‘…wrong and improper…’ ‘…cheap and tawdry…’ ‘…legacy…’

“Bloody hell! Bloody hell!”

He smacked the palm of his hand against his forehead twice. He was desperate to commute the information. He wanted to understand it all.

“Oh, Charlie, I’m so sorry.”

He hadn’t realised that Barbara had come back into the living room behind him. For a split second, he wanted to hide the fact that he was holding the letter (her letter) like a child with their hand in the biscuit jar. He quickly realised that there was no point in hiding it. Barbara had seen him and, besides, he wasn’t ashamed of the fact that he’d read it. He needed information. He had questions.

He turned to face her.

“What the bloody hell is THIS all about?” he waved the letter. “And THIS!” he gestured over the table that the other items were on.

Barbara’s eyes were red and puffy. Her face was wet with tears.

“Charlie. I’m so sorry.”

“Don’t keep saying that!” he shouted “Just tell me – what the fuck is this all about?”

This was a stressful time. He would NEVER swear in front of a lady but he was frantic.

She apologised again.

“Stop saying that!” he was really shouting now “Tell me what this is all about!”

“Charlie, please. Please calm down…”

“I’ll bloody calm down when you give me some answers! What’s going on? What does this all mean?”

“Oh, Charlie. I never wanted you to find out like this. WE never wanted you to find out like this…”

“Find out what?” he yelled.

"Please Charlie, sit down. Please. I'm trying to talk to you. Please."
Charlie sat down slowly on 'Barbara's' chair. She sheepishly shuffled over to the sofa, still sniffing back tears.
Once she'd settled, she visibly was trying to compose herself.
"Charlie, no one ever wanted to hurt you or upset you. We kept things a secret to protect you. To protect everyone…"
"What are you talking about? Just come to the point!"
"Charlie, I don't know how to begin. I don't know how to say this. Years ago, before any of us had children, me and Derek were very good friends with Bryan and Katie. We used to hang out together, even go on trips together…"
"I know all that. I've always known that."
"I know, Charlie. Look, no one planned what happened, it just sort of happened. Early one summer, I'm sure you can work out roughly which one, it turned out, well, I sort of found out, through Bryan, I mean, he told me, err, that him and Katie were having problems. They hadn't fallen out or suchlike, they weren't splitting up or rowing or anything, it's just that they weren't that close, at that time. They were going through a rough patch, that's all. It was a couple of years after Don was born. They still loved each other but, it was just that…they weren't that close at the time. Look, Charlie, we didn't plan anything, we didn't mean for it to happen, it just sort of happened…"
Charlie knew what was coming. It was quite a shock. He knew his Dad was a bit of a ladies' man but he really didn't want to know details, especially when it involved a 'family friend'.

"Charlie, I'm so sorry you had to find out like this but…your Dad and I, well, we, you know, we had a thing for a bit…"
"You mean you had an affair. Why can't you just say it?"
"Oh, Charlie, that makes it sound all cheap and tacky. It really wasn't like that. We gave comfort to each other through a difficult time. We didn't want to wreck marriages or anything like that…"
"So, you had an affair, with my Dad, behind my Mum's back but you try to justify it by saying it 'wasn't tacky'? You 'Gave comfort'? Bloody hell."
"I'm sorry Charlie. I know this must be shock to you and, please believe me, I never wanted you to find out like this."
"I don't reckon you EVER wanted me to find out!"
"I'm sorry. I'm so sorry. We did all we could to keep it all a secret, even afterwards. Especially afterwards. You see, Charlie, that's not all of it. There's more. There's more that you should know."
"Oh Christ, more? We've really opened a can of worms now, haven't we?"
"Charlie, it was a strange time. You see, me and Derek were also having our problems. Our whole marriage was like that, on and off. We were in separate rooms at that time and not talking much. That happened from time to time. We always got over those problems, until the next one came along.
Anyway, during this time, Bryan and me were, you know, seeing each other and, this is so difficult to tell you, this is when, well, how can I say it. I fell pregnant."
Charlie was stunned for a second. He sat bolt upright. He was desperate to make sense of what she just said. He had to be sure about it.

"Fell pregnant? What are you saying?"
"I'm saying I fell pregnant; we didn't mean for it to happen; it was an accident."
"Yeah, that's what they all say. Hang on hang on. I'm trying to get my head round this. What are you actually saying?"
"Charlie, I'll just say it. I'll have to just say it. Bryan is Elaine's father!"
"WHAT? WHAT? Jesus! You're kidding me! What? Oh Christ! Are you sure? How can you be sure?"
"We're sure, Charlie, it's definite, one hundred per cent"
Charlie leapt up off the sofa. He was almost hysterical. Her words had hit him like a hammer. He was reeling. "Dad? Bloody hell! Elaine?" he was screaming inside his head.
Barbara looked genuinely afraid. Charlie was raging, shouting. He yelled
"I can't believe this. You're telling me…Fuck!"
"I'm so sorry Charlie. You should never have found out like this."
"Oh my god, all these years! I never knew. I definitely never knew! I can't believe it!"
"I'm sorry Charlie, it is true. That's not all of it. You have to hear it all…"
"I don't want to hear all the sordid details! I think you've said enough. Jesus, all this time…Elaine! Bloody hell, me and Elaine…this is terrible. How could you do this to me?"
"Charlie, please…"
"Just shut up! Stop talking! I can't stand it! Christ, I can't take it in! bloody hell"
He marched across the living room towards the hall. He caught a glimpse of the gallery of Elaine photos on the sideboard. He looked at her 'official' Tyrrells primary

school photo. Jet black hair.
"Was there a resemblance? Does she have Dad's jawline, like Don? Or am I imagining it?"
He leant on the sideboard on his palms, his arms rigid, checking out each photo, looking for something, he didn't know what, exactly.
He sprang into life, rushed down the hall and struggled to open the 'new' front door. He could hear Barbara coming behind him, pleading.
"Charlie, please. Don't go. We must talk about this. We must talk about all of it!"
He finally got the door open and was off down the garden path.
"Shut up! Shut up! I don't want to hear it! I've heard enough. Just leave me alone!"
This time, the garden gate was definitely loud as he slammed it behind him in a rage. As he quick-marched along the walkway towards his car, he could hear Barbara at the gate, pleading, crying.
"Charlie, we must talk about all this. Please Charlie!"
As he got to his car, he paused. He knew Barbara hadn't followed him. She couldn't chase him. He'd 'escaped' her words. He was too shocked. He couldn't take any more. He leant on the roof of his car, his head on his hands.
"Elaine? Oh Christ, all this time…Shit! You know what this means? I've been...with my own sister! Oh, bloody hell. Why didn't anyone tell me? Why didn't anyone stop me? Why didn't they keep us apart?"
He tried to analyse what she had said to him. He tried to get his head round it. It was too much of a shock. His mind was in a spin. Racing.
"No wonder they kept it a secret. Shit! What if Don found out? He couldn't have known. Don definitely would have said something. Something along the lines

of 'Ha-ha! You're shagging your own sister!' Oh Jesus, that's just it, I was! All this time. How could they keep it from me? What if me and Elaine had got proper loved-up and wanted to get married? To have kids? Bloody hell, I bet someone would have stopped it. Someone would have said something then"

There was too much going on in his head. There was too much to take in.

He finally climbed into his car and drove off. It was one of those drives that, when you get to your destination, you can't remember anything about the journey. You can't remember how you got there. He kept hearing Barbara's words in his head.

His destination, that he didn't remember the journey to, was their old family home in Bodmin Road. Bodmin Road was a long, curved road that cuts right through a large estate in Springfield. It was right in between the primary school - Tyrells and the secondary school – Boswells. The buildings in Bodmin Road varied from small blocks of flats to large, expensive, six-bedroom detached houses. The Mills family home was mid-range. It was a three-bed semi. Dad was a firefighter; he wasn't going to be able to afford one of the bigger places. It was a lovely house though, in really good condition. Dad always kept it immaculate. His attention to detail was such that the décor was perfect. Charlie found it reassuring that the 'new' owners maintained his Dad's standards. It was a house with many happy family memories (apart from when Don was acting like an arse, of course.)

Charlie sat in his car, staring ahead, still trying to come to terms with what he'd just heard. He started to put some pieces together in his head.

The watch, the Saint Christopher, both must have been 'secret' gifts that Barbara gave to his Dad. Sentimental

keepsakes to 'commemorate' what they had together. Not necessarily the 'sordid' affair but a child, their "gift", their 'legacy', Elaine, his sister.
The photos, they were obviously discreetly given to Dad by Barbara to give some sort of a record of their time together and of Elaine growing up.
He couldn't understand this. The families were good friends. WERE good friends. Surely Dad would have been able to witness Elaine's progress.
The trouble was, Charlie surmised, that they had to be careful to keep the secret from everyone, especially Elaine, so, yes, they HAD to be discreet.
This was too much information for Charlie to process. It was too much coming at him at once. The hangover certainly didn't help, nor did the raw emotions of the last week or so. He actually felt as though he was suffering from a form of shock!
He turned to look at their old home. He had loved it there. It was a great house in a lovely area. He had great childhood memories of that place. Were they now tarnished after what he'd just found out? Apart from the photos that he'd just seen, he just couldn't picture his Dad and Barbara together. Really together. He wondered if his Mum knew about any of this. He then recalled that Elaine was only a few months older than him. It all was so disturbing for him. It was all so confusing for him. He couldn't get himself to hate his Dad or to even be angry with him. He just knew that it would take time to get used to the situation, to fully understand what he'd been told and the implications. It was too much information, shocking information, to take in. He needed time.
As he headed back to Steve's he desperately tried to focus. He had to work out what he was going to do

next. He wanted to come to terms with Barbara's shock revelation and to know how to deal with it.
As he sat in his car outside Steve's house, he thought he'd worked out his next move. He decided that he did not want to stay in Chelmsford right now. Although there were things he needed to do, (sorting out Dad's affairs, mainly) "Dad's affairs" When he was to use those words, from now on, he almost let out an ironic laugh. "Affairs" Bloody hell.
He was going to head home, to Poole. As soon as possible. Was he running away? That's one of the things Don would often accuse him of, when Don was being particularly vindictive. 'Running away from responsibility' Don would say.
"Sod Don. Sod what anyone thinks. I need time to get my head round all this. Being here, with all these memories, nostalgia trips, old faces, stories and shock revelations is not helping me. It's not helping my mental state."
He left Steve a note, along with the spare key that he'd borrowed, on the kitchen table. He'd ring him later.
When he eventually got on the 'bastard' M25, he almost felt relieved. No more shocks. No more things that he didn't want to hear. Perhaps Don was right about running away from responsibility. He felt like he was burying his head in the sand or was behaving like a child, with it's hands over it's ears shouting "Can't hear you! Can't hear you!"

Chapter Nine Don

During the drive home, with all that had happened (Barbara's revelations, the funeral, the booze) Charlie was surprised that he kept thinking about Don.

What Don would make of it all. What Don would say. How Don would have a go at him, belittle him. Don had a way with words, he would always seem to find the words, the expression that would really hit home. His 'opinions' could really humiliate Charlie and make him feel so uncomfortable.

Charlie assumed that Don kept cropping up in his mind because he was 'running away' and Don would be straight on to that fact and have a go.

Looking back and trying to analyse his relationship with Don, Charlie had a theory.

When they were growing up, Don, being the older brother (by three years) was quite domineering, starting from when they were both very young. They had different personalities. Don being over-confident, cocky and quite self-opinionated. Charlie was quite shy, sensitive and self-conscious.

When they were both at Tyrrells Primary School, Don would, on occasions, be in trouble with his teachers and the Headmaster for being a bit of a bully whereas Charlie would be more likely to be bullied, by other pupils that is. Don would save his torture (physical and mental) for when they were at home.

This was Charlie's theory: -

He believed that because Don was so full of himself and often critical of him that he spent his childhood years (and most of his teens) consciously and sub-consciously, stressing about getting Don's 'approval'. He realises now (but not at the time) that he would worry about everything that he said or did in case Don would berate him for it. Charlie had lost count of the times, over the years, that Don had tutted and mumbled "Stupid idiot" after Charlie had done or said something. He was surprised that he wasn't a nervous wreck – perhaps he was!

A few childhood memories of Don flashed through his mind.

He remembered how, when they were much younger and Charlie had a friend round after school, Don would usually poke his nose in, tease them both and often demand a 'wrestle-fight' with Charlie so he could make him submit or hurt him so that he cried in front of his friend.

When they were young teenagers, they were both invited to a joint birthday party. (The party was for brothers, one from Don's year, one from Charlie's) Charlie recalled that he was going through the 'awkward, self-conscious' period that young teenagers have (His seemed to last for years!) At the party, there were older teenagers (Don's year) and Charlie found that intimidating. There were also girls! Charlie was very awkward around girls. During that Saturday afternoon, one of Charlie's friends produced an envelope of photos taken at sports day and on a school trip. His friend held up a photo of Charlie taken outside York Minster. He said -

"Look at this, Charlie, it's a good one of you!"

Don looked round then shouted across the room -

"Yes. It is a good one of him, it's a bit blurry so you can't see his spots"

Charlie wanted the ground to swallow him up. He went bright red, he felt as though everyone in the room was looking at him, laughing, judging him. Don just laughed out loud. Moments like that can have a lasting effect on a child growing up.

Charlie began reminiscing about both their childhoods and as to why they both 'turned-out' the way they did. Charlie recalls his own personality traits that he seemed acquire as a child and then as a teenager. Although he wasn't that confident, he seemed to want to be the class clown, taking hardly anything seriously, answering teachers back with 'witticisms'. This behaviour got him into trouble quite a bit and could have derailed his entire school process. Now he can look back and be objective, he assumed that, as he was sub-consciously vying for Don's approval, this feeling of inadequacy spilled over into all aspects of his life. He was also sub-consciously trying to get the approval of his classmates by getting laughs or showing-off and subsequently being disciplined by the school.

Now he can be totally honest with himself, he cannot recall ever going through the 'horrible teenager' phase. Apart from Don being there, he felt that his home life was pretty good. He remembers getting on well with his parents (although they had a tendency to embarrass him, as parents will invariably do) His Dad was a good laugh and got on well with his school friends and he felt that he was pretty close to his Mum.

Don, however, certainly was the stereotypical nasty teen. Charlie could remember Don and his parents having so many rows. He also remembered eavesdropping and hearing them talking about Don when Don wasn't there and hearing them getting upset. His Mum would occasionally cry due to the stress and the worry.

Charlie could think of many occasions when his parents and Don would have the standard parents/stroppy teenager exchange: -

Mum/Dad "So, where are you off to tonight, Don?"

Don "Out, just out."

Mum/Dad "Oh, right. Who are you out with?"
Don "People, just people. No one you'd know. Stop asking so many questions! Stop hassling me!"

As soon as Don started at Boswells secondary school, he seemed to get in with the wrong crowd. He went off the rails for a bit. Charlie recalls his Dad getting letters from the school, Dad going to the school to see the headmaster (with Don) and, on the odd occasion, Don would get in trouble with the Police.
Charlie remembered that the only time that he ever got into bother with the Police, was because of Don. Charlie was in the final year at Tyrrells primary school (Therefore Don was in his second year at Boswells) One of Charlie's mates had found a dis-used warehouse on the edge of an industrial estate. He'd sneaked around the back and found a wooden office door. He'd carefully removed the lower door panel so it could be put back in place (or appear to be in place) and crawled through. The inside seemed cavernous. It was empty apart from a few pallets scattered around and some battered office furniture. This lad told Charlie and a couple of others and they used to go there some evenings. It was like an exciting adventure to four ten-year-olds. They would just hang out in there; they would sit on the knackered furniture and talk. They even made a den from old pallets. All perfectly innocent (If you disregard the trespassing issue!) It all went wrong when Don got involved. Don and one of his mates had wandered over near the industrial estate to have a crafty smoke. Don spotted Charlie and his friends and decided to discreetly follow them. He rumbled their 'secret place'. Charlie could never figure out how Don and his mate squeezed through the 'door

panel' entrance but they did and they took great delight in surprising Charlie and his friends.
Charlie was shocked -
"What are you doing here?"
Don had an evil grin on his face -
"Well well. What have we here? I was wondering what you lot were up to. Is this your secret hiding place then? Is this where it all happens?"
Charlie felt a mixture of shock, embarrassment and anger - "Look, we just hang out here sometimes. It's nothing to do with you. Why can't you leave us alone?"
Don was in his element -
"We have just as much right to be here as you. Come on, let's have a look round"
As he began his exploring, Don casually pushed over the den made from pallets.
"Oh, bloody hell Don! What's the matter with you? Why can't you just leave it?"
Don just laughed. He picked up a lump of broken concrete and threw it at some windows that were high up, near the ceiling. The noise of the shattering glass echoed through the empty warehouse. Don liked it, so he did it again, then again, each time laughing raucously.
What none of them realised was, the warehouse next door, on that side was in use and the smashed windows (and lumps on concrete) were falling onto some cars parked there and, obviously, the owners were not amused.
Don and his mate wandered into the office area, looking to see if there was anything of value whilst Charlie looked at his friends with an apologetic shrug.
What none of them realised was though, the neighbouring workers had called the Police and they

soon arrived. They forced open the back door and came in shouting. They rounded up all the boys. Charlie remembers being very afraid (this was during an age when youngsters had a respect and fear of the Police) Not so much Don. Charlie recalls the defiant expression on Don's face and his reluctance to co-operate. The policemen took everyone's details and Charlie and his mates complied. Don later used this against Charlie, calling him a 'grass' or a 'copper's nark'. The youngsters were split into two Police cars and were driven to their respective homes. Charlie later realised that this was just a tactic to frighten them, they were never going to be prosecuted. It worked with Charlie. He was in the kitchen with both his parents and a Police Officer and whilst the Officer was telling Charlie's parents all about what had happened, Charlie burst into tears and was full of remorse. Don, however, remained defiant and unmoved, even during the rollicking they both got from their parents after.
Charlie was always amazed that Don never had a criminal record. He thought that it was quite ironic that Don ended up with a job in security where they would have thoroughly vetted him (and obviously found nothing. If only they knew…!)
Charlie fully accepted that he was no angel, he wasn't perfect but he never got up to anything like the dodgy things that Don did. Don pulled some strokes, got up to 'mischief' yet always seemed to get away with it. Not so funny when it sometimes resulted in both their parents going up the wall with worry or in tears after another row with him.
Don's first serious girlfriend caused their parents more heartache. When he announced that he was seeing Jackie Keelan, it raised a few eyebrows. Jackie had a reputation. She was well-known for 'putting it about',

usually with older, married men but there were also stories of her behaviour at a couple of parties, involving a few of the local lads. (That terrible nickname 'Town Bike' was often used to describe her!) Charlie had heard these stories and was more embarrassed than horrified. Their parents also got wind of her reputation but couldn't decide whether or not to interfere. Don however seemed to revel in it. He didn't seem to be bothered about her reputation, he liked the fact that everyone else knew that he was having regular sex (to a teenager like Don, that gave him a certain kudos) Obviously the relationship didn't last. Jackie dumped Don (without actually telling him) and was seen out with a slightly older lad who had come into some money. She liked his sports car and designer clothes. Don made out that he wasn't bothered but it was obvious that he was heart-broken. Charlie recalls that he offered him no sympathy because, by then, Charlie saw Don as a selfish individual with not too many redeeming features.

When Don met, and subsequently married Carol, to most people's relief, he seemed to mellow a bit, to conform, to stop being such an arse. To Charlie though, he could see that it definitely caused Don to change in many ways, he still found him to be obnoxious, rude and domineering.

At first, Carol seemed to be a really pleasant girl. She was always polite and friendly and she 'tamed' Don and 'kept him in check'. She changed when she inherited some money. It was, apparently, a tidy sum (Charlie never found out exactly how much, he thought that it would be better if he didn't, it might depress him) and it went to her head, she thought it made her somehow superior to everyone else.

Charlie had ‘come to terms’ with his relationship with Don. When Charlie moved away, became an adult (he matured mentally) he discovered how to handle Don. Obviously, the fact that they lived so far apart and hardly saw each other, helped but Charlie knew that Don could now longer dominate him or intimidate him. Charlie was quite prepared to stand up for himself (if he was totally honest, he actually quite enjoyed it)
With their Dad passing away, it meant that Charlie and Don had to be in contact, they had to liaise but it proved to Charlie how much he had grown. He was no longer going to be pushed around. He would not allow Don to take over or walk all over him.
Charlie almost felt guilty about the fact that he was glad that when all his Dad’s ‘affairs’ were dealt with, he really didn’t need to have anything to do with Don and Carol. ‘Almost’ felt guilty, but didn’t, he was just being honest with himself.

Chapter Ten Nottingham

Charlie thought, that once he'd got home and settled, he would be overcome with a feeling of relief. No chance. The Elaine situation wasn't going away just because he'd 'run off'. For a while though, it did seem a bit more 'surreal'. Whether that was because he was, somehow, coming to terms with the shock or the fact that he was away from Chelmsford, away from the people and the places involved, he wasn't sure.

He was back in his flat. He went back to work, he was glad of the distraction, any sort of distraction to, hopefully, take his mind off it. The problem was, it was always there, eating away at him.

He compared this with the shock he felt when he got that phone call, telling him that Dad had died. That also hit him like a bolt from the blue, (he can remember that night, vividly) but this was different. Obviously, he was devastated that his Dad had died and he was still mourning that loss. Barbara's news was different. He began to wonder if the problem was, that he was just being selfish. Was he so upset because of how it affected him? His Dad has just died and all he seemed to be really stressed about, was something that happened fifty years ago. That theory didn't help. Of course, it was a big deal. His Dad having an affair, having a child as a result, a child that grew into a girl that he was in a relationship with. He desperately tried to blot it out but there no getting away from it – he had sex with his own sister! Not knowingly but he still did. What would happen if this information got out? Could he be locked up for the incestuous relationship? How would this information ever get out? Barbara wouldn't say anything (she's kept the secret for fifty years) and he certainly was not going to ever mention it to anyone!

What about Elaine? Does she know? Surely not. Or does she? Can she keep the secret? If she knew, there's no way she'd ever want it to get out – she had sex with her brother.

Charlie was tormenting himself. This was torture. What was he supposed to do with this information? That is a good point. What WAS he supposed to do with this information? It's not as if he was going to keep bumping into Barbara or Elaine. The secret was pretty safe (as far as he knew) He just had to man-up, deal with his mental issues, stop feeling sorry for himself and move on with his life. There, that's it sorted. Simple as that.

Yeah, right.

Charlie accepted that that knowledge was always going to be there. He was determined, however, that he must not let it screw him up and ruin his life.

He knew that eventually he was going to have to go back to Chelmsford. He still had his Dad's affairs to sort out. ('Affairs' ha-ha!) There was the flat, the Cortina, the writing desk… the envelopes… The envelopes! He still had two more envelopes to deal with. He resigned himself that once he'd opened the next envelope, or the one after, he'd be bound to have to go back to Chelmsford (much sooner than he wanted to) However, he had no choice. He had to deal with the envelopes. The news of Dad's affair should have no bearing on that. But what if they revealed another affair? Or something even more shocking? That's all just speculation. The envelopes, and the instructions within, should be dealt with. He owed that to his Dad.

Charlie pulled his suitcase from off the top of his wardrobe. There inside, as he knew they would be, were the fifth and sixth envelopes.

He replaced number six and took number five over to his bed where he sat down, full of expectation.

Envelope Five.

He tore it open and shook the contents out, onto his quilt.

The contents: -

The usual A4 sheet with a message from his Dad and the 'instructions'

A cheque (made payable to Mr C. Mills) for £150

A smaller envelope addressed to "Paul Chaplin, Red Watch, West Bridgford Fire Station, Nottingham".

Charlie unfolded the A4 sheet, it was, as expected, a letter from his Dad with some instructions.

Paul Chaplin, Nottingham.

Charlie,

Please carry out this request, it's important to me. I'd like you to go to Nottingham, to West Bridgford Fire Station (There's a few Fire Stations in the area but I'm sure you'll find the right one!)

The enclosed cheque will, hopefully, cover the trip. I want you to get in contact with a Fireman there: Paul Chaplin. He used to be in Essex, he transferred up there a while back. I want you to give him the enclosed letter, personally. I can't really say any more as it's quite a sensitive matter. He may talk to you about it, he may not. If he does, please be a good listener (I'm sure you will be, as well as being sensitive and sympathetic)

If he doesn't, please don't be offended, it's quite a delicate business. He may not want to talk to you (or anyone else) about it. You'll just have to let it go. My letter to him is important to me.

Sorry, I don't have his home address, I lost contact with him when he moved up there. I'm pretty sure he's on Red Watch, West Bridgford Fire Station.

Be nice to him, Charlie, he's been through a lot. I know I can count on you.
Regards,
Bryan.

Charlie read the instructions a couple of times. He couldn't help but be intrigued as to why this man was so 'troubled'. He knew, however, he had to respect his Dad's wishes and he had to respect this Chaplin bloke's response.
He began to prepare for his trip. He was shocked to discover that the train journey from Poole to Nottingham was going to take around six hours!
"Not a day trip, then!"
Charlie decided to make a long weekend of it. He arranged leave for the Friday and the Monday and booked himself a room in a Travelodge in Nottingham. The cost of the train ticket shocked him but he had no choice.
He believed that this long weekend would be a good way to attempt to blot out Barbara's revelations, well, he could try. At least he was getting away, a change of scenery and all that.
He'd always understood that Nottingham was a nice place. He googled 'West Bridgford and one post called it "…the posh part of Nottingham…"!
He had an early start on that Friday. The train journey was, as he'd feared, long and tiresome. It actually felt like six hours (it was!) Charlie passed the time with a combination of reading, looking out at the countryside whizzing by and dozing. He was irritated because, every now and then, he found himself going through his conversation with Barbara. He found himself analysing and over-analysing all her words. He was so hoping that he would stop doing this.

His train pulled into Nottingham Station just after midday and it was a shortish taxi journey to the Travelodge.
Once in his room, he threw his bag onto the end of the bed and wandered over to peep in the bathroom. He always did this at hotels; first thing, check out the bathroom.
"Doesn't everyone do that? Is it clean? How modern are the fixtures? Does it look like it's got a good shower?"
He came out and fell back onto the bed.
"Not bad. Quite comfy"
He tried to relax; it had been a longish journey. Straight away, however, he felt restless.
"What am I doing? Wasting time like this. I'm here for a reason, I have a purpose"
Charlie leapt up, grabbed his jacket, made sure he had the 'Paul Chaplin' letter and marched out.
West Bridgford Fire Station was another short taxi ride away. When Charlie arrived, he stood at the front of the building.
"Is it me, or do all Fire Stations look the same? I know they all have a tower out the back and they have those bays where the fire engines park, but the actual buildings all seem to look similar"
Just at that moment, Charlie had a flashback to that night he returned to Chelmsford Fire Station for that COFFs meeting. However, this time, he didn't seem to have any nerves.
He approached the door marked 'Visitors' and pressed the doorbell.
There was no noticeable sound.
"Is it working? Do I press it again? What if it's ringing inside and I can't hear it? Will it annoy them in there if I keep ringing?"

Whilst he was contemplating this, he noticed, through the glass, a figure coming through the inner door who then open the outer door.
What greeted Charlie, was a tall muscular man, with a shaven head and tanned face, sporting a goatee beard. His Fire brigade T shirt was soaked in sweat and Charlie noticed beads of sweat all over his head, trickling down.
"Yes, Sir, can I help you?"
"Err, hello. Sorry to bother you. Could you tell me if a Paul Chaplin is on duty? I believe he's on Red Watch"
The big man thought for a moment –
"Paul? Erm, sorry, he's not on at the moment. Red Watch… err, oh yes, they're on tomorrow at nine. It's the start of their tour"
Charlie was hastily re-arranging his plans in his mind –
"Oh, right. What do you think would be a good time to come back?"
"Well, probably between nine-thirty and ten. Around then. It will give them a chance to complete all their checks and that"
Charlie smiled –
"Great. Thanks for your help"
"No problem. Oh, by the way, sir, I must apologise for my appearance. I've just been in the gym"
"Okay, ha-ha! I thought as much. I hope it was worth it!"
"Oh, I don't know. I might be getting too old for this gym lark!"
Charlie laughed. That firefighter seemed to be in pretty good shape to him.
He again thanked the man who went back inside.
Charlie ambled back to the pavement at the front of the Fire Station. He had the rest of the day to himself. He decided to have a wander and explore. Earlier on, he

had made a mental note of which directions things were, in relation to the Travelodge and the Fire Station so he roughly knew which way to head off.
He enjoyed his walk. He passed through mainly residential areas, through suburbia until he realised that he was on the edge of the city. He eventually noticed, above all the rooftops ahead, some floodlights. As he got nearer, he realised where he was; this was Trent Bridge Cricket ground. He was quite pleased with himself that he'd stumbled across this famous test match venue. He walked around the perimeter and as he came round the other side, he noticed the stands of another stadium. He knew, straight away that it was The City Ground, home of Nottingham Forest Football Club. As he wandered past the main stand, he thought about the history there and he pictured Brian Clough and two European Cups. He came to the banks of the River Trent. He remembered his geography lessons at school; 'The Trent is the third longest river in the UK.' He looked up and down the river. He then spotted another football ground.
"That must be Notts County's ground, Meadow Lane. Blimey, they're close. Just across the river from each other. That's three stadiums so close together"
He was feeling surprisingly chilled. He was enjoying being somewhere different, away from the usual.
He had a meal and a couple of pints in the, aptly named, Test Match Pub; a lovely old-fashioned pub (which Charlie liked) with loads of cricket memorabilia on the walls.
He headed back to the Travelodge feeling quite relaxed.
The next morning, after a good night's sleep, a hot shower, (his bathroom inspection was accurate; the shower was efficient) and a hearty breakfast, another short taxi ride brought him back to that Fire Station.

He rang that doorbell on the ‘Visitors’ door and waited. A firefighter opened up the doors to greet him.
Charlie cleared his throat -
“Hello, good morning. I wondered if I could speak to a Paul Chaplin, please”
The firefighter half-smiled –
“That’s me. I was told, or fore-warned, that I’d be getting a visitor this morning. Can I help you?”
Charlie reached out to shake his hand -
“I’m Charlie Mills. I feel I should explain why I’m here”
The Firefighter looked troubled. In fact, he looked that way the whole time Charlie was with him. He seemed to have a permanent frown and he had bags under his eyes. His grey hair was receding somewhat and he had a pigeon chest that was covered by a, somewhat ill-fitting, Fire Brigade T shirt...
“I’m the son of Bryan Mills. I believe you knew him in Essex. He’s asked me to come and see you”
It took a moment for Paul to register what Charlie had said. Charlie noticed the ‘penny-dropping’ moment.
“Oh, please, come in”
Charlie followed him through the two sets of doors into the building.
“Are all Fire Stations the same?”
The walls of the foyer were covered in old Fire Brigade photographs, some looked very old. There were also cabinets containing polished brass stand-pipes and nozzles next to fire helmets from the ages. Charlie’s memory told him that Chelmsford’s foyer was similar to this.
Paul led Charlie to an area by the foot of some stairs. There were a couple of leather-look ‘comfy’ chairs next to a low table.
Paul indicated to them –

"Please Charlie, sit down"
They both sat on the low chairs and shuffled to get comfortable.
"So, Charlie, I'll admit to being quite surprised at you visiting like this. It's very unexpected. You are correct; I knew Bryan when I was in Essex. That seems like ages ago. He must be retired by now. How's he getting on?"
Charlie gulped –
"Paul, I'm really sorry to tell you this but Dad passed away recently"
Paul's face dropped.
"What? Oh no! Charlie, it's me who should be sorry. That's shocking. I'm so sorry for your loss. Bryan was a cracking bloke"
"Thank you, Paul. That's what everyone seems to be saying to me"
"I bet they do. Wow. That's so sad. Please Charlie, I'm slightly confused. Have you come all the way up from Essex to tell me that sad news?"
Charlie smiled –
"Err…Poole in Dorset, actually"
Paul looked shocked –
"What?"
"Paul, if I could explain; Part of Dad's Will was: He left me a pile of numbered envelopes. Each of them containing instructions and details of people or organisations he wanted me to visit or contact. The latest one has your name and details in it"
Paul frowned, (more than usual) his shoulders seemed to slump –
"Oh, I suppose you know all about me and why Bryan was involved"
"No, not at all. He said in his instructions that it was a somewhat sensitive matter, that's all. He said I was to

understand if you didn't want to talk about it. He left this; I was to hand it to you personally"
He held out the envelope to Paul.
Paul nodded slowly, a troubled look on his face. He reached out and gently took it. For a moment, he stared at his name on the front before calmly and slowly tearing it open. He unfolded the A4 sheet.
Charlie felt slightly uncomfortable, almost intrusive. He started to feel the same way he felt when Barbara opened her letter and read it. This reading also became emotional, just like Barbara's.
Paul hadn't read much when Charlie noticed that his eyes were welling-up.
"Oh, Bryan! You didn't have to say that. There's no need. You did the best you could. None of it was down to you or your fault..."
Charlie felt even more awkward.
Suddenly, Paul put the letter down on his lap. He looked up, his eyes were darting around that reception area. He quickly stood bolt upright.
"Charlie, can you give me a minute? Please excuse me, I'll be right back"
Paul turned and briskly walked through some double doors, still clutching his letter.
Charlie shuffled in his seat. He wondered what was happening. He was concerned that Paul was clearly upset. A couple of minutes went by then Paul came back through the double doors.
"I'm so sorry, Charlie. Please, follow me. I've spoken to my guvnor and he said we can use his office"
Charlie followed Paul along a short corridor until he was ushered through a big heavy door into a small office.
Paul gestured to a chair –

“Please sit down, Charlie. I’m sorry about this. I think we need some privacy, it’s too exposed and public out there. Look, Charlie, your Dad was correct, this is a sensitive matter. Well, it is to me. I feel I should explain…”

Charlie interrupted –

“Please, Paul, you don’t have to. You’re not obliged to. If it is that delicate, it’s okay. It was between you and my Dad, I completely understand…”

It’s okay, Charlie, you’ve come all this way, I think you deserve an explanation. Besides, you’re Bryan’s boy. Bryan was so good to me, I feel that you should know, especially as we’ve lost Bryan”

Paul sat back in his chair, deep in thought, he then leant forward to face Charlie –

“You have to understand a couple of things; I haven’t spoken about this to anyone for…well…years. It might not seem a big deal to you, I don’t know. It was to me…and a few others. You also have to understand that I’m very religious. I come from a very religious family. I suppose, with my surname, it had to be… You know, Chaplin?”

Charlie smiled and nodded –

“Which branch of religion are you and your family?”

“Err…I’d rather not say. I don’t want your opinion of me and what I’m about to tell you to be influenced or prejudiced by your view of my faith”

Charlie felt a bit put out –

“Whoa! Paul, I promise you, I’m not like that. I wouldn’t judge in any way. But, it’s okay, everyone’s faith and religion are their business. That’s fine”

“Sorry Charlie, I meant no offence. I hope you understand how this matter affected me”

He paused, staring at the wall behind Charlie then leant forward and looked Charlie straight in the eye.

"Now, where do I begin? The beginning, I suppose. I was at Training School, Fire Brigade training School, years ago. You have to understand what it was like back then. It was almost like the military. We had twenty or so weeks of really strict discipline; it was double everywhere, you know, run don't walk. It was: - come to attention, yes Sir, no Sir. We had to follow the orders given by the training officers, without question. If you hesitated, had an attitude, questioned anything, they could have you. If they didn't like you, they could have you. When I say 'they could have you', I mean they could virtually sack you on the spot. You'd be out, no Fire Brigade, no job, no comeback. It became instinctive to do exactly as you were told"
Charlie nodded –
"Yeah, Dad told me what it was like. Like joining the army"
Paul leant even further forward –
"Yes, but I'll bet, in your Dad's day, the training officers were decent, experienced firefighters who wanted to give something back. When I was there, they were relatively inexperienced. Some of them were almost certainly using the position to get on the promotion ladder as well as it being an ego thing; they got to shout at, and order about, twenty-odd blokes. Anyway, there was one particular training officer; Warren. Some, in the brigade, knew him as 'Bunny' Warren. Later, there were loads of lads who just called him Warren, they refused to use the 'Bunny' part. If you used his nickname, it sort-of implied he was a good bloke or a mate. Well, Warren certainly was not either. All through our twenty-odd weeks at training School, Warren was the strictest, in fact, he was really a bully. He seemed to enjoy shouting blokes down, he relished

humiliating them. He always acted the tough guy, boasting how hard he was. He loved being intimidating. A few days before we were due to leave Training School, we had a PT session. We had all had our showers and were in various stages of getting dressed. There were twenty-one of us left in our training squad. Anyway, all of a sudden, the locker room door flew open and there stood Warren. Normal procedure – the first recruit to see a training officer enter would shout 'Stand up!' Everyone stood to attention by their lockers. Warren was different this time; he had a weird look on his face. He strutted into the locker room and shouted

"Right! It's time for your short-arm inspection!"

We were confused, no one knew what that was. Warren stood at one end of the room and yelled

"Everyone! Drop your trousers and underwear…NOW!"

You have to understand, Charlie, we'd had twenty-odd weeks of blindly following orders, instantly, without question. It became like, automatic. We had to do it; we had no choice. everyone complied. I'm well aware, if any officer tried that at a Fire Station now, he'd be told to eff-off. But, we were recruits, desperate not to be sacked. Warren moved forwards. It was then we noticed what he'd been hiding behind his back; it was a feather duster, on the end of a stick, roughly two feet long. I can't believe what he did next… he went round to each of the twenty-one recruits, individually… he took his feather duster and he… prodded, lifted, tapped and poked everyone's…err…erm…genitalia. He made comments. Comments like:

"Don't tell me your missus is satisfied with that?"

"Yours looks like a whelk"

"I can't even see yours, are you sure you're not a girl?"

And such like; really, anything derogatory that he could think of. It was horrible. All the time, he had this look on his face; all wide-eyed and a madman's grin. It was awful, so embarrassing, humiliating, degrading. I honestly cannot remember what he said to me. I was mortified, crushed. I just wanted the whole thing to be over.it was probably more traumatic for me because of my faith"

Charlie felt so embarrassed, he felt so sorry for Chaplin. He'd noticed that he never swore (presumably because he was a religious man) and that this was so difficult for him to talk about.

Chaplin's hands were shaking as he wiped tears from his cheeks. He was obviously distressed.

"Paul, it's okay, you don't have to go on, you don't need to…"

"No Charlie, I should. I shouldn't bottle things up, I feel I should talk to you, I feel I should tell you"

Charlie didn't know what to say, he fell silent. Paul sniffed and tried to pull himself together –

"The bloke next to me, Hawkins, he was an ex-Para, he just shrugged it off. But, the others around me were really put out, they knew that Warren's actions were, at the very least, out of order and probably even, well, you know…

Eventually, he'd finished interfering with all twenty-one of us, he laughed and sauntered out, slamming the door behind him. Everyone just stood, frozen, not knowing what to do or how to react. I think it was Hawkins, he just muttered a swear word and got dressed. We all, sort of, awkwardly did the same. Someone, over the other side of the locker room tried to break the tension, the awkward silence. He said –

"I think we've just been part of Warren's homo-erotic fantasy!"

There was some nervous, fake laughter then everyone just carried on.
Charlie was stunned –
"Bloody hell, Paul! That was so out of order. Not only was that clearly an abuse of authority; a training officer taking advantage of recruits, that also has to constitute sexual assault"
Paul had that ever-troubled look on his face –
"I know. Those were virtually the same words that were used. But, not until YEARS later. Anyway, during the last few days at Training School, it was barely mentioned. I think everyone was shocked. We just wanted to get away from Training School, away from Warren and go to our postings, to our Fire Stations"
"Wow. So, Paul, you said something about years later…"
"Yes, we all went to our respective Fire Stations to begin our careers. I was quite happy with my posting, got on well with the lads and did my best to be a good firefighter. Anyway, we heard about Warren's career path; He got his promotion, as he'd planned, at Training School and went to a station as an officer. The story was, he had got a taste for promotion and power. So, in order to get on, he wangled an office job at Fire Brigade Head Quarters, threw in his Union membership and boot-licked and brown-nosed. We had three or four disputes and he worked through the strikes, you know, scabbed. And management like snaky scabs like that. They soon worked-out how they could best utilise a nasty piece of work like Warren. As well as his clerical position at HQ, they appointed him to a made-up role of Discipline Enforcer. Basically, if there's been any hassle or trouble at a Fire Station, Warren and his sidekicks would go there to investigate and intimidate"

Charlie noticed that Paul had calmed down a bit and obviously wanted to tell him the whole story.
"However, one day, this, sort of, rebounded on him. He'd been sent to a Fire Station where management had got word of some horseplay that, they believed, had got out of hand. Anyway, Warren was standing in front of the relevant watch doing his best 'management hard-man' act. He was shouting at them, saying that they were 'professional firefighters' and should 'behave as such' and 'respect each other'. Remember Hawkins? The ex-Para who was in that locker room with me? He was on that watch. He'd had enough of Warren's nonsense, so he asked him-
"Remember what YOU did to twenty-odd recruits at Training School with your feather duster? Was that professional behaviour? Was that respectful?"
At first, believe it or not, Warren denied it, it was only when everyone laughed at him and backed-up Hawkins, that he realised he'd been rumbled. Apparently, he had a look if horror on his face. The story goes, he 'tactfully' withdrew, fled that Fire Station and went straight back to Head Quarters. He then requested a meeting with the senior management. He confessed everything to them but, his defence was, a claim that worse things happen at Fire Stations (a highly doubtful accusation) Now, you think about it, if he'd been an ordinary firefighter, a Union member, a 'nobody' who went to management and confessed to sexually assaulting forty-odd recruits at Training School, yes, forty! We discovered that he did the same to the squad that came after ours! If he'd confessed to that, well, he'd be sacked on the spot! Or at the very least, suspended, investigated, charged and sacked. Not Warren. He was one of theirs; a scab, a boot-licking brown-nose and all that. Guess what? He was put on

'gardening leave'. Basically meaning; he was allowed to hide away at home, do nothing, have no investigation and to still receive full pay. Unbelievable. The Union got wind of all this and sent a delegation to meet with senior management to discuss his offence and ask them what they were going to do about it. They were just fobbed-off and nothing happened. Soon after, we can only assume thanks to a whistle-blower, the police got involved. It was a surreal time. They sent detectives to the homes of all the recruits that were assaulted. Apparently, some didn't want to get involved but there were a few who gave statements"

Charlie found all this compelling –

"Paul, I'm guessing they came to you?"

"They did. The detective was actually a really nice guy. He was sympathetic and understanding. As you've probably noticed, I find the incident so difficult to talk about…"

His voice was cracking.

"…however, my faith compels me to always tell the truth so, all I did, was to give my honest account of the events, no matter how embarrassing, humiliating or degrading the facts were"

"So, what did the police do?"

"Well, it got passed on to the CPS; the Crown Prosecution Service, and they decided to prosecute Warren. I'm told, if the CPS believe that they have a seventy percent chance of a successful prosecution, they'll go ahead. The Police came to me and added my name to a list of several lads who would be prepared to testify in court. The Union decided to support all those involved, they wanted to support those who were going to court and they were worried about a possible backlash from management, you know, 'cos we dared to stand up to one of their own. That's when I met

Bryan; your Dad. He was assigned to buddy-up with me. Lovely bloke. He often came to my house and to my Fire Station. He was always phoning, making sure I was alright. He seemed to understand, straight away, what a big deal it was for me to even talk about it, let alone to stand up in court and talk about it, in front of all those people. He was so supportive; I was very lucky to have him assigned to me"

"So, Paul, what happened to Warren in court?"

"Ha Ha! 'Warren in court'? Right. You won't believe it. We couldn't believe it. You couldn't make it up. About a week or ten days before the court date, we all got the phone call; the CPS decided not to pursue it, they dropped it"

Charlie was shocked –

"What? After all that? How come?"

"Well, we'll never know for sure. Some say the CPS had decided that it wasn't a good look for them to be prosecuting a serving firefighter, even someone as vile as Warren. Some lads reckon it was the old boy's network, you know, Freemasonry. Lots of top coppers are Masons as are a lot of the Fire Service management. Some say they 'came to an arrangement'. Whatever the reason, Warren was off the hook, he'd gotten away with it. There were stories going around that, up until the case was dropped, he was stressed, depressed almost suicidal. You have to ask yourself; why? Guilt over what he'd done? Or, the fact that he'd been rumbled? I know which one my money would be on! Don't get me wrong, my faith doesn't allow me to be vindictive or vengeful. However, we do believe in a person facing consequences for their actions. If someone commits a crime, they should be punished accordingly. No chance in this case. Bryan was so supportive, he helped me a lot. But, Warren getting off, after I've given a statement and agreed to appear in court was too much for me. I had a bit of a breakdown; I was off sick for a while. Bryan arranged for a lot of medical help and psychiatric help for me. Thing is, I knew I had to get away. He helped me, he pushed management and they eventually agreed to fast-track a transfer up here to Notts for me. I managed to get temporary accommodation until the house move finally came through"

"Wow. All of that must have awful for you. I hope the transfer and the move helped you. I have to ask; what happened to Warren?"

"Warren? Well, part of me didn't want to know, part of me did. Again, you wouldn't believe it, you really wouldn't. Management look after their own. So, despite the fact he'd ADMITTED to sexually assaulting forty-odd recruits, they allowed him to stay on 'gardening leave' for months and months. Then, get this, they arranged for him to retire, on his full pension. There was also a rumour that he even got a medically enhanced pension because he was so 'stressed'. I hope that's not true. Not bad for a bloke who should have been sacked and should have lost his pension and everything. I've no idea what he's doing now, I don't want to know, not interested. I imagine he's living the life of Riley, not a care in the world"

Charlie and Paul sat in silence for a short while. Charlie didn't know what to say. Paul broke the silence –

"Oh yes, this! Incredibly, Bryan has sent this letter, apologising, yes, apologising for what happened to me! And for not doing more for me! He's unbelievable. None of it was his fault, he did so much for me. I can't believe he'd apologise, what a guy! He really put himself out for me. Charlie, I'm sorry to have gone on a bit, all full of self-pity and that, it's just that I wanted you to know how good your Dad was to me and why he asked you to come here"

When Charlie left that Fire Station, he went for a stroll on his own, deep in thought. He felt so sorry for Chaplin and all he'd been through. He was angry that Warren had got off Scot-free after his abuse of authority and sexual assaults. Mainly, though, he felt so proud of his Dad. He'd known that his Dad took his Union duties seriously but obviously he often went above and beyond to help others, like Chaplin.
Paul Chaplin had walked Charlie to the front door and when he gave him a firm handshake, Charlie could see the tears in Paul's eyes. It was all very moving.
Charlie just hoped that Paul could find some happiness and contentment in a different environment, away from where he'd been traumatised.
During Charlie's stroll around Nottingham's suburbia, he realised that he now just wanted to go home to Poole. He came to the conclusion that there was no point in hanging around for the sake of it, even though he liked Nottingham and West Bridgford. He decided to cut short his weekend away and travel home on the Sunday, he knew that he had a six-hour train journey to mull over all that he'd discovered because of that particular envelope.
From the window in his train carriage, watching the countryside whizz by for six long hours, Charlie thought about Paul's torment and humiliation. He really felt for him. Charlie's mind inevitably drifted back to Barbara's revelation about Dad, her and Elaine. No matter what he did, those thoughts kept coming back to him.

These envelopes are throwing up some shocks for him. He had a weird feeling in his stomach when he reminded himself – there was only one envelope left.

Chapter Eleven Dublin

Charlie sort of understood his own mind. He knew that he was procrastinating, in a way. He did this sort of thing when he got right into a box-set and was enjoying it; whether it was a DVD box-set or one he was following on television. If he was really enjoying it, when he got towards the end, he consciously or sub-consciously put off the finish. There were occasions when he only had one episode left and he delayed watching it for a while. It was as though he didn't wish to face the inevitable, he didn't want it to end. Obviously, and inevitably, he had to face reality and watch it. It was as though he didn't like the finality, the conclusion, the fact that there were no more.

He was aware that that was what he doing as regards the envelope situation.

He knew he only had one left.

Despite the fact that some of the envelopes had been, perhaps, too revealing and sometimes shocking, he'd found them to be compelling.

He knew that it was inevitable. He had a duty to his Dad to complete his requests.

He actually put off even considering envelope number six for several days following his return from Nottingham. Once he'd pulled himself together mentally, he got the envelope down from that suitcase and felt surprisingly emotional as he held it.

It was the final one.

Envelope six.

Charlie opened it and found inside, the usual hand-written A4 sheet and three cheques (undated)

Michael Hunter – Dublin.

Charlie, I would like you to carry out this request. As I'm sure you'll realise, it is important to me.

Please contact an old friend of mine – Michael Hunter. The best way to contact him is via email. His email address is –
michael.hunter45@hotmail.roi.com
I would like you to arrange to meet Michael. This would mean for you to travel to Dublin. I enclose a cheque for you for £250 to cover your trip.
I would like you to communicate with Michael, he's an old family friend from my past.
Please give him the other two cheques that are made payable to my two favourite charities.
Thank you, Charlie.
Enjoy your trip!
Bryan.
"A trip to Ireland!" thought Charlie "Did not expect that! I know Dad was proud of his Irish heritage but I had no idea he'd want me to go there for him."
Charlie re-read the letter, to make sure he had got all the information. When he got to end though, he felt strange.
"This is the final envelope. Dad's final envelope. He's just signed-off with 'Enjoy your trip, Bryan' On his final set of instructions, that's how he signs off. That doesn't seem right. It seems a bit cold, or am I reading too much into that?"
He examined the three cheques. Sure enough, one was made payable to Mr. C. Mills (for £250) one was made payable to 'Focus Ireland' (for £1,000) and the other one was made payable to 'Respond' (also for £1,000)
Charlie knew that he had to see this through. It was his duty for his Dad and, after all, it was the final one (he still couldn't get over how his Dad signed-off though)
Later that day, he duly emailed Michael Hunter.
Dear Michael,
I'm sorry to message you out of the blue like this.

My name is Charlie Mills, I am the son of Bryan Mills.
He has requested that I contact you with a view to coming to Dublin to meet up.
He wanted me to communicate with you and he has given me a couple of cheques to donate to his favourite charities.
Hopefully, between us, we could sort out the arrangements.
Thank you.
Yours, Charlie.

As soon as he'd sent it, Charlie suddenly panicked, slightly.
"What if Michael doesn't know that Dad has died?"
He re-read his email.
"I have given no indication, in that message, that that has happened. How can I get round this? I can't just send him a supplementary email with 'by the way…' Also, I can't just meet up with him in Dublin and say something like 'Here, did you know…"
He needn't have worried. Later that evening, Michael replied.
Dear Charlie,
Thank you for the message.
The fact that I have received it, tells me that we've lost Bryan.
Charlie, I'm so sorry for your loss. Bryan was a wonderful man and has been a good friend to me ever since we were children. Even though he and his family moved to England in 1956, we always stayed in touch and we met up on the odd occasion.
It would be great to meet you, Charlie. Please let me know when you are coming and we'll sort things out.

Yours, Michael.

Charlie felt a bit relieved. Obviously, Dad had been in contact with Michael and told him of his illnesses.

"Wish he'd told me about how ill he was. Perhaps it wouldn't have been such a shock when he died!"

Charlie and Michael had a few 'back and forth' emails arranging the trip, dates etc. Charlie booked his flight so, just a few days later he was off to Dublin.

It was so handy for him that he could fly from Bournemouth Airport, just twelve miles away.

It was a late afternoon flight and Charlie spent most of the journey wondering what was in store for him. He tried desperately to blot out the Barbara/Elaine business and wanted to focus on Dad's Irish heritage. He'd always wanted to go to Dublin, he could remember his parents went on some trips to the North and South but he'd never been. He'd booked two nights in a small hotel near the city centre and was looking forward to a bit of sight-seeing as well as the 'envelope' business.

He arrived at Dublin Airport at six thirty pm.

He'd already told Michael about his arrival time and Michael had said that he wasn't going to be able to meet up until later in the evening. He left some specific instructions as to when and where.

Michael had arranged for a friend to pick up Charlie from the airport. He greeted Charlie with a cardboard sign at arrivals.

He was a short, chubby man with a jolly face, he was wearing a brown, checked suit, that had seen better days. He had 'cigarette' breath and Charlie noticed the nicotine stains on both his hands.

"Charlie? Pleasure to meet you. I'm Johnny, Johnny Murphy. My friends call me Murf. So, I'll let you call me that. Ha-ha! Listen, Michael's told me a few things about you. I'm really sorry to hear about your old man.

He was a bloody good bloke by all accounts."
He spoke so quickly, with a very strong Irish accent (obviously) Charlie had trouble understanding him, or keeping up with him.
Murf walked deceptively quickly, for a man with such short legs.
"You're in luck, Charlie. I'm actually a cabbie, that's my profession. So, I know where your hotel is, I can take you on the scenic route, without fleecing you! Don't worry, the meter's not running! Haha!"
Charlie instantly warmed to Murf. He was clearly quite a character and was very friendly and upbeat.
Murf was true to his word. Once they were in his Mondeo with it's taxi plates, he certainly took the 'scenic' route.
Charlie was almost overwhelmed with information, historical facts and figures. Murf was relentless with his knowledge of all the famous sites and landmarks around the city.
Murf showed him a beautiful cathedral (Charlie was sure that Murf said it was 'St. Patrick's') He took him past Trinity College (another lovely building) He paused at Dublin Castle but bombarded Charlie with so many facts and dates that he struggled to recall any of them afterwards.
"…King John…" "…seat of British rule…"
"…1922…" "…Big fire…". It was hard to take it all in.
Murf showed Charlie the entrance to the world-famous Guinness factory (Charlie had fully intended to go there during his stay.)
Murf was in full flow -
"When you finish the tour of the factory, at the top, they give you a free pint of the black stuff. I tell you something, Charlie-boy, that will be the best pint you'll

ever have. Straight from the factory, you'll notice how good it is!"
As Murf was driving alongside the river (The Liffey) he pointed across at a building -
"See that? Bono owns that hotel."
"Really?" said Charlie, "Does he live in the penthouse or anything?"
Murf laughed -
"Don't be daft, he doesn't live here. He's a tax exile"
Charlie was surprised.
"A tax exile? I thought people CAME to Ireland to be tax exiles not LEAVE it! Hang on, Bono is a multi-millionaire but he's a tax exile from his own country, a country that has favourable tax laws, because he wants to save a few more quid? Sorry, Euros"
Murf agreed
"I know. These people are so fookin' greedy, I mean, how much money do they want? How much money do they need? If Bono lived here, as a multi-millionaire and paid his proper amount of tax, he still be a multi-millionaire. Just one who pays a little bit more tax. And he could be content in the knowledge that his 'extra' tax could be making this a slightly better country. You know, better healthcare, better Police, Fire Brigade, roads and the like. I tell you something, Charlie-boy, it's the likes of you and me that should be dodging tax. We're struggling to get by and that could help us a bit. The irony is, the rich bastards, who could easily afford to pay their taxes, are the ones who hire clever accountants to help them avoid it! We can't do that! We can't afford the accountants and besides, our income tax is taken at source, we can't do a thing about it!"
"Even taxi drivers?" asked Charlie, half joking.
"Ah no" laughed Murf "Not taxi drivers, I'm self-employed so I have to sort out my own tax affairs. If

I'm a bit 'creative' with my book-keeping, let's put it this way, I don't think it will wreck Ireland's economy!"

As they drove further along, Murf pointed out 'The Spire of Dublin' a 120m high 'needle' of stainless steel.

"It's also known as 'The Monument of Light' because it lights up at night. However, the locals generally call it 'The Stiffy on the Liffey' ha-ha!"

As they drove along the Liffey, Charlie noticed a walkway, suspended just below the wall along the side of the river.

Murf explained -

"That is 'The Liffey Boardwalk'. It's a fine thing, a good idea. The only problem is, it only goes up one side. On a few occasions we'd had drunks rolling out of pubs or clubs, showing off, jumping over the wall onto the Boardwalk. Only to find that the daft bastards are on THIS side of the river where there IS no Boardwalk. The Fire Brigade, just up there, they've got a small motorboat and they come along a fish the silly buggers out!"

Charlie felt thoroughly entertained on his journey. Murf was a good laugh.

Murf shouted back -

"I'll show you one more place because we're nearly at your hotel."

He slowed down to a crawl outside a beautiful, grand-looking building.

"That, my friend is The Dublin Post Office. Scene of the famous 1916 Easter Uprising. Quite a historic place."

"I've heard of that" said Charlie "Dad must have told me about it. A big battle, wasn't it?"

"Yes, son. It did kick off. A hundred-odd years ago and people still talk about it. Some of the bullet-holes are still there."
When they finally crossed a bridge then pulled-up outside the hotel, Charlie was almost sad that the journey was over. He thought Murf was great.
"Thank you so much, Murf. I don't think I could have hired a better tour-guide anywhere! I really enjoyed that."
"You're welcome, son. I hope you enjoy your stay here. You'll like Michael, he's a good bloke. You're meeting tonight, aren't you?"
"Yes. He assured me that it's in walking distance, just over there." He pointed back across the bridge, into the city.
They said their goodbyes then Murf roared away, back across the bridge.
Charlie wheeled his suitcase into the hotel lobby to check-in.
He thought he didn't have too long to faff about. He dumped his case in his room, a quick shower, down to the hotel bar for a burger and chips "Not a typically Irish meal" but he was in a bit of hurry (So he thought)
He set off into the city to meet Michael but, as usual, he was ridiculously early. He had, in his pocket, a print off of the email Michael had sent. He had highlighted the important part.
…meet outside –
The Temple Bar Pub
47/48 Temple Bar
Dublin D02 N725
9.00PM
Once Charlie realised he was so early (what a shock) and that it would take him no time to get to The Temple

Bar, he decided to have a wander (not too far off as he mustn't be late!)
He found himself wandering along Grafton Street. He peeped in the windows of some of the pubs and they looked pretty lively. He stumbled across a statue outside a place called Bruxelles Pub. He remembered reading about it. The statue was one of Philip Lynott. Charlie was chuffed. He was a big fan of Thin Lizzy so he was well pleased to see this. He would have loved to have his photo taken with it but as usual, he didn't have the confidence to ask anyone. Daft really as most people there seemed so friendly and approachable.
He ensured that he was 'nice and early' to arrive at The Temple Bar. As he waited outside, he could hear music and laughter coming from within.
The Temple Bar Pub was an old-fashioned looking building on the corner of a junction. The window frames and wood panelling, all around the pub were bright red, it really stood out. He had read about it after Michael sent the instructions. It was renowned for it's signature dish of Oysters and Guinness. Inside there were a number of bars around a central courtyard and there was always live music going on in there. Although some locals may have thought it was a bit 'touristy' and a bit pricey, it was popular with Dubliners and tourists alike.
Charlie was just thinking that he could do with a pint, he was wondering if he had time for a quick one before meeting Michael. The bar looked so inviting and he was loving the sound of the music coming from within.
His thoughts were interrupted by a booming voice.
"I'm guessing you must be Charlie? Charlie Mills?"
Charlie turned and was greeted by a giant of a man. He guessed that he must be at least six feet four and probably seventeen/eighteen stone. He had a mop of red

hair and a full beard of a similar colour (with a lot of grey mixed in) He was wearing the full 'double denim', the jeans faded and worn, especially on his knees. The jacket was completely done up to his throat. On his huge feet, he was wearing black DMs. Charlie did think, however, that for a man who must have been in his early to mid-seventies, he seemed to carry-off that look.

"Yes, yes, I am. And you're Michael, Michael Hunter?"

"Indeed I am."

They shook hands and Charlie noticed that his own hand was engulfed by Michael's huge paw. Charlie felt his hand being effortlessly crushed by this Irish giant.

"Good to meet you, Charlie. Sorry I couldn't meet you earlier, at the airport and that. I hope Murf looked after you."

"That's okay, Michael. Yes, Murf was brilliant. Great bloke. He showed me some of the sights on the way in."

Michael laughed.

"Murf is a good lad. When he drives his cab, he loves taking tourists round the city. He knows his stuff and enjoys telling them about HIS city. You should see the tips he gets. They love his banter and his knowledge. Anyway, how are you Charlie? Are you okay? I'm sorry for your loss. I have to tell you that me and your Dad have been friends since childhood. Even though he and his family moved to England, we always stayed in touch. He and your Mum have come over a few times to visit me. They used to have family in the north too. Sorry, I'm talking too much. I tend to do that. Do you fancy a drink?"

"That would be great, I'd love one. How about in here?" He pointed at The Temple Bar.

"We could have a couple in here, if you like, Charlie. It's a bit noisy though. We should have a chat, at some stage."
Charlie realised that Michael was correct. They do need to be talking.
"Oh, sorry, Michael, we can go somewhere quieter, if you'd rather."
Michael laughed
"It's okay. If you've not been to Dublin before, you should experience a place like this. It has a great atmosphere, they serve a lovely pint of Guinness and the music's great, if you like that sort of thing."
"I love it." Said Charlie, enthusiastically "I really fancy a Guinness right now too!"
Michael ushered Charlie in. it was very busy inside, consequently it was hot. Charlie thought that they might have trouble getting served but the crowds seemed to make way for Michael's huge presence and the bar staff acknowledged him straight away. They got their pints and moved away from the bar to a (slightly) less crowded area.
In one corner of the room, there was a band playing. The band consisted of a guitarist, two fiddlers and a man playing just one drum with a double-ended drumstick. Charlie thought "This is not what some people would call 'diddly-diddly' music, this is quality. Top musicians." He loved it.
They had their two pints of Guinness whilst enjoying the band (It took Charlie a bit longer to get served than it did Michael.) They managed to shout some small talk to each other, over the noise of the band and the crowd. When they had both drunk-up, (obviously Charlie took longer than Michael) they nodded at each other and made their way out.

"I loved it in there" said Charlie, once outside "Great atmosphere and that band was brilliant!"
"I'm glad. You can't beat a bit of live music."
They walked slowly down the darkened street and Charlie was surprised how lively that area was.
Michael was very interested in Bryan's funeral and wake. He seemed pleased that there was a good turn-out for him (that expression again!)
Michael eventually led Charlie into a proper old-fashioned bar. It was dark inside. Charlie looked around. There was very basic wooden tables and chairs. Charlie thought that they wouldn't have looked out of place in someone's kitchen or maybe in a 'greasy spoon' café. He looked at the four or five blokes who were sat near the bar. They looked like, who Charlie would imagine to be, 'serious' drinkers. One bloke, at the far end of the bar was wearing a long coat and a cloth cap. Beside him, on a lead was a small terrier, waiting patiently. Two old boys were playing darts in another corner.
"Shall we sit here, Charlie? I'll get them in."
Michael pointed to a table next to the front window. Charlie liked that. He could 'people watch' out the window, as well as talk to Michael.
Michael returned with two pints of Guinness and loads more questions. He wanted to know all about Bryan's life in England. The house, the flat, what happened when his Mum was killed, everything. He told Charlie that, although Bryan had told him of these things, he wanted to hear Charlie's point of view. He said that he felt that Bryan had often 'played things down' or not told him everything so that he wouldn't worry. Charlie was as honest and as 'blunt' as he could be with his replies. He didn't want to 'sugar-coat' anything as he felt that Michael deserved the truth.

When Charlie got to his Mum's death, her funeral and how it devasted Dad for quite a while, Michael seemed genuinely moved, almost close to tears. Charlie desperately didn't want it to be all doom and gloom. Dad's life really wasn't like that. His Dad was a really funny man and was always having a laugh and a joke. He managed to move the conversation around to COFFs, the Fire Brigade, The Tulip and all the funny stories that he's heard from those people (the ones that he could remember) Michael was laughing, a couple of times he ROARED with laughter, so much so that most of the people in that bar looked over.
Charlie told Michael all about the envelopes and the instructions within. He told him that he felt that it was his duty to follow them all through. (He left out the part about Barbara's revelation though)
He felt himself get a bit emotional when he told Michael about how his Dad signed off the final set of instructions.
"I was a bit surprised and disappointed. It just said 'Enjoy your trip, Bryan'. They were his final words. I don't know what I should have expected. Something a bit more… I don't know. I just felt it was a bit cold and unfeeling."
"I'm sure he has his reasons, Charlie. I reckon it must be a bit difficult to know what to say in that case. Maybe he didn't know that that was to be his last one, I don't know. Thing is, he wasn't a poet or anything like that. Perhaps you were hoping for something too profound or quotable. It's hard to know what he should have said. Maybe we shouldn't read too much into it."
Charlie had to ask -
"Tell me, Michael. How did you know that it was me, outside The Temple Bar? I could have been just anyone."

"Well, Charlie" He looked Charlie up and down "You look so…English. You have that look about you."
Charlie felt a bit puzzled, he thought -
"Look English? What does he mean?"
Michael chuckled to himself. He had made up that part about 'looking English'. What he didn't say was that Charlie was the only bloke outside the bar at the time, looking lost and 'innocent'.
Charlie then asked -
"Do you think I look like my Dad at all?"
Michael stared for a moment then replied -
"No. If anything, you remind me of Katie, your Mother. I think you take after her."
"That's what most people say" said Charlie.
He felt so relaxed in Michael's company. He sensed that they were getting on really well and he felt that Michael quite liked him. His lack of confidence issue hadn't surfaced and he was, hopefully, being himself. Michael was clearly a warm and friendly bloke who genuinely cared for his Dad and subsequently was being so good to him.
As the evening wore on, the Guinness flowed and they really did get on like a house on fire. Charlie realised why his Dad had always kept in touch with this man. He genuinely was a lovely fella.
When it came time to 'call it a night', they were standing in the street, right near The Temple Bar. They shook hands, Charlie's hand was crushed. He tried to disguise the pain. He thought his Dad would be saying "Don't let on that you've been hurt!"
"Charlie, do you know what. I like you. I'd love you to meet my family. I'd love it if you'd come to my house tomorrow. You could meet my wife, Joan. My daughter Sandra has been back with us for a while since her

divorce. I'd love you to meet them. You could tell them all about your Dad. And yourself. What do you say?"
"Tell you what, Michael, I'd love that, that's really good of you. Thanks very much."
Charlie had originally hoped to be a tourist on the following day, see some sights. However, he wasn't disappointed in the slightest. Michael was a great bloke, a true friend to Dad and it would be good to go to his house and meet his family. He began thinking how strange it was that he seemed so confident and comfortable here. Normally, if someone, anyone, was to invite him round to 'meet the family', he'd be quite nervous and uncomfortable about it, sometimes he'd been known to make his excuses and not go. Here, however, he was very happy about it, actually looking forward to it.
"Can you write down the address? Do you have a pen and a bit of paper?"
"Charlie, we live on a big estate on the outskirts of the city" He pointed in one direction, thought for a moment then pointed in another direction.
"You'd never find us. Tell you what, I'll get Murf to pick you up from your hotel tomorrow morning, say at eleven? Would that be okay?"
"That's bloody good of you, Michael. Are you sure Murf would be okay with that?"
"Oh, he'll be fine. Besides, he owes me. So, I'll see you tomorrow, son."
The 'crushing' handshake that followed, turned into a big embrace. Charlie was engulfed. Michael squeezed and Charlie felt there was some genuine affection between them (or was it Guinness induced?)
As Charlie wandered back through the streets towards the bridge that led to his hotel, he took in the atmosphere.

"What a lovely place this is" he thought.
"Everyone seems to be out having a good time without that underlying sense of potential violence that you feel in some pubs at home. Having said that, I know that there are Irishmen who enjoy a good punch-up, same as anywhere I suppose. Anywhere where there's booze and women." He remembered his Dad telling him, when he was talking of his own Irish heritage, that there's always a fight at every Irish wedding or funeral!
That night, in the hotel, in his large bed, Charlie had quite a good night's sleep. He felt so relaxed here. He didn't seem to be suffering with his usual lack of confidence, his shyness, his insecurities. The 'Barbara' business was pushed to the back of his mind (sort of) and he was enjoying the genuine warmth and friendliness he'd experienced since he'd been in Dublin.

Chapter Twelve Michael's House.

The following morning, when Charlie woke (too early, as usual) he felt a bit of a hangover. Only a bit. Nothing like the post 'Tulip/wake' hangover that he'd had.
He was in luck. When he came down, he spotted on the hotel's breakfast menu 'Full Irish Breakfast'.
"I'll have some of that!"
It was a very good breakfast. Nothing like the same size as the one Steve had made him but there was plenty. The only difference (apart from the size of it) was that instead of black pudding, they serve up white pudding. He later discovered that white pudding was an oatmeal and breadcrumbs-based dish as opposed to the blood-based black pudding.
As he was early (as usual) he realised that he had time to nip out and get some gifts for Michael and his family. What could he get them? Obviously, he'd never met Michael's wife and daughter so he couldn't know what to get for them and, even though he'd met him, he was struggling to know what he could get for Michael too. Just up the road from his hotel was a supermarket of sorts. Whilst he was flitting round the aisles, he got a little panicky. What could he get them? He felt, eventually that he, sort of copped-out. He opted for a bottle of Irish whiskey for Michael and bunches of flowers for the ladies. "How original" he thought, his insecurities possibly rearing up again.
Sure enough, on the dot of eleven, Murf's Mondeo pulled-up at the front of the hotel. (Charlie had been stood there for ten minutes previously but didn't let on)
Murf leapt out
"Hello Charlie! How are you doing?"
He spied the flowers

"Oh, Charlie, you shouldn't have. We hardly know each other. Ha-ha!"
Charlie jumped in and again, as Murf drove through the city, he went into his unofficial tour guide act, pointing out places of interest and landmarks etc.
"That's the 'Molly Malone' statue. You know the song? #In Dublin's fair city, where the girls are so pretty…# You must know it! #Crying 'cockles and mussels, alive alive oh'#"
"That there is Croke Park. That's the stadium where we play our Gaelic games. There was a time when we played our rugby there, and we always used to stuff the English! Ha-ha!"
In no time they were heading out of the city into the suburbs. As they drove onto a sprawling estate, Charlie realised that Michael was right, he would never have found this on his own. He could have got a taxi but that would have been expensive, he imagined. Good old Murf.
They turned into a cul-de-sac and pulled over in front of, what looked like a former council house that had been bought and done-up. It had been 'done up' very well. Charlie later found out that this was the case.
"Thank you so much, Murf. Here, please take some Euros."
"Don't be daft. Happy to help out. Hope you have a good time. Michael and his ladies are good people."
They exchanged pleasantries and then then Murf did his usual roaring off in his Mondeo.
Charlie walked up the steep path to the front door and before he could knock, the door was flung open and there was Michael and his wife, both with big smiles.
"Hello Charlie! Won't you come in!" They both seemed to say in unison.

Michael was, once again, in his jeans and boots but now was wearing a dark blue shirt (buttoned right up)
"This is my better-half, Joan"
"Lovely to meet you, Charlie. Michael's told me a lot about you."
Joan was quite a tall, slim lady, Charlie guessed, aged late-sixties. She had light-brown hair and, what Charlie would call, a smiley face. She looked taller in the doorway because, Charlie assumed, she was wearing a long black skirt topped off with a beige cardigan.
Charlie moved forwards to shake hands but he was surprised when Joan came forward and hugged him and kissed his cheek.
"Everyone seems so friendly here" He thought.
"These are for you" He handed Joan one of the bouquets.
"Ooo! Thank you, Charlie, they're lovely. Who are those ones for?"
"These are for your daughter. Hey, Michael, I got this for you," He handed him the whiskey.
"As if we haven't got enough booze in this house! He'd be better off with the flowers!" joked Joan
"Thank you, Charlie. You didn't need to do that. I'm afraid Sandra's not here at the moment. She'll be back soon. Anyway, come in, come in."
They all went in. The hallway was brightly decorated with many colours leaping out. Charlie noticed a crucifix on the wall as well as a picture of The Pope. Not the current Pope but Pope John Paul II, the Polish one that died in 2005.
They showed Charlie into their living room. Again, a myriad of bright colours met him. None of the colours seemed to match, even the three-piece suite but it didn't seem to matter. It was cosy and homely.

Joan was straight in with the hospitality
"Would you like anything to eat, Charlie? Have you had any breakfast? Would you like me to do you some sandwiches?"
"Oh, no thank you. I had a big Full Irish at the hotel."
"Okay. Can I get you a nice cup of tea then?"
"That'll be great, thank you."
Joan soon came back in the room, carrying a tray. She served up tea for the three of them from a tea pot into China cups (with saucers) Charlie guessed that this tea set is only kept 'for best'. He felt honoured.
"So sorry about Bryan, Charlie. So sad. Brian and Katie came here and stayed with us a few times. They were lovely. We were very fond of them, both of them. So sad."
"Thank you. I know Dad was very proud of his Irish roots."
Joan asked about Bryan's funeral and wake and Charlie proceeded to tell her, fully aware that, to Michael, he was repeating himself. Michael didn't seem to mind, he sat there smiling and nodding.
Charlie threw in a couple of the famous amusing stories that everyone enjoyed and, once again, they went down well.
They chatted for a while and Charlie was enjoying their company, they were so friendly. They were always smiling or laughing.
Eventually Joan looked at her watch -
"I don't know what's happened to our Sandra. She's gone to the shops for some bits and she was getting some stuff for me for dinner. You will stop and have some dinner with us, won't you Charlie?"
"That's very kind of you. I'd love to"

Charlie then remembered his Dad's requests. He produced the two cheques from his pocket and told Michael and Joan about his Dad's wish.
Michael took the cheques.
"Oh yes. 'Focus Ireland' That's a very good charity. It's a charity that looks after the homeless in Ireland. They'll be glad of that. What was the other one? Respond. Oh yes, that is a charity that helps to build affordable homes for the not-so well-off. Another good charity. Your dad was a good man. I know he cared about these things. I can forward those cheques."
Joan then stood up.
"I'll make some sandwiches and stuff for us. I don't know where Sandra has got to. Will you give us a hand, Michael?"
They both went off into the kitchen and whilst they were 'preparing' stuff they put music on, loud, and were singing. Charlie laughed. He loved how happy they were.
Charlie then heard a knocking at the door. He waited. No movement from the kitchen, just plates rattling, music and singing. The door knocked again. Charlie thought that he'd better get it.
He wandered out, down the hall and opened the front door. There she stood, loaded down with shopping, he presumed it was Sandra. She was rummaging through her handbag.
"Sorry, I forgot my key again. This bloody…oh, hello!" She'd looked up and seen Charlie.
She was a very attractive woman. Late forties? Charlie noticed, straight away that she was wearing long black leather boots. She had on some 'unfeasibly' tight jeans and a black leather flying jacket. Her long strawberry-blonde hair wasn't a surprise when he thought of her parents' colouring. She was immaculately made-up.

"Hello. I'm Charlie. Sorry, your parents are busy in the kitchen."
"They've put the music on again, haven't they? Nice to meet you, I'm Sandra, the prodigal daughter."
Charlie helped her in with the shopping. She called him 'a gentleman'. She led him into the kitchen. Her parents were just about to come in with plates, loaded down with 'nibbles'.
Joan smiled
"Ah! You're home at last. You've met Charlie, I see. Did you like the flowers?"
"Flowers?" said a puzzled Sandra.
"Oh, hang on," said a slightly embarrassed Charlie.
He nipped in the living room a brought back the bouquet. He handed it to Sandra. He felt himself blush a little bit.
"Oh, thank you, Charlie. That's so good of you. What are you trying to do, seduce me?"
Now Charlie was blushing a lot.
"Sandra!" said Michael and Joan, in unison.
They all filed into the living room and Charlie couldn't believe how much food they kept carrying in from the kitchen.
"I got you a lager, Charlie. Hope that's okay." Said Michael, carrying two pint glasses in for them.
They all sat and ate and drank together. They were chatting about life in general. Charlie was interested in what life was like in Ireland compared to England. He noticed that Sandra was very 'forward'. She made one or two 'racy' comments and was a bit flirty (or was she a wind-up?) No one seemed to mind. Everyone was enjoying themselves. There was plenty of laughter.
After a while Michael stood up, he had a brain-wave.
He popped in the kitchen a came back with a large lemonade bottle.

"Ever tried this, Charlie?"
"Lemonade? Yes, once or twice." quipped Charlie, a little confused.
"No, you daft bugger. That's only the bottle. It's Potcheen. Ever tried it?"
Charlie had heard of that. He knew that it was Irish moonshine. He knew that it was made from fermented potatoes (and other ingredients) and was known to be LETHAL.
"No, I've never tried it. Is it right that it's deadly?"
"Well, it's got a bit of kick to it! I'll get you a glass."
When Charlie took a swig, he knew it was strong. He got an initial taste, that he could only describe as, like pepper. It did, as Michael said, have a kick to it!
They all had a glass and toasted each other. That, along with the lager, meant that a couple of them were getting a bit merry.
Charlie heard himself talking, what he thought was, drunken crap.
"My Dad was always so proud of his Irish roots, his heritage. Did you know about our middle names?"
"I know your Dad's middle names" replied Michael
"He was 'Bryan Michael Collins Mills', wasn't he?"
"He was."
"Charlie, do you know who Michael Collins was?"
"Err, I think so. He was a famous Irish rebel, wasn't he?"
"He was more than that, you know" said Michael.
"Oh God. Here we go!" said Sandra, as though she's heard it all before.
"He was a revolutionary" Michael continued "He fought against the English to try to free Ireland. He was involved in the Easter uprising and went to prison for it. A prisoner of war. When he came out, he was part of the government of the Irish Free State. He was only in

his early thirties when the bastards murdered him. Your Dad had those middle names, a bit ironic when it's fairly likely his surname 'Mills' probably came over from England sometime in the past! My Mum said I was named after Michael Collins too."
"Dad had told me a few things about that. You know my middle name is Oscar, after Oscar Wilde? I don't mind it now. The bloke was a genius with words, bloody clever bloke. Didn't like it when I was at school. When they got wind of it, all I got was #You're named after a poofter, you're named after a poofter#. Not very PC but kids can be cruel, can't they? Having said that, when they realised that my initials are C.O.M. they called me a commie. Kids, hey? Don, my brother, his middle name is Behan"
"Brendan Behan?" said Joan "He was my favourite poet, ever. He wrote some wonderful stuff. Beautiful words. Liked a drink though. Did you know he was in the IRA? I think a few people hold that against him."
"I don't blame you for not knowing too much about Irish history, Charlie" said Michael "I know it's not really taught in schools much in England. It's funny, isn't it? They tell English kids to learn about their nearest foreign nation and tell them it's France. The thing is, their nearest foreign nation is actually joined on to the UK, it's The Republic of Ireland! Perhaps the powers that be, in England, are a little bit embarrassed about their own history and behaviour over here."
"He's off!" said Sandra, like she'd heard it all before "You can tell he was a teacher, can't you?"
"Shit" Thought Charlie "All that time I spent with him last night and now today, I never once asked what he used to do. He must think I'm a right ignorant git."
"Really? You were a teacher? Where did you do that?"

"I worked at a local secondary school." continued Michael "It didn't pay that well but I loved it. Most of the kids were pretty good. Pretty receptive. The thing is, when I was at Uni in Dublin, I did my degree in British History, so, Ireland featured quite a lot. It was an eye opener, that's for sure. Don't get me wrong, Charlie, I'm not one of those blokes who hates the English for all they did in the past. There are a few people who are like that but thankfully not many. That's a bit sad, being like that. That's like hating all German people now for what the Nazis did seventy-odd years ago. What I don't like is, though, when history is denied or ignored. These things happened. They shouldn't be just forgotten, they should be talked about, learnt from. The trouble is, as they say, most history books are written by the victors so, for example, there seems to be a very distorted record of what the British did here and with their Empire."
"I know what you mean, Michael" Charlie joined in "I know there are some proper 'Little Englanders' who still think, or wish, that we still had an empire. They think that somehow that makes them superior to all foreigners. There are also some looney right-wingers who think all Irish people are IRA terrorists."
"You're not wrong, Charlie. I know some ignoramuses call us 'Thick Micks' or 'Bog-trotters'. Amazing when you think, that ninety-nine per cent of people in Ireland, north AND south are ordinary, decent human beings who hated the troubles, the violence. Decent people who are sick of this insane bigotry. In England, it's never taught in schools about how, in the past, the English came here and stole land and resources. They hardly mention the famine, the potato famine where so many died or suffered. They don't talk about the cruelty, the killings, Churchill sending over the Black

and Tans… I could go on. It's like I said, there were some horrible people, on both sides, but I'm not all knotted-up with bitterness now, I would just like the truth to be told, not denied."

"You've got a point" said Charlie "I know it was a bit difficult for my grandparents, my Dad's parents. My granddad was from the south and my gran was from the north. The problems THAT caused! Some of their family, from BOTH sides, virtually disowned them. The ignorance, the bigotry is quite shocking."

Michael leant forward.

"I'm glad your Dad told you about all that. You should know about your ancestors, so to speak. I'm sure you noticed that Bryan and Katie never brought you and your brother over here on their trips. They were desperate to protect you from the troubles. They'd visit here and they'd also go to the north, to Portadown, where your Mum's from and to where they met, Laurelvale. You must have noticed that you and your brother always stayed at an 'auntie's' or at friends whenever they came."

Charlie nodded. "My Dad's family were from Birr, weren't they?"

"That they were, Charlie. It's in County Offaly. If you look at a map of the Republic, it's pretty much right in the middle. I'm sure you've heard their story, haven't you? They moved to Laurelvale for work. County Armagh. There was a factory they worked at called Hoffmans. They made ball-bearings there. My father worked there too, that's how we all met. Me and Bryan were great friends as kids. Well, Hoffmans had a factory in England, in Chelmsford and Bryan's parents really wanted to move there but, obviously the war came and, eventually, went and they moved there in the fifties. Me and Bryan were, like, pen pals, we kept in touch all those years. Well, eventually, me and my family moved here to Dublin, mainly for work but also to get away from the onset of the troubles. And this is where we stayed. Your Dad's family had a beautiful house in Laurelvale, big place, I believe they rented it out when they moved to England. Probably not sure if they could make a go of it or not. Something to fall back on."

Charlie was loving this chat. Obviously, he was devastated to lose his Dad but ever since, he'd discovered so much about him, his past, his history. Most of it was fascinating, loads of it was really funny and, of course, there was that one almighty shock. There was no way he could ever get himself to confide in anyone, to reveal Barbara's dark secret. He really liked Michael and felt so relaxed with him but he could never even try to tell him about it or try to make him understand.

That afternoon, the lager (and the Potcheen) flowed. Charlie sort of knew that it would happen. His Irish friends 'coped' better with the alcohol than he did. He was 'merry' and beyond. They didn't look as though they were affected. Joan even disappeared into the kitchen to prepare dinner, Michael soon followed. Charlie felt a little awkward around Sandra (even with the alcohol in him) She seemed quite flirty and suggestive, or was it his imagination? Perhaps she meant nothing by it, it was just her way, or was she coming on to him? He quickly realised that this is how he always was with women. He could never read the 'signs' properly. He thought about the times that he'd got it wrong and really made a fool of himself.

"So, Charlie, are you courting at the moment?"

"Sorry? Am I what?"

"Courting. Are you involved with anyone at the moment?"
"Oh, no. Not at the moment. Had some bad luck with women lately."

"Well, that's a waste, Charlie. Good-looking fella like you. Someone should be enjoying all your… pleasures."
She looked him up and down as she said the word 'pleasures'. He felt himself blush.
She continued -
"None of us are getting any younger, are we? How long is it since you've been with anyone?"
Charlie was panicking. He thought -
"What does she mean 'been with'? Shit. What do I say? Don't get me wrong, she's a very attractive woman but she lives in Dublin and Michael is a good friend and, err… Perhaps it was just a perfectly innocent question and, as usual, I've got hold of the wrong end of the stick. Err…how do I answer that?"
"If you'd like to come through, Joan is just dishing up." Michael had perfect timing. "Please make your way to the dining area." He amusingly tried to put on a posh English accent.
"Thank God" Charlie heard himself blurt out.
"Oh, sorry Charlie, are you hungry? You should have said. Me and Joan would have done you some sandwiches."
Charlie felt himself blushing again
"Oh no. I meant to say 'thank you Michael' err…for err…your hospitality."
As he stood, he glanced at Sandra. She had a 'knowing', almost 'evil' smile on her face.

They served up a huge dinner and even more alcohol. By the time Charlie got back in the living room and sat in the armchair, he could barely keep his eyes open. Just as he was lowering himself into the chair, Sandra, who had already sat on the sofa, was patting the seat next to her, inviting him to sit next to her.
Charlie sat back and mumbled -
"Oh, it's alright, thanks. I'm just err… I'm okay here, thank you."
Sandra was giggling. She seemed to be enjoying tormenting him.
Michael and Joan came in the living room.
"Charlie son" Michael said "Why don't you crash here for the night? I know you've got your hotel room and that but you don't really want to be going all the way back over there now, do you? It's paid for whether you're there or not. We'll look after you. What time's your flight?"
"Yes" said Sandra, sultry "We'll look after you."
"Err…thank you, Michael. Very kind of you. My flight is at eleven. Trouble is, my stuff is my hotel room."
"Don't worry, Charlie" said Michael, thinking "I'll get Murf to pick you up in the morning, he'll run you to your hotel for your stuff and checkout and that and then get you to the airport on time. Don't worry about it, he owes me big time."
That was settled then. Charlie was staying. It was a good thing, he was very tired, a bit drunk and full of good Irish food. He told Michael that he wanted to turn in.
"Okay, Charlie. I'll show you your room. Joan has made the bed up."
He went to say his 'goodnights'. Joan stood and gave him a hug and kissed his cheek. He went over to Sandra. She stood, slowly and embraced him. She

kissed his cheek and whispered -
"My room is at the end of the landing, just for your information."
As she said that, Charlie felt her hand reach down and squeeze his buttock.
He was shocked, embarrassed, panicky. He looked round but neither Joan or Michael took a blind bit of notice. Or perhaps they didn't realise it had happened.
When he got in his room, he locked the door. He couldn't take any chances.
He needn't have worried. He was undisturbed during the night (as far as he knows.) He was 'out for the count' very quickly so even if 'someone' had tried his door, he wouldn't have known.
The next morning, he awoke early, as he always did. Michael must have heard him moving about because he knocked. Charlie gingerly unlocked then opened the door.
Michael put on his funny Irish voice -
"Top of the morning to you, Charlie! Hope you slept okay. Here's a towel, there's the bathroom. Have a nice shower. When you come down, Joan's doing you a Full Irish."
"Thank you so much, Michael"
When Charlie got in the bathroom, he again made sure the door was locked behind him.
"You daft twat" he said to himself "What do you think is going to happen?"
When he eventually came down to the kitchen, showered and refreshed, Joan had indeed made him a Full Irish. A big one. He was certainly eating well here (and drinking well)
He stuffed his face again. He sat back in his chair.
"Thank you so much for looking after me. You've both been so kind. You're such good people. I can see why

my Mum and Dad had been friends with you over the years."
Michael and Joan both looked pleased. Joan came over and hugged Charlie.
"You're very welcome, Charlie. It was lovely to meet you. Your parents will be very proud of you, wherever they are." She crossed herself.
Michael gave him another very firm handshake then also hugged him.
"That's right. You're welcome here anytime. You're a good lad, just like Bryan. I hope we can keep touch. I don't want to rush you, son but Murf will be here in a minute."
"Oh, okay. Of course, I'll keep in touch. Err… is Sandra about?"
"Jesus, don't be daft" Michael laughed "She won't be up for ages. Her majesty needs a rocket up her arse sometimes. She needs to sort herself out. Now her divorce is all finalised, she should have a word with herself. Tell you what, Charlie, if, or when, you come back here to see us, I'm sure Sandra could look out for you. She could show you a thing or two around Dublin."
Charlie laughed. He thought -
"I bet she COULD show me a thing or two!"
Murf duly pulled up outside and honked his horn.
"Oh my God!" thought Charlie "He'll wake the whole neighbourhood!"
He said his final goodbyes and as Murf drove him away, he looked back at Michael and Joan who were stood on their front step waving. He got quite emotional, really choked with his eyes welling up. Natural emotions or hangover induced ones? He wasn't entirely sure. They were certainly lovely people. He was so glad he met them. He thought that they had a

wonderful relationship together. he wished that, one day, he could be in a relationship or marriage like that. They were so happy, so suited. He was attracted to Sandra but she did intimidate him somewhat. On purpose? Was she just having a laugh? Was it normal behaviour for her? How would he ever know?

Murf drove way too fast. Although Charlie was glad because he liked to be early for everything, Murf did frighten him a couple of times. He was full of his usual banter.

"I'll bet you had a good time there, didn't you, Charlie? Lovely people, Michael and Joan. I bet they looked after you. Hey, look Charlie, there's the biggest fire station in Dublin. Tell you something, they're so well trained, those fellas. As well as being firemen, they're also fully-trained paramedics. How about that? Soon be at your hotel. How did you get on with Sandra? She's a girl, isn't she?"

Charlie had no idea what Murf meant by that and certainly was not going to ask.

He was dropped off at his hotel to grab his stuff and check out. When he came to get back in Murf's Mondeo, he felt like a bank robber getting in a getaway car. No sooner had he thrown his case on the back seat and climbed in the front, Murf roared off.

Another terror-drive ensued. Charlie forgave Murf as he got him to the airport in plenty of time.

"Murf, thank you so much for all you've done for me. Please take the last of my Euros."

"Don't be daft, Charlie. Happy to help. You know, a friend of Michael's… and all that… You come back and see us soon, won't you?"

"I certainly will. Please Murf, I really want you to have this. Perhaps look upon it as Guinness tokens, with my gratitude."

"Okay, Charlie. Thank you. Safe journey."

During his flight back to Bournemouth, Charlie reflected on what had happened. He was so glad of his Dublin trip. He really needed that. After the shock and subsequent mourning when Dad died, the 'sorting' of the envelopes, Barbara's mind-blowing confession, he was so glad that he went to Ireland. He had met some genuine, warm, friendly people. They obviously were very fond of Dad and, during his stay, they seemed to take to him too. He decided that he would like to go back there one day, when all the dust had settled in Chelmsford.

It had been the last of the envelopes but he knew that he still had loads to do.

Chapter Thirteen Organising.

Charlie didn't know whether to laugh ironically or to let rip with a sweary rant.
"It's EVERY bloody time! It's always the bleeding same! This is why I hate coming up here – the bastard M25! Just look at the queues! It doesn't matter which way I go, they get me. It's like all these cars and lorries wait for me to come on this shitty journey so they can come out, slow me down and aggravate me!"
Sweary rant it is then.
He'd put this trip off for two weeks after Dublin but he knew that he'd have to go back to Chelmsford at some point. Besides, there was some things that needed to be done, to be sorted.
He had decided to travel down on the Friday, early afternoon and spend the weekend in Chelmsford to get on top of things.
He did laugh ironically, in the end. He thought that he'd travel at this particular time on a Friday to avoid the traffic. After all, it is 'Poet's day' (Piss Off Early, Tomorrow's Saturday)
"…avoid the traffic… ha-ha! Just bloody look at it!"
He was travelling in a Transit van that he'd hired. Obviously, Dad had wanted him to have his writing desk and there might be some other bits and pieces to take back home so a van seemed logical.
There had been a lot of phone calls, back and forth during the week to get everything organised for the weekend.
He'd contacted Steve, good old Steve. Steve was more than happy to put him up on Friday and Saturday nights. Steve had said that he wanted to talk to Charlie about the Cortina situation. Charlie was relieved. He

didn't have a clue about how he was going to do it up and was glad that Steve seemed to have a theory. During the previous week, he had the pleasure of ringing Don. There wasn't too much small talk but Charlie was glad that Don had agreed to meet him at Dad's flat on the Saturday. They needed to sort through Dad's stuff, to decide what they were keeping and what they were binning and so forth.

Charlie had also contacted a local estate agent. The agent would be round the flat on Saturday to value etc and set the wheels in motion. It would make sense to get it on the market sooner rather than later.

So, everything was sorted and organised. Dad would be proud.

The bastard M25 continued to annoy Charlie. His left calf was aching due to the endless clutch work from going from first gear to second, back to first and so on. His thoughts turned to Chelmsford.

He was looking forward to seeing Steve. They would have Friday evening together for a beer and a chat. Saturday. Great. Don. Still, it had to be done. What was Don going to be like? Would he be agreeable? Or obnoxious? Charlie knew which one he would bet on. He knew that they'd have discussions about everything in Dad's flat and have to come to some sort of agreement. That could be interesting.

Then there would be the estate agent. Not his favourite type of person but it had to be done. In Charlie's experience, they were like politicians – professional liars. He'd been in an estate agents' office before when one of the agents was telling the office junior to lie to a customer, literally. He'd also heard stories (from reliable sources) that they even sell out their own customers just to get a sale

"Look, I know Mr. Bloggs has his house up for three-

hundred thousand but I happen to know he'd accept two-eighty"
Thanks, Mr. estate agent, for getting me the best price! Still, they're worth every penny, aren't they? A few photos, quick description, stick it on the internet then wait. Oh, they might have to show a potential buyer round -
"…and this is the kitchen…" No shit.
Charlie decided that he had to stop this negative attitude, this 'downer' he had on estate agents. This one might be alright.
It was never too long before his thoughts turned to Barbara and what she'd told him. He really did not want to run into Barbara, or Elaine, for that matter. It comforted him to think that there was very little chance of bumping into either of them.
After the torture of the bastard M25 (and the A12 this time, too) Charlie eventually got to his old home town, or city, as it is, of Chelmsford.
He really didn't fancy doing a mini nostalgia trip on his way through. Not just because he was tired and a bit miserable after the crappy journey but he just did not want to run into, or even see, any old faces. He laughed to himself as he pulled up onto Steve's driveway as he'd rushed the last part of the journey, almost with his head down to avoid being recognised.
"You really are a pillock sometimes." He said to himself.
Good old Steve was in. He got off early so he could meet Charlie (It's good to be the boss)
"Nice Transit, is it yours?" he asked.
"No mate. I wish. I've just hired it for a couple of days."
When Charlie went in, an amazing aroma met his nostrils.

"Now, that smells good. What is that?"
"Charlie, just for you, I'm making one of my famous curries. It's been festering on the stove all afternoon. Hope you don't mind if it's a bit spicy."
"Oh, mate. You're a legend. I love a good Ruby and that smells like a good one. I like it quite spicy. I'd say almost up to a Vindaloo. Almost. Anything hotter than is just, well, punishment."
He peeped into the kitchen. There on the cooker was a largeish pot of curry, gently bubbling away, giving off exotic smells.
"I brought some beers, they're in the back of the Tranny."
"Good man. Reckon we'll have a good night, then!"
A good curry, a few beers and a few laughs with a mate are great ways to get a shitty road journey out of your system. Charlie was feeling chilled. The beers were going down a treat and Steve was making him laugh, as usual. He was full of amusing stories and jokes.
Just as Charlie was really relaxed, laughing, having a good time, Steve ruined it. He inadvertently killed the atmosphere, for Charlie, anyway.
"Here, I bumped into Elaine's Mum last week. She said that you'd been round, couple of weeks ago. I told her that you'd stayed at mine. I asked her how Elaine was, you know, to see if I could get any clues for you, if she was separated or single or whatever. Mrs Robson got a bit upset. She said she really wanted to talk to you, said it was important…"
"Shit! You didn't give her my phone number or address or anything, did you?"
"No mate, calm down. I'd never do that. I'd talk to you first. She really…"
"You didn't tell her I was coming round here this weekend, did you?"

"Bloody hell! No. I didn't. I just thought that as I was seeing you today, I'd tell you about it. Then you can see her if you wanted. Jesus. What are you so worried about her for? She's alright. She's a nice lady. Look, in case you're worried about it, I'm sure she knows that you were shagging her daughter all those years ago!"
Charlie felt himself blush, slightly. He had to put Steve off the scent. Scent? What scent? He could not possibly know about the incest controversy. He knew for certain that Barbara would not have said anything about it.
"I'm not scared of her. Don't be bloody daft. That was all in the past. I just don't want to get bogged down with having to see her this weekend when I've got so much to do. Don't know why she's getting so upset. Besides, Elaine is married and that."
Charlie then got worried. Was he 'protesting' too much? Was he being too defensive? Was he giving the game away?
"Oh, for Christ's sake!" he thought "…'giving the game away…' What game? You bloody idiot. Calm down. Steve would never suspect anything. Not the truth, anyway. He will just think I'm paranoid or something if I keep over-reacting like that."
He looked at Steve. Steve appeared to be taken aback, only slightly but enough for Charlie to feel bad about snapping at him. Better diffuse the situation, change the subject or something.
"Anyway, why would I want some old dear having a go at me, getting all upset and crying and that? That was the first time I'd seen her in years."
"No, you don't need that. She was keen to talk to you, though."
"Oh well, never mind. Can't be that important. Hey, Stevie, you mentioned that you've got an idea about what to do with the Cortina?"

"Oh, yeah. Just a thought, an idea I had. What do you reckon about this? How about, I do up the Cortina, smarten it up, get it roadworthy?"
"Really? What do you mean?"
"Well, I've got a garage in the block round the corner. We could move it here and I could, you know, tinker with it. It could be a project, a hobby, if you like."
"That's what Dad used to call it, his 'hobby', his 'project'. Are you sure about this, Stevie?"
"Yeah. I reckon I'll enjoy that. A weekend thing. Might take a while, though. I won't be on it like I've got deadline or anything."
"That's really good of you mate. Christ, there's no deadline. Just tinker with it in your own time. There's no hurry for it. Tell you what, I'll only agree to this if…I cover any expense that you might incur. ANY expense. You know, parts, a tin of paint, tyres, a screw, anything. Is that okay? Is that fair?"
"Sounds fair to me, mate. I reckon I'll enjoy that. Love those old Cortinas. Look, I've got a low-loader at work. We use it to pick up cars to take to the workshop. I could get the Cortina out of your Dad's lock-up and bring it here. I can do that sort of thing 'cos I'm the boss!"
"Why don't you come up there tomorrow? I'll probably be there most of the day. Err, just one thing. Sorry, I'll have Don with me."
"Right, that's it! Deal's off! Great. Don. I won't hang about long then, don't really want to spend long in that man's company."
"Me neither. Unfortunately, I've got most of the day with him!"
Although Charlie was glad to get off the subject of an upset Barbara, he was perhaps more pleased with Steve's suggestion. It was a weight off his mind. It

made good sense and he knew he could totally trust him. He could trust him to good a good job and to not rip him off.

Charlie enjoyed another evening with Steve. They didn't get hammered and didn't turn in too late so Charlie thought he might be ready for everything that was happening the next day.

Charlie aimed to get to Dad's flat around eleven the next morning but, as usual, he left early. Ten-fifteen. Forty-five minutes to get across town? Even Charlie was beginning to think that he had a problem!

As he was leaving, Steve also set off. He explained that he was popping to his workshop. He had a couple of 'admin bits' to sort out then he would come to the flat in his low-loader a bit later on.

As Charlie turned into the cul-de-sac and saw the block where his Dad's flat was, those feelings started to come back. He felt a dull ache in his stomach. It was similar to butterflies but not pleasant in any way. There was no getting away from this awful sadness.

He'd arranged to meet Don at the flat around eleven-thirty to twelve. He even thought of telling Don that it was ten-thirty so that, even with his usual lateness he might turn up at the time Charlie wanted. He didn't do this because he thought that this would the one time in his life that Don would actually be on time, he wouldn't be there and Don would be Mr Angry. It didn't take much to set him off.

Charlie didn't mind that he was early. He could go in the flat on his own, with his thoughts and memories before Don came rampaging in, being too assertive etc.

Charlie parked the Transit round the back, in the allocated space and thought Don would probably moan about that, somehow claiming that he was more entitled. That's what he was like.

He wondered if he'd see Stan. He even contemplated knocking on his door but, perhaps selfishly, decided not to as Stan would talk all day and he had loads to do.
He let himself into the flat, closed the door behind him and let out a sigh (just like the last time) This was not going to be easy. None of it. It's got to be done though. He tried to ease his feelings of guilt and of being intrusive by saying to himself that every family has to go through this when they lose a parent. That didn't help much.
He wandered round the flat, looking at the photos, thinking about Dad. He realised that he was behaving virtually the same way as he had done on the last time he was here.
He sat at the desk. He realised that he hadn't 'gone through it' before as once he came across the envelopes, he was away. He unlocked it and lifted the lid.
There was a space in the middle where he had taken the pile of envelopes. The rest of that area was so tidy. There were small pots of pens, pencils and rulers. There was a stapler, a hole punch, some marker pens, books of stamps, small envelopes, all neatly laid out.
"That was Dad" thought Charlie "Neat and tidy. 'A place for everything and everything in it's place'. I should have known."
He looked in the drawers at the front. In neat bundles were all his council tax bills, his electricity bills, gas bills etc.
Charlie then spotted some bundles of correspondence. When he examined them, noticed the postmark 'Dublin ROI'. These were all the 'pen pal' letters that he had received from Michael. Charlie really wanted to read them but he wondered if he should. Should they be regarded as private? He carefully placed everything

back where he'd found them. He decided that he was taking the desk anyway so if, in the future, he did think that it was okay to read those letters, he had the option to.

Once again, he found himself moving around the flat looking at every photo. He found some albums in a box in the bedroom and was enjoying the emotional roller-coaster of going through those, preparing to get really emotional when the doorbell ringing made him jump out of his skin.

"Bloody hell, don't tell me Don's actually on time!"

Obviously not. When he spoke into the door-entry intercom, it was Steve's voice that greeted him.

"Hello mate, only me!"

He trotted down the stairs to meet him. Steve had parked his low-loader right across all the garages.

"Sorry mate, I didn't know which one was Brian's."

"No, I'M sorry Steve, bad news. Don's not here. You won't be able to chat with him!"

"Oh no, what a pisser! Okay, let's get this Cortina loaded and away before that lovely bloke gets here."

Steve was very good, very professional. He backed his vehicle up to the appropriate garage, after Charlie had opened it, and in no time had rigged up the cable to pull the Cortina onto his low-loader. With a lot of revving and whirring the Cortina moved up onto the back. Steve chained the wheels and before too long, it was ready to go.

"Charlie, much as I'd love to stick around to see that lovely brother of yours, you know, I reckon I'll head off."

"Nice one, Stevie. Thanks a lot. I'll see you later on."

With a bit of manoeuvring and two and froing, Steve turned his low-loader around and with a wave, pulled off.

Charlie laughed and thought -
"Lucky bugger, he gets away without seeing Don!"
He wandered back into the flat and tried to resume with the photo albums.
The doorbell made him jump again. He looked at his watch. Probably too early for the estate agent (they'd agreed an afternoon appointment) so it must be…
"Take your time! I thought no one was in! Look, am I alright parked here? Some prat has parked a Tranny in Dad's space."
The intercom amplified his voice unnecessarily.
"I'll come down."
When Charlie got down the stairs, he saw Don perched on the front wing of his Range Rover. It made him think of Jeremy Clarkson in his most arrogant, pompous act on 'Top Gear'.
Not too unsimilar. Don often claimed to have a thirty-eight-inch waist and wore (unsuitable) jeans accordingly. The only trouble was, Don wore them low enough so that they fastened underneath his very large stomach which hung over the front. Today, he was also wearing a very white T-shirt with a large 'Levis' logo on it. Charlie guessed that Carol had made him wear this combo. She probably thought it was 'work gear chic' when in reality it was more 'sad old man in denial'.
"Hello Don. Actually, the Tranny is mine. Hired it for the weekend."
"Oh, Jack's alright then. Where am I supposed to park then?"
Charlie somehow knew it would be like this.
"You could park in Stan's place, number sixty-eight. He doesn't have a car."
Don just sighed and Charlie thought he heard him do one of his famous tuts. He obviously didn't like the

incredible hardship he had to endure in moving his car along, one parking space.
When he was done, he joined Charlie and they wandered into the block of flats. Charlie was so tempted to say
"Do you want me to point out which one is Dad's?"
But he didn't.
"Glad you've come to your senses about that old Cortina. That's what I'm gonna do with those two old bikes. I'll flog them or get someone to take them off my hands."
"What are you on about?"
"I just saw the Cortina being taken away on a low-loader. Must have been Dad's. You don't see many like that around now."
"That was my mate, Stevie. Steve Gates. He's taking it to his lock-up and he's going to restore it for me."
"Really? Oh, I couldn't be bothered with all that. Did you know that there's no petrol in either of them? They're completely empty!"
"That's just Dad being careful. If you leave fuel in the tanks for too long without using it, it starts to rot through the metalwork."
"Oh, right, I did think that was a bit strange. Besides, we've got nowhere to put them."
"What? 'Nowhere to put them'? You've got that big house with a double garage."
"Oh, no, no. We use one half of the garage for storage and Carol likes to park her BMW in the other."
"And Dad left them for you. To do up. To enjoy."
"The thing is, I'm sure Dad would be just as happy if we made some good money selling them and did something nice with it."
Charlie was fuming. He should have known that Don would do this.

He thought -
"…'Dad would be just as happy…' like he'd know. I bet Carol's behind this. She wears the trousers in that house 'Ooo, we don't want those old things. I think we should sell them'. And, of course he'd go along with it. He'd be too scared to do otherwise."
They both went into the flat. Don marched down the hall, hardly looking at the photos, straight into the living room. He went over to the three-piece.
"Pretty good furniture, this."
"Yes, it is. I thought we could try to sell it but that's a bit of a pain because neither of us can be here for buyers and that. I thought that we could give it to a charity shop, there's a good local one that would almost certainly take all the furniture from here."
"Oh, hang on, Charlie. I reckon this would go nicely in our new conservatory. You know we've just had a new conservatory built, don't you?"
"Oh, have you? That's nice."
"Yes, it's pretty big. I can just see me and Carol sitting on these, looking out across our lawns. I think Dad would have been pleased that it was going to good home."

Charlie nearly shook his head with despair.
'Dad would be pleased…' How the bloody hell would Don Know? Still, it would save them from trying to sell it. Charlie had already decided to be 'easy-going' and agreeable about the stuff in the flat. He knew that Don would be demanding so he would let him have his way until they might come across something that he really wanted. He would have room to manoeuvre, he could just become assertive about that, rather than about everything.

"Not sure about that coffee table or that little dining table combo. Don't really like the look of them."
Charlie thought but didn't say -
"Oh, you don't think Dad would have wanted you to have those, then? Just the newer stuff."
What he actually said was -
"Well, he specifically left the desk and it's contents to me. I tell what, I'd really like to have his mounted Fire Brigade axe."
Don looked round at it. He then walked over to it and picked it up to examine it.
"I wonder if it's worth anything."
"Oh my God" thought Charlie. Time to be 'assertive'.
"I don't think it's worth anything in monetary terms," he lied "I think it's more for sentimental value. That's why I'd like it."
Don continued to examine it.
"Oh, okay, I suppose you could have it then."
Charlie thought -
"That's bloody good of you"
He pointed towards the bedroom.
"There's some clothes of Dad's in a wardrobe and a chest o' drawers in there. I don't know if you want to go through them. If not, I've got rolls of bin bags in the Tranny. I was going to take them to a charity shop I know in Poole. I've also got a pile of collapsed cardboard boxes too, for anything else."
Don seemed quite distant. He was gazing around.
"Yeah, yeah, probably a good idea. What else is there?"
"Well, there's bedding and towels, they can go in the bags with the clothes. There are a few photos. On the wall and in albums."
Don looked around, finally taking notice of the photos on the walls. He moved around the flat, taking three or four down, as if claiming them. When Charlie checked,

it seemed that Don was taking the photos that he himself appeared in (along with other family members)
"I'll just take these for now. Don't really have time to go through the albums. Perhaps when you do, you could sort some out for me."
"Yes, of course."
Again, Charlie lied. He had no intention of pulling photos of Don out from the albums for Don's ego.
"I'll just nip down to the Tranny and get the bin bags and boxes and we can make a start."
"Oh, yeah, okay."
Don's lack of enthusiasm was pretty obvious.
Charlie wandered down the stairs thinking that this ordeal would be over fairly soon. He was always on edge around Don, ever since they were kids. He was determined that Don would not get to him anymore.
As he slammed the back door of the Transit, with arms loaded down with flattened cardboard boxes and bin bags, he noticed a skinny lad, wearing a grey pinstriped suit that looked to be too big for him, coming around the side of the flats. The lad then took a photo of the block on his phone camera. Charlie knew that this had to be the estate agent.
"Hello. Are you from Churchman's? Estate agents?"
"Mister Mills? Good afternoon. My name is Duncan, Jordan Duncan I'm from Churchman's, as you pointed out."
"Did they get you out of retirement for this job?" joked Charlie.
The lad looked, to Charlie, to be aged about seventeen. He had gelled hair and a touch of acne.
"I'm sorry?" said the lad. That quip went completely over his head.
"Anyway, how do you do?"
He reached out to shake Charlie's hand before realising

that Charlie could not respond because of the stuff he was carrying.
Charlie felt bad about 'leaving him hanging'. The lad was clearly a bit nervous.
"Come in, Jordan. We're on the first floor. You can have the pleasure of Don."
During their 'journey' into the flat, Jordan took some more photos. He was like a tourist at The Tower of London.
He escorted Jordan into the flat.
"Don, this is Jordan Duncan. He's from the estate agents."
"Oh? Right. Hello."
Don's indifference was bordering on rudeness. He seemed too busy picking up ornaments and examining them, presumably for value.
"Okay Jordan, do your thing." Said Charlie, trying to lighten the mood.
"Sorry?"
"Err, you can carry on and do your 'estate agent' stuff now"
Charlie left Jordan to it. Jordan had a laser measurer and his digital camera on his phone. He was noting stuff down on his iPad.
"So high tech, these days" Charlie thought.
Charlie got stuck in. he loaded all Dad's clothes and bedding into bin bags. A lot of bin bags. He put the photo albums into some of the cardboard boxes.
He called out to Don -
"I'll start taking these down to the Tranny, Don!"
"Okay"
"I'll do it all then, shall I?" Charlie muttered.
After a few trips, up and down the stairs, the boxes and bags were all in, or by the back of, the Transit.
Charlie went back to Don.

"Don, can you give us a hand to take the desk and chair down to the van?"
This time, Don actually did tut. And sigh.
The writing desk wasn't too heavy, more awkward really. They eventually got it down the flight of stairs (during which time they did the obligatory 'To me – to you' joke, that everyone does now.)
Charlie tried to explain his plan to Don.
"I thought I'd put the desk in the middle there, then load all the bags around it. They'll protect it a bit and stop it sliding about."
"Oh, right." Said Don, already heading back to the flat.
Charlie laughed then carried on. When he was done, he went back upstairs.
"Now look here Duncan, these flats have got to be worth three-eighty, three-ninety. What the bloody hell are you on about 'three-fifty'?"
Don was beginning to raise his voice.
The poor lad looked terrified.
"I'm only going by current market values and one very similar nearby was sold for three-fifty recently."
"Well, we'll see about your valuation."
Charlie intervened -
"Calm down Don. Jordan here, his name's Jordan, is only doing his job. I'm sure he knows what price we could get for this place."
As Don went into the kitchen, tutting and sighing, Charlie smiled at Jordan, nodded and winked, as if to say don't worry about that gobshite, we'll sort this. Jordan seemed to understand.
Once the poor lad had gone, Charlie realised that he and Don were virtually finished in the flat. Charlie gave Don a set of keys to the flat (and the lock-up) so he could come back to get the three-piece (and the 'unwanted' bikes)

Amazingly, Don seemed reasonably content with the arrangements. He obviously thought he would be a 'pain' to come back again but he knew that he needed to return with a suitable vehicle, to transport everything and some assistance to help him move the furniture and the bikes.
Charlie knew that Don wouldn't hang about. Don said his goodbyes and was off downstairs to his car, with his 'claimed' photos tucked under his arm. Charlie peeped out the window and saw Don, in his Range Rover, on his phone. Charlie just knew that Don was 'reporting-in' to the Ice Maiden. Eventually, he saw him pull away. Charlie couldn't help wonder when he would see Don again. Maybe when the flat was sold, they may need to both sign paperwork etc. Probably not in a social way, though.
He decided to have one last look around the flat. This would almost certainly be the last time he would ever come here. Although he never lived here, it was a special place because it was where Dad had spent his final days. Straight away, upon realising this, he felt all those emotions coming to the fore again. As he slowly walked around the flat, he pictured his Dad in every room, in different scenarios, from his memories. There were no more photos on the walls, no more memorabilia apart from a few items of furniture.
Charlie stood in the place where his Dad's desk stood. He looked out the window, from where his Dad would have done. He felt tears running down his cheeks. He felt the pain, the pain of mourning in his chest. He had to accept that he'd never see his Dad's face again. His Dad who always seemed to be laughing. He'd never be able to ring his Dad again. His Dad was always so pleased to hear from him, always so keen to find out he was getting on. He had to be strong and cope with it but

it was not going to be easy. It would take time. He wondered how much time it would take for this pain to recede.
He was in no hurry to leave. He walked very slowly down the hall, pushing his Dad's old office chair, imagining the photos that had been on the wall.
When he finally shut the door to Dad's flat, he felt that 'thud' reverberate through him. Choking back tears, he carried the chair down the stairs, outside and into the Transit.
This time, as he drove away, for almost certainly the last time, he did not look back. He couldn't get himself to do it. It was a symbolic moment, he knew he had to move on and not wallow. Easier said than done. He sniffed back tears and headed back towards Steve's.
He certainly didn't rush across town. He took his time. When he eventually pulled up on Steve's driveway, he turned off the ignition, sat for a moment, took several slow, deep breaths before climbing out.
"So, how was that lovely bloke Don, then? His usual self?" Steve was quite chirpy, that gave Charlie a lift.
"Err…usual."
That's all that was needed. Steve knew what 'usual' meant.
Steve could sense that Charlie was a bit down. They sat in his kitchen and had a chat over two or three beers. Charlie explained the estate agent conversation and the furniture situation, how Don had claimed the good stuff and the rest would go to a charity.
"Charlie, I know a really good local charity. They come and clear everything out. Not like the actual 'house clearances', this lot load ALL the furniture onto vans and take it away to a big warehouse. They'll go through

it. Some stuff would go to families in need and the rest, they get rid of."

"Tell you what, Steve, that would be a bloody good solution. And, Dad would definitely approve. He had a thing for these sorts of charities in Ireland."

"I'll give them a ring on Monday, if you like. See when they can come round."

"For God's sake Steve, make sure you tell them that the three piece is spoken for! You know what Don's like!"

"Charlie, you don't have to worry about Don now. You'll probably hardly EVER see him from now on. Look, if you leave me a set of keys, I can be there when they come to clear everything out. I can help liaise with the estate agent too, if that will help. I can be your 'man in the middle', your 'go-between', if you like."

"That's bloody good of you Steve. That would really help me out. You've been such a good mate."

"I hope that doesn't mean that we have to do one of those 'man-hug' things now, does it? I'm not really into that sort of thing!"

"No, you're okay Steve. Let's just have another beer."

They had a good, chilled evening. A few beers, a bit to eat, chatting and laughing. Charlie missed this. He didn't really have a 'best mate' in Dorset. Not like Steve. One who he went way back with, one who he could confide in. Confide NEARLY everything, NOT everything. The Elaine business would remain 'buried'. Not even a best mate could know about that!

The following day, Charlie left to head home. He decided to go mid-morning, he felt he'd imposed on Steve quite enough.

As he hit the bastard M25, he reflected on the previous day. He felt relieved, somewhat. Everything seemed to be getting sorted, without too much drama. Although he would be miles away, in Poole, he was content that the

wheels were in motion. Dad's affairs (ha-ha) were being dealt with and he could now try to move on with his life.
He smiled.
"It's Sunday, the bastard M25 isn't too bad. Shouldn't say that, it doesn't take too much to turn this into the biggest 'carpark' in the world!"

Chapter Fourteen Wendy.

"Hello Charlie! Fancy bumping into you. Haven't seen you in a while. How are you?"
Charlie was squatting over a shopping basket, re-arranging it so that the milk he was about to put in didn't squash the loaf already within.
He looked up and in just a few milli-seconds had, what he later decided was, a hot flush (the muscles in his shoulders and neck seemed to tighten and his head felt hot. He may have blushed but hoped he hadn't) At the same time, he concluded that he also felt cold! Not necessarily a 'blood running cold' moment but still a strange, almost indescribable phenomenon.
There in front of him, looking quite 'glammed-up' was, the nervously smiling, Wendy.
Charlie hadn't laid eyes on Wendy since the day he moved out of the flat they were sharing. He occasionally wondered how he would react if they ever ran into each other (he wondered how she would react too) Now, he was finding out! He felt as awkward as he imagined he would (again hoping, praying that he wasn't blushing) Whereas she gave the impression of someone who was calm and in control. He thought that was somewhat ironic, considering she was the guilty party who had wrecked their relationship. He slowly raised himself up from his squatting position, knees creaking slightly, desperately trying to think of a cool, witty or clever response.
"Oh, hello Wendy. How are you doing?" was the best that he could muster.
"I'm fine, thank you. So, what brings you to this area then, Charlie? It was Poole you moved to, wasn't it?"
"Oh, I occasionally treat myself on my days off and come to the big city, or Bournemouth town, as it's

known. It's like a grand day out for us bumpkins from Poole."
He realised that, as he was nervous, he was making a sad attempt at humour.
Wendy smiled. She was a very attractive girl, tall, slim, long legs and a mass of curly, strawberry-blonde hair. When Charlie thought about it, he knew that she was the only girl who had ever actually broken his heart. He recalled some tin-pot expert on a TV show saying - "You haven't lived until you've had your heart broken". Charlie often thought that the so-called expert had been talking crap as that was a pain that he could have done without.
He met Wendy through an internet dating site. His relationship with Lisa had fizzled-out and he was, in a way, lost and alone in Bath. Lisa had originally persuaded him to move there with her from Chelmsford but it didn't take long for them to realise that there was no real spark between them and she only really wanted to live there to be close to her family. It left him in limbo, somewhat. He loved the place but had no social life, no close friends, so he thought that internet dating might be a way to get his life back.
Although he was still living in the flat with Lisa, he didn't feel uncomfortable about trying out that internet dating lark because they had become more like flatmates, like friends. Fortunately, they were in a two-bedroomed flat so they could do their own thing. The way things developed, at that time, meant that they hardly saw each other. It wasn't a deliberate thing, it just worked out that way. They were both content with the fact that there was no ill-feeling between them, they both accepted that it was just one of those things. (Charlie, was secretly proud of the way that he didn't throw in Lisa's face the fact that he had moved a

hundred and sixty-odd miles from his home town, just to be with her but her real motives, maybe subconsciously, were to be closer to her family. He wanted to be the bigger person and didn't see the point of bickering about it now they were just 'flatmates')
He remembers being quite excited when he was about to set up his profile on the dating site. The site was called 'Fishing for Love' and, as if the name wasn't corny enough, the logo was a cartoon cupid, holding a fishing rod and, on the end of the line was a large heart! His excitement soon turned to, almost, despair when he came to describe himself. He then realised how dull he probably was. He found it so difficult to write a profile to make himself seem even slightly desirable. He knew that it was just like a CV. Everyone 'exaggerates' or 'bigs themselves up', it's expected. So, whenever he tried to compose his profile, he felt it looked really sad. He would wonder what women would think. His profile, despite being apparently over-stated was still disappointing! It turned out, however, that he was being particularly hard on himself. He decided that it was best to be honest. He knew that, if he described himself as a 'Patrick Swayze lookalike' or having the physique of Arnold Schwarzenegger, (it was the late nineties!) he would be setting himself up for a fall. He imagined the look on a girl's face when she would meet him for the first time. That look of disappointment or even of horror!
"Patrick Swayze looks?!"
"What muscles?!"
Best to be honest (not brutally honest, though!)
He eventually got his profile out there on the 'Fishing for Love' site. He included the best two photos of himself that he could find. It did cross his mind to include one that was 'blurry so you couldn't see his

spots'! (It's a good job that incident hadn't stayed with him over the years, he sarcastically chuckled to himself.)
Surprisingly, it wasn't long before he got a response. He was more surprised with the fact that a lady had contacted him. He assumed that the site was like it was in society, men had to make the first move (and run the risk of being shot down in flames) He realised that he was a bit out of touch and some women were different, more forthcoming.
He received a message from Kim from Bristol. He was pleasantly surprised with her message. Her grammar and spelling were good and she wrote a charming message, with a small amount of humour. He checked out her profile. She only showed one photo, it was a sort-of head and shoulders one. She had a pretty face and, he couldn't help noticing, a very impressive cleavage. He resisted the temptation to make the sexist joke about Kim from Bristol with the Bristols. He realised that he was being shallow and crass and she was probably sick of such remarks. They exchanged messages for a while, then phone numbers. She was very friendly on the phone and they chatted for some time. During one of these conversations, Charlie mentioned his theory about honesty. He stressed that he felt it was vital. He believed that someone might lie or exaggerate to make themselves seem more attractive, more interesting, more exciting. The problem is, they would get found out and look ridiculous AND the other person would also know that they were prepared to be deceitful.
Eventually they arranged to meet. They sorted out the details over the phone and Charlie did think that it was bit odd that the last thing that Kim said was "Just to let

you know, I'm no gym bunny."
He struggled to figure out what she meant.
They arranged to meet in a country pub situated between Bath and Bristol. Charlie wore trousers and his best shirt (he decided that a tie would be OTT) and took a bunch of flowers. He got to the pub early as he believed that a lady shouldn't be expected to go in a pub alone.
Kim arrived soon after and Charlie, when he was honest with himself, was actually quite shocked. She came in the door and straight away, he noticed that she was enormous. Not just over-weight but huge. This is what she meant by 'not a gym bunny'! Charlie tried to disguise his reaction and was polite but his mind was racing. Firstly, he thought back to the profile that she had put on the site, it said 'build – medium' (the other options were: - 'petite', 'athletic' and 'could lose a few pounds'. Straight away he realised that she was either deceitful or deluded. Then he started to question himself – Was he being shallow and obsessed with image? Was he expecting Michelle Pfeiffer to walk in? (late nineties) Was HE deluded? He tried to defend himself, in his mind, with the thought that, for a relationship to have any 'legs' there has to be certain amount of attraction and he knew that he wasn't attracted to the larger lady.
Charlie was polite and they had a couple of drinks and a chat. They were there for a couple of hours. He knew that this wasn't going anywhere but he also knew that he had no understanding of dating site etiquette. How or when should he tell her? If not now, what should he say at the end of the evening?
He ended up full of guilt and self-loathing. He took the coward's way out. He found himself saying-

"That was a lovely evening, we must do it again. I'll give you a ring."
The following day, he sent a cowardly text saying that he'd had a 'change of heart' and although she was 'very nice', he 'wasn't ready for a relationship'. He was fully aware of how pathetic that sounded.
The experience failed to put Charlie off the internet dating world. He decided, however, to be a little more cautious next time, to 'do his homework'.
He spent a couple of evenings trawling through profiles on 'Fishing for Love'. He had put in for a search of a radius of thirty miles around Bath and the site gave him plenty of potential 'dates' to look at.
One girl caught his eye. Her name was Tracey and she was from Trowbridge, only about eight miles away. What struck Charlie was, as well as having a very attractive face, she also had, like a mane, of thick, jet-black hair. He studied her photos and noticed that she was in pretty good shape too. He decided to go for it.
He wrote a message to her, re-reading, correcting, spell-checking etc until he was happy with it. She responded the following day and they sent each other two or three messages until they inevitably exchanged phone numbers (this was normal dating site etiquette)
Eventually they arranged to meet. Charlie said that he would go to Trowbridge and meet her outside a coffee shop just off the main square. He had a good feeling about this one. She seemed very friendly and he definitely found her attractive.
Again, Charlie dressed smartly. Again, he took flowers and was early. Again, he was disappointed. A lady approached him, looked him in the eye and asked -
"Charlie? It's Charlie, isn't it?"
He studied her. To his shock, he realised that it was Tracey. It was Tracey but and older version of Tracey!

She had a bit too much make-up on for his liking, a lot of foundation to cover, he realised, her wrinkles. Her mane of jet-black hair was turning grey in places. Charlie realised that her photos, on her profile page, seemed as though they were probably around ten to fifteen years out of date! He frantically thought -
"How old is she, exactly? Has she lied about her age?"
He was so close to asking her -
"Is your daughter coming?"
He was despondent. He asked himself if this was normal for dating sites. Dishonesty, deceitfulness, falsehoods just to get your 'foot in the door'. He was not expecting this. However, if he was honest, he didn't know what to expect but surely, he thought, honesty is a prerequisite.
"Yes, yes, it is. You must be Tracey. Nice to meet you."
He had to be polite, he had to act like a gentleman. He couldn't possibly confront her over her out-dated photos.
They went into the coffee shop and chatted over some over-priced, bizarrely-named cups of coffee.
Charlie thought that she seemed okay, she was bubbly and enjoyed a laugh but the only problem was that she was a bit coarse for his liking. She frequently dropped some swearing into general conversation (Charlie always believed that a lady shouldn't really swear too much, only when stressed or hurt or only when quoting someone else. Perhaps he was old-fashioned. He always did his best not to swear in the presence of a lady) She was also quite suggestive, Charlie thought that she was bordering on vulgar. Not that he was totally against that (he was no prude) but not on a first date. First impressions, and all that!
After a couple of cups of expensive coffee, they decided to go for a stroll. Charlie was glad of it, he

didn't care for the pretentious coffee house. They ambled for a while, exchanging small-talk when, out of the blue, Tracey announced -

"Do you know what, Charlie? I live just over there" She pointed. "Do you fancy coming round for a coffee and that?"

"That would be nice but please, no more coffee!"

He surprised himself how swiftly that he agreed to go to her flat. He wasn't exactly smitten and he hadn't been making too much of an effort to be charming but she was definitely keen.

Before they got to her flat, she came out with the "You'll have to take it how you find it. I wasn't expecting visitors" line. As soon as they entered, Charlie realised that she certainly wasn't! It was very untidy but not dirty. Clothes strewn over most items on furniture, washing hung in many places. Tracey cleared the stuff off her sofa and she and Charlie sat down. He felt slightly awkward, she was being quite forward.

Looking back, Charlie couldn't quite recall how the next sequence of events took place. Somehow, he found himself kissing Tracey (he knew for certain that she had initiated this) and it got more and more passionate. Before he knew it, she had manoeuvred herself so that she was straddling him, she then proceeded to grind herself on him. In hindsight, Charlie knew that he should have perhaps attempted to slow things down a bit but he had a reasonably attractive girl astride him, who was getting more and more physical and he couldn't help but get a bit 'excited' which she clearly noticed. Again, he couldn't remember it happening or how it happened but the next thing he knew they were in her bedroom, frantically undressing each other. Even then, Charlie, in the back of his mind, was saying to himself that he shouldn't be doing this. This was a first date; he didn't really feel that he wanted a proper relationship with this girl and she was WAY too forward considering that they had just met. He also knew, however, that he was a typical bloke, she was a sure thing, he was definitely going to have sex with her (and he'd 'been without' for a while) and, besides, he was really fired up now so he couldn't stop himself. She again straddled him. She insisted on staying on top the whole time. He remembers that she was quite domineering, almost aggressive, as she hurriedly, and forcefully bounced upon him. Consequently, it was all over very quickly and Charlie recalled, straight away, feeling guilty, used, even a bit dirty. He almost chuckled to himself -

"Hang on, it's the girl who's meant to feel like this! I'm the bloke! I'm supposed to not give a shit! Bloody hell, next I'll be asking for a post-coital cuddle and a discussion about feelings!"

He couldn't remember any conversation they might have had as they eventually got dressed (perhaps there wasn't any) but they must have had some sort of exchange because he recalls them both sharing a bottle of lager back on her sofa. Charlie felt bad because all he wanted to do was to leave and when he finally felt it was ok to mention that, Tracey didn't seem that bothered that he was going.

He could just about remember saying, as he was going out the front door - "It was great to meet you, be seeing you."

He was sure that all Tracey said in response was -

"Yeah, you too. Bye."

He realised straight away that neither of them even hinted at being keen on having a second date. Although Charlie wasn't completely au fait with dating site etiquette, he knew that it was strange that neither of them made any effort to discuss their next move (or lack of it)

It was an uncomfortable walk back to his car. Once he was pulling away onto the Bath Road, he had a nagging urge to have a shower. Did he feel dirty? Or was it to wash away the guilt? He experienced strange feelings and he was almost tormenting himself with his thoughts and over-analysis.

Had he behaved like a right bastard and just used her for sex? He decided that, basically, he had. However, in his defence, he never intended, originally, to go to her flat. He never intended to have sex with her. It was her who initiated it.

If they were never to see each other again, (he was pretty sure that both of them knew that they wouldn't) had he just used her? Would she be upset about that fact that he'd had a 'one-night stand' (or 'afternoon' stand) with her and then would not be in contact with her? He mulled over this all the way home. The journey was only around eight miles but it was bugging him. He stopped outside his flat and thought for a while. He made up his mind. He came round to thinking that they were both adults, they knew what they were doing. He didn't rape her or force her to do anything that she might not want to do. If anything, it was her who pushed for sex (obviously he didn't fight her off!) She was pretty clear that she wasn't interested in them seeing each other again, he was equally not that bothered too. Although it wasn't like him to have sex on a first date (on an ONLY date) he could have called a halt to it at any time but didn't.

His conclusion, about all this, was to put it down to experience. He had sex with a girl and it meant nothing.

He was fully aware that this sort of thing goes on all the time but, not in his world. He began to question himself. What was he worried about? Isn't it every bloke's fantasy to get casual, no-strings sex? The blokes he grew up with would all be proud of him. Or would they? He pictured the lads with whom he knocked about with in his late teens, usually beered-up, sat around a table in The Two Saxons pub. Did they really mean all the things they said or was it all macho talk? The constant misogynistic attitudes. The claims of sexual conquests. The lack of empathy with anyone who displayed any feelings. He wondered how fake that all was. He certainly wasn't like that. He was actually quite sensitive and never felt the desire to just 'use' a woman. He then hoped that he'd not joined in with their loud, cold-hearted blustering (Well, not too much, anyway)

He wandered into his flat and was relieved when he realised that, once again, Lisa was out. He wanted to be alone, he couldn't be bothered with their usual small-talk, he wanted his own company. He knew that he was always over-analysing things and ending up torturing himself. He decided that usually it's not the end of the world to make a mistake, provided that you learn from it (and hopefully not balls-up again.) He knew what he wanted from this bizarre dating site and a girl like Tracey was not it. He was determined to find someone on that dating site that he could have a 'normal' relationship with.

It was only a couple of weeks later that Wendy came into his life.

He decided, that evening, after the Tracey encounter, to spread his search radius. In his wisdom, he thought that by just searching the local area (thirty miles around Bath) he was restricting himself. He philosophy was that this expansion would give him more of a chance to be more selective. It was then he started to doubt himself. He was concerned that as he was a bit dull and no pretty-boy, why would any girl be interested in travelling any distance to see him? He decided to carry on with this new approach as he had nothing to lose (nothing except his dignity, his self-respect, his fragile confidence etc)

Charlie spent a couple of hours on that site, most evenings, scrolling through so many profiles of ladies, it was starting to get on his nerves. Although it was an exciting voyage of discovery, he was getting frustrated. Any woman, that he stumbled across, that was very attractive, he immediately thought that she was out of his league and couldn't possibly be interested in him. Any that weren't that attractive, (in his opinion) he was not going to pursue. He then felt guilty about his attitude. He was sure than none of them would consider him to be exactly Tom Cruise (it was the late nineties) so who was he to judge?

Wendy's profile leapt out at him. He instantly noticed her blonde, her strawberry-blonde, hair and she was very attractive (he was aware that he was being shallow but he really liked the look of her) The fact that she was from Bournemouth (not exactly 'local') was irrelevant to him. He read and re-read her profile. It was so different to all the others that he'd been through. She had been very witty, with sarcasm and irony and it made him laugh. She also had hinted that she was tired of this internet dating game as she'd encountered:

"...too many stereotypical rats..."

"...wide boys, just after one thing..."

Charlie was determined. He wanted to get in contact with her, charm her and prove to her that not all men are the same. It wouldn't be an act, he really was sensitive, caring, attentive and actually interested in a 'proper relationship'.

It took Wendy a couple of days to reply. Charlie thought that he'd missed his chance but she explained that she was cautious and really was on the verge of giving up. She told him what it was like to be a female on one of these dating sites. Often, she explained, blokes would send crude messages like - "Nice tits" or

"Do you shag on a first date?"

On occasions, they would just send a photo of their genitalia. There are some weird people out there.

Charlie couldn't help wondering, does that approach ever work? Are there women out there who would think that behaviour was 'cool' and the perpetrator to be desirable? Surely not.

It reminded him of another vulgar 'line' that he'd heard 'lads' use. When a female was bent down or kneeling down near them, they would say - "While you're down there, love…"

Surely, there can't be woman on Earth who would like that and would think -

"Ooo, he's lovely, isn't he? Now he's shouted that remark, I feel that I'd like to be in a relationship with him but first, I should perform oral sex on him because he implicated that."

He wondered if perhaps there were girls who would 'put up' with that boorish behaviour. Chavvy girls, perhaps. Maybe, if the gobshite was a 'pretty-boy' and/or possessed pots of money, there would be girls who would put up with it (but surely not 'embrace' it?)

Charlie decided to be totally honest, right from the start. He told Wendy everything about his home life, the situation with Lisa, his crappy two dates that he'd had through this site (he did leave out the part where he had a naked romp with Tracey, too sordid, it would put Wendy off) She seemed to appreciate his honesty and over the course of the many messages, (they were both taking it slowly) they appeared to hit it off. When they eventually got around to exchanging phone numbers, they experienced several epic phone conversations. They both had plenty to talk about and they made each other laugh. Then came to the meeting-up part. The distance between them was going to be a bit of an issue, Bournemouth being over sixty miles from Bath and they discussed this many times.

He will never forget the first time that they actually met. Wendy suggested that he came to Bournemouth and they would meet at the entrance to Boscombe Pier. Charlie thought that this was a great idea and, obviously prepared himself meticulously. Even though that he was determined that this date should be different to the others, he still dressed well, took flowers and arrived way too early.

This time, he was actually quite nervous. He realised it was because this one was important. Wendy was different, she was a bit classy, well-spoken, intelligent (and gorgeous) He did not want to mess this up, he wanted to, at least, try to make a go of it. (He had decided all this before he'd even met her!) When she came strolling down the Promenade, Charlie spotted her, straight away. She was slim, tall, had excellent posture and the wind was blowing her mass of curly hair around. To him, she was like a vision. He always remembered the way she gently held his shoulders and kissed his cheek as she greeted him. A short while after, she used her lacey handkerchief to wipe her lipstick mark from his face. He loved this closeness, this intimacy, the fact that she was quite tactile.

They had a fabulous first date, they really hit it off and it was obvious to both of them that they were more than compatible. They laughed a lot; they shared some quiet conversations and there were some lovely moments of tenderness. It seemed that they both couldn't wait to arrange to see each other again and this they did. Charlie was so happy. He knew that this relationship was just what he had wanted and he was fortunate to stumble across this lovely girl. The distance between them, at first, seemed like an obstacle but they got used to it. It was usually Charlie who went to Bournemouth where he often stayed with Wendy (she had her own flat) The only time that Wendy came to Bath was when Lisa was away for a long weekend with her family (His new relationship was still a secret from her)

Over the next few weeks, they became very close. Before every phone call, before each time they met, Charlie was getting butterflies. He couldn't wait to be with her and she soon confided with him that she felt the same. As he was spending more and more time with her in her Bournemouth flat, it was decided that he was to have a space in the wardrobe, a drawer to himself in her bedroom and his own area, for his toiletries, in her bathroom. Once this was established, the conversation inevitably came around to the possibility of co-habiting. Although it was relatively early in the relationship, Charlie was all for it (he disguised his enthusiasm and excitement for fear of appearing too keen) It made sense to him as he was spending so much time there and there was nothing really for him in Bath. To him, it was a logical step. He even, discreetly, applied for jobs in the Bournemouth area, using Wendy's address as his own, knowing that he'd soon be living there. He didn't tell Wendy about this until he'd got an interview because, again, he didn't want to appear too presumptuous. (There are those anxieties again!) She did, however, think it slightly odd that he was receiving post at her flat!

His successful application for a clerical job at Dorset County Council was the catalyst for his moving in with Wendy. They both, in their wisdom, decided that it was 'fate' or 'destiny' so it accelerated the process.

When he finally informed Lisa about what was to happen, she actually seemed quite sad. She wasn't hostile or resentful, more philosophical (the cynic in Charlie could deduce that she was more concerned about losing his share of the rent but maybe he was being harsh with her)

When moving day came around, Charlie actually felt a tinge of sadness. He thought Bath was a lovely place but he knew his future was in Bournemouth. He didn't have too much 'stuff' to move into Wendy's flat and she was relieved that there weren't loads of 'bloke crap'.

Charlie, for once, could actually say that he was enjoying life. It was great living with Wendy. They were both quite 'loved-up' and 'into each other' (these were expressions that he found himself using) His job, with Dorset County Council was, although not that exciting, reasonably interesting, reasonably well-paid and not too demanding. He liked the area, in fact, the only time he seemed to leave it was when he made the journey to Essex to see his Dad.

He loved his home life. He and Wendy were getting on so well and they couldn't keep their hands off each other. They seemed to have plenty in common and used to laugh a lot. This was wonderful for Charlie, this was what he had been looking for. It appeared to be too good to be true.   Unfortunately, as Charlie realised through experience, if something appears to be too good to be true then…

He remembers that it was a Thursday lunchtime. He got on really well with his line manager at work. He was Jimmy McGoldrick, lovely bloke, not far off retiring. He knew the job inside out and had hit it off with Charlie from day one. This was a good thing because when Charlie had told him, that day, that he was feeling unwell, Jimmy knew that it was genuine and he wasn't just trying to skive. Jimmy told Charlie to have the rest of the day off and to see how he was on the following day. Charlie headed home, feeling a bit sorry for himself.

He thought that it was a bit strange, when he got back to the flat, that the front door was on the latch. He then was trying to remember who was last out, him or Wendy. He wandered in and, as he was feeling a bit rough, he neglected to close it properly. He kicked off his shoes and they bounced along the wooden floor towards the shoe rack. That was when he heard Wendy's voice from another room -

"Come on in, baby. I left the door open for you!"

He stopped in his tracks. He wondered what was that all about. He knew that he hadn't told her that he was not well and coming home. Besides, he assumed she was at work. As he stuck his head around the door to their bedroom, her face told him all he needed to know. She looked shocked and her face went bright red. She was laying on the bed with just a thin top-sheet covering her nakedness.

"Charlie!"

"I don't think you were expecting me, were you?"

"Oh, Charlie! I, err, oh, bloody hell!"

"Thought not. Just who were you expecting then?"

Right on cue, Charlie heard a noise behind him. He turned around to see a familiar face coming in through the front door. It was Ken. Ken suddenly stopped dead once he noticed Charlie and his face also became a complete giveaway! Ken was a plumber; he was a friend of a friend of Wendy's who was recommended to her when she needed some work done on the central heating system. Charlie had met him a few times but not, obviously, under these circumstances.
"Hello Ken, how are you doing?"
Ken looked flustered. Charlie almost admired the cheek of the bloke. Almost.
"Oh, hello Charlie. Is, is Wendy about? I, err, she, wanted, err, a quote and..."
"Oh, fuck off, Ken! Don't even go there!"
There followed a, sort of, Mexican stand-off. Three people in the flat, no one knowing what to say next. Charlie could feel his heart thumping. He knew that his whole world was crashing down around him. He found himself just staring at Ken. Ken could not make eye contact with him. In the end Charlie broke the silence -
"In fact, just fuck off, Ken. I mean, actually fuck off. Right now!"
Ken scurried away, shutting the front door behind him. It came open again.
The flat fell silent. Charlie just stood, in exactly the same position as he was when he confronted Ken, he was already contemplating his future. Eventually, he slowly moved across the hall and gently closed the front door, properly. Looking back at that moment, he reckoned that it was probably more uncomfortable for Wendy due to the fact that he didn't rush in and start shouting and screaming at her. The fact that he calmly strolled into the living room, sat down and mused, must have been like mental torture to her. He now could

picture her, as she realised that the big confrontation wasn't coming, eventually, self-consciously, getting up off the bed and nervously getting dressed.
She sheepishly crept into the living room and sat on the sofa on the other side of the room, awkwardly hugging her knees up to her chin. He noticed that she had real trouble making any sort of eye contact with him. They just sat there, in silence for what seemed like an age. Wendy, not knowing what to say, Charlie, deliberately prolonging it to, hopefully, make her suffer a bit.
Eventually, it was Charlie who caved in -
"Well, that's that buggered then, isn't it?"
She began to cry. He felt nothing. Normally, he felt very uncomfortable around women crying but, not now.
"Oh, Charlie, I'm so sorry…!"
"What? What for? Sorry you've been shagging Ken? Or sorry you got caught?"
She began to sob.
"Charlie, I don't know what to say!"
"No, I don't imagine you do. There's nothing you could say, right now, that could, you know…"
There followed more silence, broken only by Wendy, sniffing back tears.
Charlie wasn't feeling well to start with but this was a real hammer blow. He really thought that he'd hit the jackpot with Wendy. She seemed so perfect, everything he wanted, he had no inkling that something like this would happen.
When they could eventually calm down and discuss things, he remembered using those phrases. Partly because they were spot on, partly to make her feel more guilty.
Over the next few days, obviously the atmosphere was terrible. Wendy was full of remorse and apologies, Charlie almost ashamedly revelled in making her feel

more and more guilty. There never was a full, 'shouting and swearing' row. Charlie always remained calm, virtually resigned to his fate.

During one chat, a fortnight or so later, after separate sleeping arrangements and silent 'ships that pass in the night' moments, Wendy actually pleaded -"Look Charlie, I know I've been so wrong. I don't want to lose you; I realise that now. What if I promised never to see him again? Can we at least try to put it all behind us?"

Charlie remained calm; inside he was so hurt. He was heartbroken. It was a horrible pain. He knew, even though before the affair she was amazing, that there was no real hope.

"I'm sorry. That can't happen. Trust is everything. That's gone. Now I know that I can't trust you, we cannot be together."

That hurt him to say that. Wendy broke down, sobbing. In her heart of hearts, however, she knew he was right.

As more time passed, they became more civil and possibly came close, a couple of times, to actually having a laugh together or a cosy evening in front of the telly. Charlie remained resolute. She had rammed a dagger into his heart, that pain was going to be there for a while, he knew that they had to part. He began to look for somewhere else to live.

He realised, quite quickly, that Bournemouth was a bit pricey so he spread his search a little wider. He remembered that during the summer he had visited Poole (about six or seven miles from Bournemouth) and thought that it was a nice place, more picturesque and property was a tad cheaper.

During his searching, (with the help of some dodgy estate agents) he stumbled across a really nice two-bed flat, in a quiet area. A bargain, mainly because it needed a bit of work doing to it but nothing that wasn't

doable (in estate agent speak "would suit a DIY enthusiast") He got lucky with a building society too. He found one that was running a promotional campaign and nabbed quite a favourable mortgage deal (They were not quite 'giving them away', as the estate agent said!) So, everything was set.
When he told Wendy about it, she was ok, no hysterics, no 'scene'. She was more accepting of the situation. When the moving day came, she was even more agreeable. She arranged it, with a friend, that Charlie could borrow a van to use for moving his stuff. He recalls, at the time, slightly stressing -
"Please don't be Ken's, please don't be Ken's!"
Charlie, all his life, felt that he was quite philosophical about things. To him, life was full of big moments, milestones in one's timeline. Here was another. After the move, he returned the van to 'Wendy's' flat and handed her the keys, he knew that this would probably be the last time that he'd see her. The last time that he'd see that beautiful girl that he actually dared to, almost, believe would be the love of his life. As he drove away, in his own car, he was sure that that would be the last time he'd ever lay his eyes on her.
Until now.
"It's great to see you Charlie, you're looking well. Listen, if you're not busy or in a hurry or anything, do you fancy going to have a coffee now and a chat? A catch-up. It would be nice, don't you think? Just like old times."
He looked her in the eye. Many thoughts were rushing through his brain. Although she was looking good and in normal circumstances, he would quite fancy her, he remembered that pain that she had caused him. He thought of being really 'loved-up' with her and her trampling all over his heart. He pictured her laying on

the bed that day (the bed that they shared) with her face bright red when he had rumbled her. He imagined Ken and her, all over each other. How could she calmly act as though none of that ever happened? Does she actually believe that they could pick up where they left off? Or that it would be 'just like old times'?

All the heartache and pain that she had caused him, he really would be fully justified to yell at her -

"Spend time with you? You must be joking, you heartless bitch! After all that you did to me? You buggered-up my life, you cheated on me! You broke my heart big time. You can just fuck off!"

That was all in Charlie's fantasy world. He smiled at her, carefully picked up his shopping basket and calmly said -

"No, thanks. I don't think so. I don't think that would be a good idea."

He wandered towards the tills, leaving her standing in the 'Milk, butter and Cheese' aisle. He didn't look back.

He knew that he'd done the right thing.

Chapter Fifteen Poole

Charlie hadn't realised that it had been six months. Exactly six months. He hadn't really thought about it. Why would he work it out like that? It was only when it was pointed out to him, that it became clear.
He was 'getting on with his life' in Poole (he always thought that was a daft expression 'getting on with your life'. What does that mean? Everyone 'gets on with their lives' that's what they do!)
He was beginning to be a bit tired of his job. At first it was funny because it was a doddle but now, he was thinking that it didn't challenge him enough. He couldn't believe he was thinking like this. It suited him to have no pressure and go through the motions, didn't it?
His love life was non-existent. He hadn't really had a proper 'serious' relationship since Wendy. He'd been with other girls but they were just 'flings', temporary, nothing concrete. He wasn't desperately lonely or anything but sometimes he wished he had a partner or companion (he can't believe that he'd used those actual words!)
Charlie was lucky, in a way. Although he lived a three-and-a-half-hour journey from Chelmsford, he didn't have to keep going back and forth. Thanks to good old Steve's help, he could sort a lot of stuff out, regarding his Dad's 'affairs', over the phone, by email or by post. Steve had arranged for the charity people to go round to Dad's flat and clear everything out.
By the time that happened, Don had already been to the flat to collect the three-piece (The one that Dad 'would have wanted him to have')
Charlie thought that was amusing. Don had hardly been there when Dad was living there and now, he was

swiftly round there again. Funny that, just when there was something in it for him and the Ice Maiden!
Steve told Charlie that the bikes had gone too. He'd bumped into Stan at the flats and he told him that he saw Don (and a friend) load them onto a truck. Don then departed and left the lock-up keys swinging from the padlock on the door. Stan took them in. Charlie wondered what would happen to the bikes. In the end he thought that he had a pretty good idea. He couldn't get too bogged down with worrying about them, it was all about Don and his conscience now.
Steve had been great with his help with liaising with the estate agent too. Charlie had finally got Don to agree an asking price (after a couple of heated phone calls) and it went on the market. It got some interest straight away and they actually had two offers. Charlie thought that one of them was acceptable, it was 'in the region of…' but Don was having none of it. He refused to consider it and the 'buyer' subsequently went elsewhere.
Some weeks later, another potential buyer came along, seemed keen and made another acceptable offer (so Charlie thought) Don was about to blow his top and rudely reject it when Charlie 'had words'.
"Don, you've got to stop being so greedy. Your half of the money from this flat will be dropped in your lap. You won't have to do anything. If you keep turning down these reasonable offers, this sale could drag on for ages. It always looks bad if a property is on the market for too long. People ask why. It will put them off. The more money you hang on for, the longer it will take for you to get anything at all. For Christ's sake, be reasonable and let's get it sold. It's bloody good money that we're getting for doing sod all!"
Don reluctantly agreed after, obviously, consulting with the Ice Maiden. Charlie was proud of himself. He only

occasionally stood up to Don but when he did, it usually ended up a shouting match and quite unpleasant (but strangely satisfying). He was pleased that he'd been assertive and he'd eventually made Don see sense. After six months (as it was) the sale was just about to be completed so Don and Carol could get their hands on the money that Charlie thought they hardly deserved. He had to resign himself to this as it was Dad's wish.
During the six months, Charlie had had a couple of email exchanges with Michael from Dublin. They were mainly of the 'how are you getting on?', 'hope you're well' and 'come and see us anytime' type of messages but Charlie was pleased that they were keeping in touch.
The people from COFFs had sent Charlie a letter. He had absolutely no idea how they'd got his address but it was okay. In the letter, they were saying 'thank you' and they had enclosed a photo take inside the recreation room at Chelmsford Fire Station. The photo was Martin Whymark and 'Diesel' man (Charlie never did find out his name!) pointing at a framed photo they'd just put up. It was of Dad in his first watch photo at Chelmsford. Charlie was pleased that it had made it on to their 'Wall of Fame'. He wondered why they hadn't put up the 'naked with snowman' one!
Although the time passing had relinquished the shock of Barbara's 'announcement', it was always there. Every now and then, Charlie found himself dwelling on it again. Thankfully, he wasn't living in Chelmsford or visiting there much so the faces and places that would remind him and make it 'real' were far away.
He still had this terrible fear of someone, or everyone, finding out the awful truth (even though, in his heart of hearts, he knew that that was never going to happen) He

imagined Don's reaction. He would find it hilarious. It would be something new to beat him with.
He'd be going on, saying something like -
"Ha-ha! I don't believe it! You were shagging your own sister! Only you would be stupid enough to do that! Bloody hell, it's not like you're living in rural Norfolk where this sort of thing goes on!"
He'd enjoy telling everyone else too.
Thankfully, Charlie thought, it would never come to that. There's no way Don, or anyone else would ever find out. It was just him who was tormented by that information.
Charlie found out that it was six months since his Dad's funeral (EXACTLY six months) when he got the phone call from his Dad's solicitor.
"Mister Charles Mills? Good morning. This is…" (Charlie forgot the name) "…from Elsworthy and Holland Solicitors. We were instructed, by your late father. Mister Bryan Mills, to contact you on this date. The date being, six months to the day since Bryan Mills' funeral. I have to inform you that there is an envelope, addressed to yourself, that has been held with us until this specific day. We have instructions that you are to collect it in person. Our instructions are, to tell you that it's contents are very important and, although it is not 'urgently' time-critical, you are advised to accept this envelope and study it's contents as soon as possible."
"Bloody hell!" thought Charlie "ANOTHER envelope! Dad loved his envelopes. AND his mysteries."
"Oh, right. Thank you for the call. I'm assuming this means me coming to your office in Chelmsford and collecting it?"

"That is correct, sir. I repeat our guidance, '…as soon as possible'. We will be sending you an email to confirm all this."
"I should have known." Thought Charlie "Solicitors have to have a paper trail. It covers their arses AND they can usually charge extra for it!"
What on Earth could be in this one? ANOTHER one! He'd thought that, six months ago, that was it, as regards the envelopes. He then started to worry about the mystery contents. Could it be something shocking or something tame? Like more instructions on people to contact, people to see? More old memories to dig up? Oh well, back to Chelmsford again. He wondered why it had to be collected in person. Why not send it registered mail? Does that mean it's 'Chelmsford related'? This is just ridiculous speculation. There was nothing else for it. He had to go. He would ring Steve and let him know that he was coming.
He had to go 'as soon as possible' so there was nothing else for it.

Chapter Sixteen The 'Final' One.

Obviously, on that three-and-a-half-hour journey, Charlie had plenty of time to think. He thought about how this particular trip was different to others that he'd done in the last year or so.

When he was coming to see Dad, he always used to feel a bit like he did when he was a child. He would get a bit excited. He would wonder how Dad would be, what he was going to talk to Dad about, what Dad was going to tell him about his life. Even though, he was often just picking Dad up and having the laborious return journey to look forward to, it was okay. His Dad would be good company and he'd always make him laugh.

The last Christmas Dad was around for, was just like that. Dad was in such good spirits, he looked forward to coming to Poole and consequently was such a laugh. He had Charlie in stitches. The downer always came though. It came when Charlie had to drive back to Dorset alone, either after visiting Dad or dropping him off.

He remembered travelling back for the reading of the will. Not a great time for him. He was still shocked about his Dad's death and that journey was so depressing. He felt that he was perhaps a bit selfish about it but the anticipation of the will reading, Don, having to go to the flat and to the funeral all filled him with dread. Surely that would make anyone a bit miserable.

The last time he went was again different. He knew that he was going to see Steve and stay at his. He also knew that he would have to go to the flat with Don, to sort stuff out. The two, sort of, cancelled each other out. He remembers having a strange feeling about him as he drove to Chelmsford that day.

This time, again, was very different. He felt strangely relaxed. He didn't feel under any pressure. It may have been because he knew that he didn't have to meet up with Don. It may have been because he knew that he didn't have to go to Dad's flat, with all the memories there. He was actually feeling a little bit excited about this new envelope. There was always that thrill of the anticipation with each one but this time, it felt slightly different. It couldn't be anything vital or life-changing otherwise it would have been included in the pile with the others and not sit in the solicitors' drawer for six months. However, he did ask himself, why wait six months? That, he could not figure out. He kept telling himself to stop speculating. Just go to the solicitors', read it, carry out the instructions and what will be, will be. His Dad had planned everything, down to the finest detail so it was bound to something that was important to him, something good and exciting.

Perhaps, the omens were good. Today it was not such a bastard M25. He went clock-wise (always a gamble) and sailed through. There was a lot of traffic obviously, there always was but, it kept flowing and didn't hold him up at all.

When he was on the A12 and then almost in Chelmsford, he purposefully did not even glance at the grounds of Hylands House to his left. He stared dead ahead. It was in vain. It didn't stop any thoughts of Elaine entering his head. Oh, yes, Hylands. That's where he had a sexual encounter with his own sister. "I didn't know! I didn't know!" he found himself shouting aloud. He felt as though he was pleading his innocence but it didn't stop the continuous torment he felt inside.

He encountered the traffic mayhem that Chelmsford city centre usually presented. He was quite calm

though. He wasn't chasing the clock. He had no appointment booked. They said that all he had to do, was pop in and sign for the envelope. No need for a sit-down meeting with anyone.
He eventually parked up and calmly wandered across the city centre. He was so relaxed. He had a wonderful feeling of tranquillity about him. He found himself smiling at total strangers. He found himself not minding the hustle and bustle of all the pedestrians (that would normally get on his nerves.)
Normally he would be doing his brisk walk for fear of being late but he amazed himself by actually taking his time!
He eventually found himself on Duke Street, outside Elsworthy and Holland Solicitors. This time there was no feeling of dread, no nerves, no stress. He calmly let himself in.
"Ah, Mister Mills. Mister Holland has placed this package here for you. Do you have a form of I.D.? Just need that and your signature. Thank you."
Charlie duly complied and the secretary handed over an A4 sized envelope with a smaller envelope attached to it with a paper clip. He smiled when he noticed, that on the top right corner of each envelope, was a number, written with, what seemed like a permanent marker. The smaller envelope had a number one, the larger had a number two. Dad was being all organised again.
Charlie gestured towards a seat in the reception area.
"Do you mind…? Would it be okay for a moment…?"
"Of course, Mister Mills."
Charlie sat on the wooden chair, took a deep breath then tore open the smaller envelope, envelope number one. Inside was a folded A4 sheet with a hand-written message.
Charlie,

Thank you so much for going along with my crazy envelope scheme. It might seem daft to you but it is important to me.
I thank you for carrying out all the instructions in the previous envelopes (I know that you have, I know that I can rely on you!)
As you're reading this, it will have been exactly (give or take) six months since my funeral and, please trust me, it will all become clear as to why I wanted it to be like this.
Please now go to a quiet place, on your own, away from anyone, where you won't be disturbed. Then I would like you to open the larger envelope. Please read its contents, in its entirety. You may feel like stopping but please Charlie, it's important that you read it all.
Once again, thank you for going along with all this.
Love,
Bryan.

Charlie sat in that chair for a moment, gathering his thoughts. Now, he was slightly concerned. There seemed to be a bit more mystery and intrigue about this one. Why '…a quiet place…'? Why would he '…feel like stopping…'? That feeling of tranquillity and that calmness was all draining away. This seemed to be quite serious. Now, he was anxious to know what was in the larger envelope. It must be something 'heavy', if his Dad thought it was enough to make him feel like stopping.
He thanked the secretary and was on his way. Once outside, it was back. The brisk walk. He was definitely in a hurry. No time for this 'smiling at strangers' nonsense. Pedestrians were getting in his way. He had to get back to his car quickly.

He rushed into the aging multi-storey car park and almost forgot to pay. He decided that he'd have to leave there and go to a quieter place. That old carpark was not the place for peace and quiet.
Once in his car, he was worried about doing the sort of drive where you don't concentrate. The one where you end up somewhere without remembering how you got there. He deliberately concentrated on his driving, his safety, even. Once he had left the carpark, he decided to head for Springfield, an area he knew well.
It came to him as he got onto Springfield Road and went past Tesco. It was like a double epiphany. The first part was, he decided to head for Timsons Lane. It was off Peel Road, right at the other end of Springfield Road. He'd parked-up there before, many years ago, when he'd wanted to be alone or to kill time. At the end of Timsons Lane was a small carpark. It was mainly used for the Rugby Club but when there was no game on, it was a quiet, out of the way place where you could park and look over Coronation Park.
The second part of his epiphany made him feel hot. He suddenly thought of why he had to go to a place where he wouldn't be disturbed and he must finish reading and all that. His Dad was going to confess all about Barbara and Elaine! What else could it be? However, why would he wait until now? Why would he reveal it to him at all? Now, the suspense was beginning to really get to him. He had to stop himself from speeding up Springfield Road or roaring round the corner into Peel Road. He turned into Timsons Lane then into the, thankfully empty carpark. Carefully, he reversed into a space next the hedge, turned off the engine and looked at the envelope on the passenger seat.
"Well, here goes!"

He took two or three deep breaths, gulped then tore it open.
Inside, he found several sheets of A4, all hand-written, all numbered.
<u>One</u>.
Charlie, thank you for your co-operation with this envelope business. I hope you understand why I did this and why it is important to me.
Charlie, PLEASE PLEASE read all the contents. ALL of the contents. Once you are done, feel free to make your own judgement, draw your own conclusions and, hopefully be tolerant and understanding.
You may think that I've taken the 'cowards' way out here, maybe you're right but I promise you Charlie, I love you and I couldn't bear to see you upset. I swear to you Charlie, I have never done anything to deliberately hurt or upset you. You have been far too important to me.
I think that you have the right to know the truth about some things that happened many years ago.
I will tell you everything, all of it, the whole truth, warts and all.
I loved your mother so much; she was the best thing that ever happened to me and that is why I've been torn up with guilt for a long time.
I'm talking about 1967/68. We had been married around four years; this was a short while after Don was born. I don't know if it was the stress of having a baby about the place, money worries or whatever (I promise you, I'm not making excuses, just trying to find possible reasons) but your Mum and me went through a bit of a rough time with each other. It wasn't nasty, there were no rows or anything, it's

just that we sort of became distant, we temporarily drifted apart, if you like.
At that time, we were very good friends with Barbara and Derek Robson (as I'm sure you know) I bumped into Barbara around that time and, I don't know why, but I confided in her about our problems. She was so lovely, so understanding. She really helped me. The thing is, I'm ashamed to say, I don't know how it happened but one thing led to another and we became more than good friends. I'm so sorry Charlie but we had a brief fling. I think half of the reason was that she also confided in me that her and Derek were also not getting on at that time. They weren't talking, they were in separate rooms and all that. They were often falling out; it happened many times during their marriage. Me and Barbara found comfort with each other. I know that sounds as though I'm trying to dress this up as something that it wasn't but we never wanted to hurt anyone. We were never going to leave our other halves. We knew it was just a temporary thing.
The thing is, I can't believe how stupid we were. We were careless. There's no easy way to tell you this but I have to tell you Charlie, that Barbara fell pregnant. There was no getting away from it. We both knew that this was going to cause massive problems. Barbara and Derek hadn't been together in that way for a while so there was no doubt that it was mine. We didn't know what to do, who to turn to. We were so scared. So afraid that we'd hurt your Mum and Derek.
"I knew it was this! I knew he was confessing this. Luckily, I already know it all so it's not such a shock. I don't know how to feel about Dad coming clean and

telling me in this way"
Charlie almost felt relieved. Almost.

Two.

We kept it to ourselves for a bit. Pretty stupid, I know, but we were scared. How on earth do you bring that up in a conversation or tell someone out of the blue?

We decided that there was nothing else for it but we HAD to tell your Mum and Derek. We decided, rightly or wrongly, to tell them together. I don't know if that was cowardly or whatever but we were beside ourselves and didn't know what to do.

I think Barbara must have been about three and a bit months gone by then so it was beginning to show. That may have been what made us own up.

Here's the complicated part, Charlie. Remember, I'm begging you to read this right until the end.

What we didn't know was that Derek had rumbled us. I don't know to this day how but he knew what we were up to. The poor bloke. He was all over the place. Anyway, he felt that the only person he could talk to about it was your Mum. When I was on nights, he went round and told her all he knew. I know that they were both devastated and probably hated us, understandably. Once they'd got over the initial shock and calmed down, they had discussions about what to do, where to go next. They had a few of these chats when I was on night duty. During this time, I know this must be hard for you to take this in, Charlie, they became close and, just like me and Barbara, they found comfort with each other. They had an affair too. I can hardly condemn them, can I? After what I'd one.

"Bloody hell! I can't believe it! It's like the bleeding plot of a soap opera! This is incredible. I'm shaking. I have to know how this played out!"
Charlie, please try to stay calm and read it all. You have to know everything and, I'm afraid, it gets more shocking for you but you have to know it all.
"Christ! That's what Barbara kept shouting after me when I legged-it away from her house. 'The whole truth'? now I'm really scared."
I was seeing Barbara for a while before your Mum and Derek got together. I just read that back, Charlie and it just sounds awful. I'm so sorry that you have to find all this out.
We arranged to meet at our house. I told your Mum that we had someone coming round and Barbara told Derek that they were going to visit friends. I think she did well to persuade him to come in our front door!
It was so awkward when we all sat in the living room. How the bloody hell do you start?
This next part may shock you even more, Charlie. I'm so sorry. I love you. You have the right to know and I hope you're not full of hate afterwards.

Charlie was shaking. That last sentence terrified him. …'full of hate…' what could that mean?
<u>Three.</u>
We, meaning me and Barbara, had no idea that your Mum and Derek had been seeing each other so it was an incredible shock for us. We tried to tell them about us, seeing each other and the fact that we'd been careless. What we didn't know was that your Mum and Derek were involved and, of all things, had also been careless.

"What? Fuck! What? Oh, bloody hell! Oh my God!" Charlie was in full panic mode. Just when he thought that nothing more could shock him, down came this bombshell. Did he have this right, in his head? Was he fully grasping it all? He had to read on, eyes wide open, mouth gaping.

We were going to tell your Mum and Derek that Barbara was over three months gone when they told us that your Mum had just found out that she was pregnant! And they were 100% certain it was Derek's.

I'm so sorry that you had to find out this way, Charlie. It must be a huge shock for you. You have to understand that – Barbara gave birth to Elaine and I am the father. Your Mum gave birth to you and Derek is the father.

With that, Charlie threw the sheets across to the passenger side and leapt out of his car. He was screaming. He found himself smacking both his hands on to his head, like some religious fanatic. He was walking rapidly round his car then back the other way. He was swearing, shouting and screaming. He fell backwards on to the bonnet of his car and lay there, staring at the sky. Once again, there was too much to take in. Too much shocking information to process all at once. His heart was racing. His stomach was tied in knots. He wasn't sure if he was thinking or actually talking out loud.

"Oh, shit! Bloody hell. This is too much... My Dad is not my Dad!... All these years! …I knew my Dad, who's not my Dad, was a bit of a, you know, he put it about, so I understand but my Mum! Oh God. At least she was my Mum… Derek, Derek is my Dad, WAS my Dad!... Oh my God, I can't get my head round all this. I can't take this in."

His head was spinning. How could he fully understand all this? What would it mean to him? How would it affect him from now on? What about his memories of his relationship with his Dad, or should he call him Bryan? What about his memories of Derek, his real Dad? Derek was his real Dad. How can he ever get used to that?

He tried to take deep breaths. He tried to calm himself. He hadn't finished reading it all and his Dad, or Bryan, was insistent that he did. What happens now? Does he have to think about Bryan any differently? Does he have to think about Derek any differently? They're both gone. So is his Mum. It's just Barbara left. Just Barbara who has to carry the burden of this knowledge. And now him.

"But…me and Don are brothers. Only we're not. Or are we? Shit! This is so confusing. Then there's Elaine. I bet she doesn't know any of this. Elaine. Bloody hell, she's not my sister! I did nothing wrong. That's why nobody stopped me. It must have been a bit awkward but not, well, illegal or incestuous."

He sat up and looked around. Fortunately, there was no one about. No one to hear him rant and thrash about like a nutter.

Dad, or Bryan said that I have to read it all before being judgemental. "Bloody hell, he was having a tin-bath, wasn't he? How could I not freak out after reading that? Surely, there can be nothing more in there that could TOTALLY do my head in!"

He tried to calm himself, compose himself. He got back into the driver's seat and gathered the sheets of paper up. He made sure that they were in order before he continued.

I know that this must have been an incredible shock to you, Charlie. There was never, ever an easy way to tell you all this.
All four of us were shocked too. It took a while for it all to sink in. we all just sat, staring, no one saying a word. In the end, I had to break the silence (me and my big gob) I said "Well, this is a bit of a pickle isn't it?"
It was weird. All four of us laughed then all four of us burst into tears.
You see, Charlie, I loved your Mum SO much (I know, I had a fling but it was JUST a fling) I felt so awful inside because I'd hurt her, betrayed her and to see her, sat there, crying, was killing me. I had to put my arms around her, she was distraught. And, do you know what? She hugged me. The tightest hug ever. I know I didn't deserve her but she loved me. It was that moment that I knew. I knew that, no matter what, I had to be with her.
Charlie got choked up reading those words. His Mum was a wonderful woman. He felt so sad that she went through all that. All that stress.
Four.
I looked over and Barbara was on her knees in front of Derek, holding his hands. They were just looking into each other's eyes and crying.
It stayed just like that for a while then, once again, old big gob here had to pipe up again.
"So, what are we going to do about this then, people? We have to deal with it, we can't ignore it. We need to talk about it, no matter how uncomfortable it might be."
It was amazing, when I think about it. We sat there, in our living room, back as couples, cuddling up and everything. We, even then, started discussing the

situation, like adults. I know we were adults but there was no animosity, no finger-pointing, no blaming anyone.

I can't remember exactly how it went or who said what but basically, we came to the only conclusion that we could.

Each couple had to bring up the child as if it were their own. Derek and Barbara with Elaine, me and your Mum with you. You have to remember, it was the late sixties. Imagine the scandal if this got out, imagine the gossip, imagine everyone passing judgement on us. I know we probably deserved it for being so stupid but the children, you and Elaine, you didn't deserve a lifetime of that. You were totally innocent.

So, that was what we did. As far as we were concerned, no one else needed to know. We kept it all to ourselves. No one was any the wiser. Elaine was born then a few months later, you were born. It was very strange at first seeing Elaine and knowing etc but as time went on and we kept up appearances and stuck to our guns, it became normal. Elaine was Barbara and Derek's, you were mine and your Mum's. And you WERE my son, Charlie. I know I wasn't your biological father but I WAS your Dad. I couldn't have loved you more. You were a wonderful child. It was so amazing to be with you as you grew up. We were so close, as I'm sure you know, I was so proud of you.

Charlie felt a couple of tears run down his cheek. His Dad, Bryan was right. What else could they do? They had to keep the secret. He never really knew Derek. Derek was always a bit aloof, a bit distant. Whereas Bryan was a wonderful Dad. He was great with him and Don, even though Don could be 'difficult' at times.

Yes, he SHOULD still call him 'Dad'. He WAS his Dad. Isn't there an old saying? 'Any fool can be a father, it takes a real man to be a Dad'
Now, he wasn't saying that Derek was a fool, he just didn't know him very well, it's just that Bryan WAS his Dad!

Five.

As time went on, we became more accustomed to the situation. It became normal, if you like. I think I can use the expression, we were like 'happy families'. I know that Barbara and Derek had their problems over the years, bust-ups and fallings-out but they loved Elaine and were good parents. Your Mum and I grew even closer and I like to think, from then on, we had a great home life. We had such fun, such great memories with you and Don growing up.
There was no conscious decision to stop being so close to Barbara and Derek, it just, sort of, happened. It happens with friends; things change over the years. Barbara was so sweet. She discreetly sent me photos of Elaine through the years (she used to post them to me at the Fire Station) and it was reassuring to me to know that Elaine was in good hands.
Then came your teenage years. We couldn't believe it when you started going out with Elaine. At first, we thought it was a little bit awkward but we grew to quite like it. Barbara was okay with it but Derek had a real problem accepting it. I'm not knocking the bloke, we're all different and, I think, he was just being instinctively protective.
Soon after that, we lost your Mum. My Katie. My world fell apart. The pain was unbearable and, for a while, I thought that I would actually go under, I was close to an awful breakdown. I really could not

cope. Do you know what saved me? You know what pulled me through? You did, Charlie. You were amazing. I don't know what I would have done without you. You were my rock. Don wasn't much use. Not necessarily his fault, that's just the way he is. You, however, dragged me up from the depths and, once again, I was so proud of you.
Charlie began to weep. Him and his Dad were very close at that time and it seemed like the natural thing to do, to support him. He had no idea quite how much it meant to his Dad.
I have to tell you, Charlie, I fully understand why you had to get away, a couple of years later. I never condemned you for moving away, I get why that happened. I often thought I was being selfish and it was all about me. It's only when I stopped and thought about it that I realised that you had lost your Mum. (as had Don) but you were so supportive to me. Don dealt with it his own way. Don will be Don (I know, you hate that expression. You think that gets him off the hook when his behaviour is 'questionable')
Even when you were miles away, in Bath and then Poole, you were a terrific son to me. I would go so far to say that you were like the brother I never had.

Six.
I know things haven't been easy for you, Charlie. You got given the run-around by those two girls. That one in Bath (can't remember her name) and that Wendy in Bournemouth. It was a shame because you're a good lad and you didn't deserve that.
Even through all that, you still looked out for me. You always had time for me. I will say it – more so

than Don. I know he's married to the Ice Maiden (please never let on that we call her that!) but there are times when he should be his own man, maybe stand up to her. Having said that, 'his own man' can be not so nice, a bit selfish but, he's my son and I'll love him (doesn't mean I'll like him all the time!)
Charlie, I hope this news is not TOO devastating for you. I know I took the coward's way of telling you and I'm so sorry for that. There was never the right time to tell you. You deserve to know the truth and I hope, when you get over the shock, you will understand why it all happened.
Charlie, I loved like you were my own son – you WERE my own son! I hope this news doesn't tarnish any memories you have of me and of your childhood. We all did what we thought was right and we did the very best we could for you.
Charlie, once again, thank you SO much for all you did for me. You're an amazing son, an amazing human being. I'm SO proud of you. I love you.
Bryan. (DAD)

That was it for Charlie. He lost it. He slumped over the steering wheel, sobbing. His Dad was a wonderful man, a great Dad so those words meant so much to him. Charlie had never had such churned-up emotions. He was still grieving. He originally had the shock of finding out that his Dad was Elaine's father (and, therefore, he had thought, she was his sister) now he had the additional bombshell that BOTH his parents had had affairs and his own real father was Derek, a man he had barely known.
This was too much for him. He probably hadn't cried like this since he was a child, except maybe when his Mum died, but it was all coming out now. He sat back

in the seat, his face soaked in tears. Though his tear-induced hazy vision he spotted a man stood in front of his car, looking concerned. Charlie waved him away, unashamedly with a face full of emotion. That poor man, just taking his dog for a walk and he spies a grown man, in a car, wailing and sobbing.
Charlie watched the troubled man disappear into the distance, the dog trotting beside him.
Charlie wiped his face, then wiped it a few more times with his sleeve. He was sniffing and breathing heavily, trying to control himself. He gathered the loose sheets of paper together. It was then that he noticed that there was one more page. He'd almost missed it as he put all the sheets together. There was a page seven.

Seven.
Charlie, I know you've probably had enough of these envelopes and their instructions. (And after all that you've just read in this one, I could understand that you must be feeling very mixed-up and emotional.)
Please Charlie, this is important. I have one more 'task' that I need you to carry out.
My Cortina.
I asked you in my will to continue restoring it and I trust that you have been. I want you to go to the Cortina, open the driver's door, remove the vinyl panelling on the inside of the door. There you will find something that I have left for you.
I apologise for the 'mystery' involved here. Please let me explain.
I'm sorry if you think that I've been testing you here but I had to be sure.

The reason I instructed that the Solicitor waited six months was to give you time to do one of these three things:

1. **To continue restoring the Cortina, keeping it, looking after it.**
2. **To sell it on.**
3. **To scrap it.**

I know you, Charlie, I know which one of those you've chosen. If I'm correct, (I'm sure I am) please carry out my wish. Please don't take too long over it (the reason will be explained to you)
If you've chosen number two, I imagine it will be very difficult for you to carry this out. Not impossible but, remember, you can't take too long over this.
If you've chosen number three, then this is all irrelevant.
I know you won't have let me down, Charlie. I've always been able to rely on you.
Go to the Cortina.
Love Bryan.

"Oh my God" thought Charlie "He's done it again! He loved a mystery. I can't believe that, even as he knew he wasn't long for this world, he took the time to meticulously arrange and plan all these instructions. I'm a bit surprised that he may have doubted me over the Cortina. Of course, I'd carry out his wish, I'm not Don! I obviously have to carry out this one. This is a really mysterious one '…you will find something I have left for you.' This is so intriguing; I HAVE to know. I wonder why I can't take too long over it. What does that mean?"
He sat for a short while, composing himself. He wiped his face, blew his nose and took several deep breaths.

He stepped out of his car and looked around. It was quite peaceful, apart from some traffic noise in the distance. He was enjoying the fresh air. He felt as though he had been through some torture. He felt raw, he felt almost as though he'd been beaten up. It was tiring, all this emotional, shocked and crying behaviour. He checked his watch. He knew that he had to meet Steve to get access to the Cortina (he was going round there anyway to see him) It was a bit too early. Steve had told him what time he was getting home so Charlie had a bit of time to kill.
He decided that he'd drive to Steve's then go for a walk around Springfield. A nostalgia trip. Perhaps he could wander past some old haunts, bring back some childhood memories. He needed some time to calm down, to properly compose himself. God knows what he was going to find in that door of the Cortina. He got back in his car, tidied up the sheets of paper and put them back in their envelope.
"No point in being untidy. No need for a mess" He laughed. That was the sort of thing his Dad would say to him. He loved his Dad. Dad had raised him properly, he had taught him well.
Charlie took his time with the short drive across Springfield. His mind still racing. There was all the new and shocking stuff that he had to take in, as well as the new, intriguing instructions that he was to follow.
After parking on Steve's driveway, he again checked his watch. It was mainly to see how far he could wander off. He wanted to be back as Steve got home. He wanted to greet him without rushing straight into the Cortina business. He didn't wish to be selfish and rude; Steve had been such a good mate.
He ambled up the road towards old Springfield. No sooner had he got to the corner but, it was there, right in

front of him. On the other side of the road stood The Tulip.
He stood for a moment, staring at it. He tried to picture how it was in 'his day'. Not easy as it had changed considerably. He looked at the large 'Tulip' sign.
He sighed and thought -
"Sod it. Might as well pop in for a quick one. I think I need a drink after all that!"

Chapter Seventeen The Saloon Bar.

Charlie instinctively made for the saloon bar but as soon as he noticed how busy it was, he turned and went in the public bar. He thought that it was a bit busy for a weekday afternoon. When he was a lad, all you would get in here during the week was a couple of old boys and a dog.

Although he liked the big comfy chairs in the saloon, the public bar was quite smart and comfortable. None of your old 'spit and sawdust' here.

As he approached the bar, he noticed Mick, the landlord, behind the bar at the other end, holding court with a couple of older men. Mick was wearing another flamboyant, ill-fitting shirt. He was obviously hot. The shirt had a couple of damp patches and his forehead, under his sweep-over, was shining with moisture.

As Charlie waited to be served, he listened in to their conversation.

Mick was in full flow.

"Well, of course they criticise the England manager. The England manager always gets criticised. The trouble is, everyone thinks they can pick a better team than him, always. They'll always find something to moan about. You must remember how they were with Sir Alf. I heard them. It was all 'Oh, he played without wingers, had a system that had no wingers, it set the English game back years!' Bloody hell! The bloke had just won us the world cup! The bloody world cup! And still they find something to have a go about!"

Charlie smiled. He had heard his Dad say something similar before.

Mick came away from his audience and approached Charlie.

"Good afternoon, sir. What can I get you?"

"Hello Mick, how are you doing? I'll have a pint of Guinness please."
"Oh, hello son! It's err…it's…"
"Charlie."
"That's it. Charlie. Charlie. I never forget a face. Names, though… You're Bryan's boy, aren't you?"
Charlie paused for a moment and thought -
"Well, actually, I'm not, as I just found out. What am I saying? Yes, I am. I bloody well am!"
"Yes, Mick. Yes, that's what I am. I'm Bryan's boy. How are things?"
Mick was the usual pub landlord chatty stereotype. He talked to Charlie for a short while about something and nothing. Pub landlords were good at small talk. They would usually have opinions about everything but not usually too controversial, for fear of upsetting the punters. It was often the weather, the price of everything etc. They even touch on the 'Going away this year?' and the 'Doing anything special for Christmas?' that hairdressers specialise in.
Charlie just went along with it and supped his cold Guinness. Eventually Mick either remembered something or ran out of 'landlord small talk'.
"Here, Charlie. Come over here, son. I want to show you something."
Charlie chuckled to himself -
"Now, if I'd said that, Mick's reply would have been something like 'Ooo, as the actress said to the bishop!'.
Mick led Charlie across the public bar to the far wall. Once there, he turned and proudly said
"Have a butchers'. I reckon you'll like these."
He pointed to the wall. There were three of the photos Charlie had brought in six months ago. They were in lovely frames and took pride of place next to the big old clock. The photos were of the cup winning side, the old

team group and the beer garden (before the extension) each featuring his Dad.
Charlie was so pleased, so proud. There were those photos of his Dad, in his 'local', for all to see, to remember.
"Thank you so much, Mick. They look great there. Dad would be so chuffed with that."
"Pleasure son. Bryan was well-loved and well-respected here. It's only fitting that there's some sort of a memorial. Football and drinking were what Bryan was all about here. And laughter, plenty of that."
They both looked closely at the three photos for a moment, not saying a word, just reflecting.
"That's brilliant Mick, I'm so pleased. Thank you."
A moment of awkwardness followed. Neither of them seemed to know how to move things along. They both stood, smiling, shuffling.
Charlie broke first.
"Well, there's a lovely pint of Guinness over there with my name on it."
"Oh, yes. Don't let me keep you from that!"
They both returned to the other end of the bar.
As Mick went round to his side, Charlie took a huge slurp of the black stuff. He needed that, it had been a stressful hour or so. (or to be more accurate, a stressful last few months!)
He plonked his glass on the bar and said to Mick
"Mick, can you keep an eye on that for me? I've just got to pop to the little boy's room."
Mick was about to serve another customer.
"Just a moment, sir." He turned back to Charlie "Yes, of course, son. Hang on, the public bar toilets are being refurbed, you'll have to go to the saloon bar ones, if you don't mind. The management apologises for any inconvenience caused. Ha-ha!"

Charlie smiled.
"Ok Mick. Bit busy through there today, isn't it?"
"I know, great, isn't it? A weekday afternoon too! It's the local W.I. They have one afternoon here, about every six months or so."
"W.I.? Oh right. All 'Jam and Jerusalem' then, is it?"
"Bloody hell, Charlie. Whatever you do don't go in there and say that. They're a bit touchy about the stereotype image that they have. Apparently, they're trying to get away from that perception that people have of them. Last meeting they had in there, I was serving and I used the 'Jam and Jerusalem' line as a joke. Christ, didn't think I was going to get out alive! Bloody hell, if looks could kill…!"
"Thanks for the warning, Mick. I'll bear that in mind as I take my life into my own hands. Hope I return safely from the clutches of a load of grey-haired old dears!"
"Don't say I didn't warn you! And I tell you what, they're not all 'grey-haired old dears', there's one or two right tasties in there. What is it you call them? MILFs, isn't it? Or GILFs? Ha-ha!"
"Oi! Steady on Mick!"
Charlie left the public bar and wandered into the entrance hall, still shaking his head with disbelief at what Mick had said.
He pushed open the door to the saloon bar and was greeted with a sea of grey. Well, it wasn't quite like that. That was what he had planned to tell Mick when he returned to his pint of Guinness. It was busy though. Not as busy as his Dad's wake but he still had to weave his way through the groups of ladies to get to the Gents.
"Excuse me, madam"
"Why, what have you done?"
Everyone is a comedian today, thought Charlie.

Just before he got to the saloon bar toilets, he passed the spot where Mick had given him the microphone to make a speech at his Dad's wake. Charlie laughed. He was still quite embarrassed about that. The incredibly loud feedback, his pathetic words. That was six months ago. It seemed like yesterday.

After he had 'pointed his Percy at the porcelain' (he still did not know why he said that!) He washed his hands. That was another thing that his Dad was hot on. Every time, as kids, he would tell them to do that, until it became instinctive. (Don always thought it was funny to 'get away' with not doing it. Charlie used to think 'Oh, well done. What a result')

As he was washing, he looked in the mirror. He wasn't happy. He looked rough. His eyes were red and puffy. The whites were bloodshot. He then became paranoid that everyone must know that he'd been crying. He splashed some cold water into his face, he was hoping to sooth his eyes. Luckily, there were paper towels in a dispenser, he couldn't see himself bending over a fan dryer!

He composed himself, had another (disappointing) glance in the mirror then decided to head back to his Guinness.

He ambled into the saloon bar and found himself planning his route through the assembled W.I. ladies.

"Excuse me. Thank you. Excuse me, thanks."

He squeezed between the groups. As he rounded the corner, to the bar area, he manoeuvred himself through another group and that resulted in him being almost 'herded' right up to the bar itself. All that was between him and the bar was a solid line of ladies along the length of the bar, all waiting to be served. Charlie edged himself through a narrow gap behind them.

As he was about half-way along, one of the ladies, right in front of him, turned to speak to one of her friends.
"Lucy, it was a prosecco, wasn't it?"
She froze. Charlie froze.
It was Barbara.
They were face to face, probably less than a foot apart. They were both frozen, just staring. Both of them were shocked and surprised. Both of their minds were racing. It was probably only a few seconds but to them it seemed like an age.
Charlie cracked first. He smiled at Barbara. He noticed tears welling up in her eyes. Her bottom lip was quivering.
He suddenly remembered how he had spoken to her the last time he saw her. He felt so guilty. She had been right, he needed to know everything, all of it, the whole truth. It must have been horrible for her, the way he shouted at her and then ran off. Then he thought about all that she'd been through, all those years ago. Although she'd had an affair with his Dad, the pregnancy, the TWO pregnancies must have been so stressful for her (and the others) They were all young. They had the massive burden of their huge secret to deal with, not just back then but in the years since.
Charlie moved forwards and embraced Barbara. He felt her arms around him, she squeezed. She squeezed so tightly.
"I'm so sorry Barbara. I'm so sorry." He whispered into her ear.
"Oh, Charlie."
"Barbara, it's okay. I know everything. About Dad, about Derek and me. You were right. I needed to know it all. I'm just so sorry about how I spoke to you, how I swore, how I just ran off."

"Charlie, It's okay, it must have been quite a shock for you. Once it came out, I thought that you should know everything. I tried to tell you. I'm sorry. You shouldn't have found out like that."

"It's okay, it's okay. There was never any easy way. It was forced on you. You shouldn't have had to be put on the spot like that. Dad left me one of his envelopes. He's told me everything."

"Charlie, I'm actually glad that you finally know what happened. You deserve to know the truth. We all did what we did to protect you and Elaine. You must understand that. You two were innocent, there was no need to expose you to a scandal."

"I know Barbara. I understand."

"You must know that you were loved, both of you, by all four of us. We just had to keep up the appearance. No one else needed to find out. But you were loved, Charlie, you still are."

Charlie gave her a squeeze. It was a lovely moment for him.

It sort of dawned on him that, there he was, in front of the bar, in a room full of older ladies, in a lengthy embrace with Barbara, whispering in her ear. He didn't know what the other ladies made of it but he really didn't care.

"Barbara, you should never feel guilty about anything. What happened, happened. You dealt with it the only way you could, you all did. You all brought me and Elaine up in the right way. We had great childhoods; we were so happy. I have to ask though, does Elaine know about any of this?"

"Oh, no. No, Charlie. She doesn't. Please, I'd really like to keep it that way. I'm not sure she could handle it, if she ever found out."

"It's okay, Barbara, I understand. I'll never breath a word of it to anyone. It will just be you and me. It will be our secret."

Charlie felt some genuine love towards Barbara. He wasn't sure if it was her vulnerability, the fact that she had had that burden alone, she was almost 'family' or it was just the fact that she was a dear, sweet, lovely lady. She'd always been like that, he recalled. So kind, thoughtful and generous.

They chatted for few moments about the future and what that could bring. She told Charlie about Elaine, her marriage, her career. He tried to fill her in with details about his life. He was worried that his story was not too interesting but Barbara seemed to take it all in. She was intrigued about the mystery of the Cortina and this made Charlie check the time to see how long he had until Steve got home.

They promised to keep in touch with each other and they both really meant it, they had a bond between them, even more so now, that no one else could ever understand and it had to remain that way.

A big hug and a kiss, and Charlie was heading back to the public bar. As he moved away Barbara squeezed his hand tightly and smiled at him, her eyes welling up again. Charlie smiled back, feeling so much affection for her. No need for any more words.

He went through the door into the entrance hall without looking back. He was so glad that he'd bumped into her. He thought to himself that she'd probably have some explaining to do to her W.I. friends.

"Who was that man? You two were quite intimate, weren't you? Was he your toy-boy?" etc.

He got back to his Guinness in the public bar. He sunk what was left of it and realised that Mick was coming over to him.

"You were gone a while, son. I was going to send out a search party for you! I thought that some of those old dears had ravaged you!"
"That was it, Mick. There are some rich old widows in there, they couldn't resist a youngster like me!"
"Really? Bloody hell!"
It seemed as though Mick thought Charlie was serious as he went over to peep into the other bar.
"I've got to go, Mick. It was great to see you. Thank you for putting up those photos. Be careful in that other bar, they take no prisoners! Ask them to be gentle with you!"
"Yes, bye son. See you again soon."
He seemed to be distracted by the thought of the 'wealthy, sex-starved pensioners' next door.
As Charlie left the Tulip and began the short walk to Steve's, he realised that he was actually feeling good about everything. Obviously, he was still mourning his Dad and he was always going to miss him but all his Dad's 'affairs', Don, the revelations from fifty years ago, Barbara, all those things seemed to be under control, in his mind. There was much less to be stressed about and he was feeling much more relaxed about life in general. He remembered that he'd felt good about things earlier that day until the envelope from the solicitors, turned that on it's head. If he thought hard enough however, he could always find a doubt, that one thing that would occupy his mind. He knew what it was now. It was the concern as to what he would find in the Cortina. Could this be a nasty shock? Why the mystery? Could it be something awful? Surely not.

Chapter Eighteen The Cortina

As he rounded the corner, he could see the start of Hillary Close. Steve's car was on the driveway. Charlie felt his pace increase slightly, unintentionally.
By the time he was coming up to Steve's front door, it had become almost a brisk walk.
He knocked and Steve answered quite quickly.
"Hello mate, I wondered where you were. I clocked your car on the drive as I got home. I got off a bit early, you can when you're the boss, but you weren't here."
"Sorry, mate, just popped into the Tulip for a quick one."

"Bet it was dead in there, usually is on a weekday afternoon."
Charlie laughed.
"Come in, mate. How are you doing?"
Charlie went in. they exchanged a bit of small talk but Charlie was so distracted and impatient. He really did not wish to be rude so he tried to go along with the pleasantries.
As luck would have it, Steve eventually gave him an excuse to get onto the subject that he was itching to get onto.
"So, I take it you've been to the solicitors' then? You said that Bryan had another envelope for you. Have you read it? What was it all about?"
Charlie thought on his feet and came out with a 'white' lie. Obviously, he wasn't going to mention the big revelation, so he left one envelope out of the thread of the story.
"Yes, another envelope! Basically, it was all dependant on me not getting rid of the Cortina. He says that

there's something hidden in the driver's door panel for me."
"Really? You're joking! Something has been in there, all this time? You've got no idea what it is?"
"No, no idea. Apparently, it's something that I've got to deal with 'as soon as possible'"
"Well, it won't be something that will go off. Whatever it is, it's been in there for over six months, maybe well over six months! That panel, it's just a vinyl cover over the metalwork. It's only held in place by these funny plastic pegs that push in."
"Absolutely no idea what it is in there, no clues, nothing. As usual, it's very intriguing."
"Well Charlie, I suggest we go up to my garage and find out. What do you reckon?"
"Yes, I think we should mate. Sorry, Steve, I don't want you to think I'm obsessed and that's all I can think about. I did come to see you as well, you know."
"Bloody hell, shut up, you pillock! This is important. I'm almost as excited as you to find out what it is. Christ, I've been working on that car for months and I had no idea. Having said that, there was no need to do anything with the doors, they'd already been done. They're immaculate."
"I thought about that. You know what I reckon? This is Dad and his planning. He'd already done the doors so no one would have any need to touch them and discover what he'd hidden there."

"Bloody hell, Charlie, you may have a point. Come on, let's go!"
As Charlie stood, he felt an attack of butterflies. This was almost certainly the last of Dad's surprises. He hoped that it was going to be a good one, something special perhaps but who knows? He thought that

perhaps he shouldn't give it the big build-up, just in case.

Steve and Charlie walked up Hillary Close towards the block of garages.

"Steve, you've got to let me know if I owe you anything for the work you've done on the Cortina. I know you've let me know about some but surely that's not all of it. It must have cost more than what you've said."

"Don't be daft, mate, I've really enjoyed it. It's virtually finished, it runs lovely and I reckon it's time to try and get it through an MOT. Seriously, there's only been a few bits and bobs. They were harder to find and get hold of rather than expensive."

"Steve, we had an agreement. I was to cover ANY expense. You have to let me know. I'll be offended if you don't."

"Okay, mate. I'll cobble together some sort of invoice or bill."

They rounded the corner and there in front of them was the block of garages. Charlie's butterflies were active again. He was convinced that his stomach was noisy and Steve must hear.

"Right, Charlie. If you'd like to just stand here, I'll get the beast out from it's err, it's lair. You know what I mean."

Charlie stood back and watched excitedly as Steve unlocked his garage and went in. Charlie could just see the very front of the shiny, light blue bonnet.

Steve started the engine. Even to Charlie's untrained ear, that sounded great. Steve is good, he thought, Steve is bloody good.

He revved it a few times, a good throaty roar, then edged it slowly out of the garage, it's 'lair'. The bodywork looked fabulous. It was really shining in the

sunlight, it looked as good as new. Charlie guessed that Steve had sorted out the engine and all the mechanics. Charlie was grinning from ear to ear. It was a magnificent sight. He spoke aloud, unashamedly.
"That is awesome. Dad would be so pleased, so proud. That looks fantastic. Oh my God!"
Steve climbed out and shouted over.
"What do reckon? Not bad, hey?"
"Not bad? It's just brilliant!" Charlie shouted back, unexpectedly getting really choked up on the word 'brilliant'.
This was Dad's dream. The Cortina was completely restored and ready to go back on the road. It was quite a moment.
Steve knocked off the engine. It all went very quiet.
"Charlie, have a look at this panel. It's different to the others. As well as the plastic pegs, there's four screws in it. Bit of extra security, I reckon. just gonna grab my screwdriver. We need to get this off."
He disappeared back into his garage then came back with, obviously, the correct sized screwdriver. Charlie wandered over. He felt that he ought to observe this. This was to be a big moment, or was it? Is he building it up too much?
Steve paused, looked Charlie in the eye.
"Okay mate, ready for this?"
Charlie nodded.
Steve made short work of the panel, he seemed to have magic fingers, Charlie thought that it seemed that the screwdriver was merely an extension of his hand.
Steve paused, sighed then gently removed the cover. There, taped to the metalwork, was a rectangular shape of part of a plastic bag, roughly six inches by four inches, wrapped in a lot of sticky tape, possibly duct

tape. It was clearly to protect the contents, to make it very waterproof.
Steve carefully peeled it off the door. He looked at it and thought for a moment. He handed it to Charlie.
"I think you should do the honours, mate."
Charlie took the package and examined it. There was a lot of tape around it. He tried to find an end to begin peeling it off. He wanted to be careful so as not to potentially damage the contents. Gradually the tape was removed, bit by bit. When it was off, what remained was literally a folded-up plastic shopping bag. Charlie unfolded it, opened one end and, low and behold, inside was another envelope. He assumed that it was A5 sized. One word was written on the front.
Charlie.
"Mate, listen. This is your thing. I think you should be alone for this. Here, come and sit here"
Steve got out of the driver's seat and gestured for Charlie to sit there. "I've got a couple of phone calls to make. I'll wander over towards my house. I'll come back when I'm done. Okay mate?"
"Thanks Steve. Do you know what? I'm actually shitting myself. I don't know why. I don't know what to expect."
"I think you need to be on your own. Good luck. Back soon."
Charlie watched Steve go, he was already dialling on his mobile as he went.
"Well, this is it."
Charlie took some deep breaths and opened the envelope. Inside were two folded A4 sheets, as usual, hand-written.
Charlie,
Thank you so much.

The fact that you are reading this means that you carried out my wish and looked after my Cortina. I promise you; I NEVER doubted you. I knew I could trust you. I hope you will understand why you had to go through all this.
Charlie, I hope you realise how grateful I am for all you've done for me, how good you've been to me. You got me through a very difficult time and since then, you've always been there for me.
Do you remember when I used to tell you tales of my childhood in Ireland? How my family moved from Birr to Laurelvale. We had a lovely big house in Laurelvale, in a beautiful setting. When we left, when my Dad moved his job to Chelmsford, he decided to rent out the house, just in case it didn't work out in England. He wanted to make sure that we had somewhere to go back to.
Believe it or not, the house has always been rented out, ever since. Obviously, it's changed hands a few times over the years! By all accounts, it's been so well maintained and is in wonderful condition.
This is the important part, Charlie.
You have one month.
You have to do this within one month of receiving that last envelope from my solicitors'.
You have one month in which you must go and see Mister Holland and he will present you with the deeds to that house in Laurelvale.
Charlie, this is my gift to you. Our old family house in Northern Ireland.
I really want you to have it. You've been a wonderful son, so kind to me and I love you very much.
If you wish, (I promise you, there is no obligation) you could sell-up in Poole and make a new start over

there. It's a beautiful place and the locals are fine people. With your share of the proceeds from my flat and if you sold your flat in Poole, I reckon you'll be doing okay!
I have to point out – if you had failed and got rid of my Cortina (I knew you wouldn't) or you don't see Mister Holland within one month, he is under instruction to arrange for the house to be sold and the proceeds would go to a couple of charities I favour in Ireland.
If you don't mind me saying, Charlie, since that girl in Bath (can't recall her name) and that Wendy in Bournemouth, I feel that you've sort of lost a bit of direction. I sense that you're not entirely satisfied with your job. This is why I'm suggesting a that fresh start across the Irish sea might do you a power of good. (Please be clear, it is only a suggestion, I promise you. It's entirely up to you.)
I've known for a few years that I wanted you to have this house. I imagine, knowing you, that you're wondering about where Don fits in to all this. Please never repeat this to anyone.
Don has been quite selfish over the years. I hardly saw anything of him in recent years (unless he wanted a favour or something) I have to say that I think he's been downright rude, on many occasions, with me and with you (don't think I didn't notice that) I have to say it – I really do not care for his wife, Carol, the Ice maiden (please don't tell them we call her that!) She has been cold, aloof and uncaring ever since we first knew her.
I have no conscience at all about not including them in this. They are quite comfortably off, with Carol's inheritance, and really, they need never know about this arrangement.

Incidentally, I'll lay odds that Don has got rid of my bikes. I bet you're laughing now as I'm correct, am I not?! He would have failed the test. He had a habit of letting me down and letting you down as well.
Charlie, the house is yours. Please go and see Mister Holland and claim it. It means so much to me that it would belong to you. Once it's all sorted, you can decide where you go from there. I'm sure you will make the correct decision.
Charlie, this is my last message to you. My final envelope. I hope all the loose ends have been taken care of and I hope you've enjoyed carrying out my wishes. It is comforting for me to know that my house and my Cortina are in safe hands with you.
I'm so sorry that I never let on to you how ill I was. I didn't want you to be worried or to make too much of a fuss. You were brilliant just as you were and I didn't want to change that.
I'll say it again, Charlie, you have been a truly wonderful son to me. I've been SO SO proud of you and my final wish is that you have a wonderful life. You deserve it.
Please enjoy the house, please enjoy the Cortina!
I love you son.
Dad.
Charlie collapsed onto the steering wheel in a flood of tears (for the second time today.) He barely made it to the end of the message before he lost it.
He loved his Dad and kept picturing him, writing these messages, that were in the envelopes, in the full knowledge that he was about to pass away. All he was concerned about was making sure that Charlie was alright, to give him information in, as he believed, the right way, in the right order. He had known that he was terminally ill and knew that he didn't have long left but

he was ordered and organised in ensuring that everything was in place, everything was arranged so that his legacy and Charlie's plans were taken care of. Charlie peered up through the windscreen and looked up at the blue sky, tears running down his face.

"I love you, Dad. I miss you so much. You were an amazing man and a wonderful father. I so hope that you're with Mum now, somewhere special. I promise that I'll do all I can to make you proud, both of you."

He was sobbing now. It was the finality of it all that was getting to him. His Dad had trusted him with the envelopes and the tasks that they contained but now, that was it. All finished. It was like a 'closure' as far as his Dad was concerned, that Charlie didn't want. It was like he was being made to let go and he was so reluctant.

It was a few minutes before he could compose himself. He wiped his face with both sleeves, two or three times. He realised that his face was a bit tender and raw and his eyes were quite puffy.

He sat back in the seat, took a very deep breath, paused, then slowly let it out. He looked down at the two sheets of paper on his lap. He thought to himself (or maybe he said it out loud) -

"Dad, that's an amazing thing that you've done. That house was a huge part of your family's history. I know how much that place meant to you and what a big deal it is that you want to entrust it to me. Of course, I'll go and see Mister Holland, of course I'll go to Laurelvale and visit the house and, of course, I'll consider everything about perhaps moving over there."

After all the emotions of the day (or, if the truth be told, the last few months) Charlie suddenly felt calm. He felt a moment of clarity. In his mind, suddenly everything was becoming clear. He felt that he could actually ‘organise’ his thoughts as opposed to his mind constantly racing, as opposed to the stressful, almost panicky way that he’d been trying to commute all that information.

He looked around. It was all quiet around the garages, no one was about. There was no sign of Steve. Charlie decided to take advantage of the serenity. It was not often that he could take it easy like this. He was under no pressure now (he knew he had about a month to see Mister Holland but that was all) and he relaxed in the seat. Whilst he was ‘chilled’ like this, he decided to analyse all that his Dad had required him to do. He wanted to make sense of it all, to really understand his Dad’s reasons and how it all worked out, or was working out.

His thoughts went back to the will reading. He remembered how he was feeling that day. Obviously, he was grieving, he hadn’t long lost Dad. At the actual reading, he remembered that the two things that stood out to him from the will, were the writing desk and the Cortina. He knew that he was different to Don. Don was very money motivated, almost obsessed about it, all he would have been thinking about was how much he was going to get, whereas Charlie wasn’t that bothered. It was probably why Charlie was never that well-off, whenever he got money, he spent it. Investments, savings, being prudent, didn’t come into it.

He now fully understood why his Dad chose him to take care of the desk and its contents (namely the envelopes) and not Don. Dad obviously knew that he could rely on him to carry out his wishes to the best of his ability, whereas Don probably wouldn’t be so reliable or could not be depended on to do so. Charlie actually thought that it was quite an honour to be entrusted with the 'envelope' duties.

He thought about when he'd gone to the flat on the following day. He was alone. Dad couldn't have known that he'd be alone, he might have assumed that Don would be there too. Charlie was glad that he had that afternoon to himself in the flat, with his thoughts and memories. He was glad that Don wasn't there being loud and seemingly uncaring.

Obviously, Don more than made up for it the next time when he joined Charlie at the flat. He was virtually pricing things up and grabbing what he could (three-piece-suite and selected photos) as well as haggling with the estate agent and trying to inflate the sale price of the flat, confirming what Charlie had suspected therefore he was so relieved that he'd had the quiet time there for reflection.

He cast his mind back to the COFFs meeting and why it was so important to his Dad that he attended it. He felt that Dad wanted the people there to remember him and to reminisce. Charlie felt so proud at that meeting, he realised how popular his Dad was and how loved he was. The photos that he donated were a good way for the people there to not forget him and to remember him in a positive way.

Charlie had a theory about what had happened at the funeral. He thought that Dad had arranged it for the priest to announce that one of his sons would say a few words (without telling him or Don about it) He thought that Dad (rightfully) guessed that Don would be reluctant, to say the least. Charlie's theory was that Dad knew that he would step up, unprepared and say a few words. Therefore, the words would not just be read off a sheet of paper but would be spontaneous, from the

heart. Charlie hoped that he'd done his Dad proud and not just waffled a load of nonsense.
As for the wake, Charlie was asked to speak to Mick so Mick would talk to him about his Dad being a regular and playing football for The Tulip. The donated photos were, again, a good legacy and people will see them and remember. Dad couldn't have possibly predicted that Charlie would meet the two ex-teammates who would chat with him and tell him those great tales of his exploits. That was a bit of a bonus.
Initially, Charlie didn't know why he was asked to visit Barbara. He thought that it was Dad's plan that they would just chat, be friendly and, perhaps, stay in touch. She was now, the last of the four of them (Dad, Mum and Derek being the others) so it meant something to Dad that she was okay. Dad could not have known that Charlie would, during that visit, suspect something, poke his nose in and discover the scandal. Well, HALF of the scandal, and storm off in a rage.
He was really glad that he'd bumped into her earlier that day in The Tulip. He'd felt so guilty about how he'd treated her before (especially now he knew the WHOLE truth) He was very relieved that he had the chance to clear the air, to make-up. Barbara was a lovely woman and he genuinely wanted to remain close to her and fully intended to keep in touch.

The Nottingham visit made Charlie feel quite emotional whenever he thought about it. Poor Paul, he was so upset about what had happened to him when he was assaulted by that instructor and it had clearly had a lasting effect on his mental well-being. Typically, his Dad went way out of his way to try to help him and then apologised when things didn't work out the way they should have. Not Dad's fault, obviously but he was just looking out for Paul.

The Dublin request had puzzled Charlie for a while. Why did Dad want him to actually go over there? He could have posted the cheques to the charities or arranged payment via his will. He guessed that Dad really wanted him to meet his old friend Michael (and Joan) and talk to them about past times, about Dad's Irish roots, his heritage etc. Maybe, Charlie speculated, Dad wanted Ireland to be promoted to him, hoping he'd fall in love with the place and the people (bearing in mind the what was contained in the final, final envelope) but that was just speculation.
Charlie kept thinking about the envelope that he'd opened earlier. The one where Dad had confessed everything, where he'd come clean. It was still quite shocking to Charlie even though he'd almost come to terms with it, surprisingly so soon. Why did Dad leave it until then to reveal it all to Charlie? Why not months ago? Maybe Dad had left it until virtually all of his requests had been carried out in case Charlie had properly freaked out and couldn't carry on with them. Having said that, when would be a good time to tell Charlie that news? There would never be a good time so his Dad thought that that would have to do. He didn't know that Charlie would already know half of it. Did that soften the blow a bit? It was hard to tell.
Charlie was glad of the time to think all these things through. Although he didn't have the same attention to detail as his Dad, he still liked to get his head around things. He believed that it was good to sometimes sit quietly, to think about situations and people, to try to see things from everyone's point of view.
What happens now? Where does he go from here?

The Cortina was great. It looked great. He knew that, once Steve got it through an MOT, he would love to be driving it. It would be his car. Besides, it was what Dad wanted.

As for the house in Northern Ireland, Charlie was definitely going to go there, spend time there and try to suss out the people and the area. He decided he had nothing to lose, there was nothing stopping him so he would go with a completely open mind. Could he make a go of it? Could he start a new life across the Irish sea? After all, he wouldn't be a million miles away from Michael, a friendly face, so to speak. Michael and his family were only in Dublin, they could visit each other. And there's Sandra. Maybe if he met her again…he stopped himself. He was being deluded, or was he? She was probably not really interested in him, just having a bit of fun. He decided to stop living in a fantasy land where women were concerned. He would always misread signs, get it wrong, make a fool of himself. It would be much better to go with the flow, see what happens, que sera etc.

He laughed to himself. He realised that his immediate future required a lot of thought and a lot of decision making. They were however, not bad problems to have and he was feeling quite optimistic about everything. Did he actually have a feeling of contentment for once in his life? Optimism and contentment, who'd have thought?

He sensed some movement and looked out of the passenger window of the Cortina. Steve was making his way back, trying to get his mobile phone into the pocket of his jeans. He walked around the front of the car and came up to Charlie's open driver's door. He put an arm on the roof and leant in.

"Well, Charlie. What was in the envelope? Anything exciting?"

The End

If you enjoyed reading **Bryan's Will** and would like to send a message to the author, please feel free to do so. You can send a message, a comment, some 'constructive' criticism, some 'nice', 'friendly' remarks etc via –

My website: www.martinketleybooks.com
Twitter/X: @Mketleybooks
Email: Martinketleybooks@gmail.com

Coming soon, my next novel**: It's Family, to be Frank**.

Also by the same author: **Best Confession**.
Available to order from: -
www.feedaread.com
www.amazon.com
www.waterstones.com

If you have been affected by any of the subject matter in this book, there are organisations and charities that can offer help and support.

For bereavement: -
www.mind.org.uk
www.mariecurie.org.uk
www.the goodgrieftrust.org.uk

For victims of sexual abuse: -
www.sarsas.org.uk
www.crisistextline.org
www.verywellmind.com

Printed in Great Britain
by Amazon

61184482R00160